TEMPTING DANGER

SINCLAIR & RAVEN SERIES

WENDY VELLA

OTHER BOOKS BY WENDY VELLA

The Lady Seals Her Fate

The Lady's Dangerous Love

The Lady's Forbidden Love

Regency Rakes Series

Duchess By Chance

Rescued By A Viscount

Tempting Miss Allender

The Lords Of Night Street Series

Lord Gallant

Lord Valiant

Lord Valorous

Lord Noble

Stand-Alone Titles

The Reluctant Countess

Christmas Wishes

Mistletoe And The Marquess

Rescued By A Rake

For John and Mary

If there ever comes a day when we can't be together,
keep me in your heart, I'll stay there forever
-Winnie the Pooh

PROLOGUE

*I*t is said that when lowly Baron Sinclair saved the powerful Duke of Raven from certain death in 1335 by single-handedly killing the three men who attacked his carriage, King Edward III was grateful. Raven was a wise and sage counsel he had no wish to lose, therefore, he rewarded Sinclair with the land that sat at the base of Raven Mountain. Having shown himself capable of the duty, Baron Sinclair was now, in the eyes of the King, to be the official protector of the Ravens.

Over the years the tale has changed and grown as many do. There were rumors of strange occurrences when a Sinclair saved a Raven in the years that followed. Unexplained occurrences that caused many to wonder what it was that the Sinclairs were hiding, but one thing that never changed was their unwavering duty in the task King Edward III had bestowed upon them.

To honor and protect the Raven family was the Sinclair family creed.

CHAPTER 1

"*M*ove, you fool!"

Had the Marquis of Braithwaite not been deep in thought, he would have heard the warning. Instead, Nicholas's reaction was delayed, and seconds later he was travelling sideways at speed.

He came to an abrupt halt against the side of a building. His grunt was one of pain as his shoulder hit the unforgiving wood. A soft body pressed into his, and his arms had closed around her to brace them for the impact.

"A-Are you all right, madam?" Nicholas knew she was female because he could feel her breasts crushed to his chest. Her scent was also soft and definitely feminine.

A shiver of awareness traveled through him as he set her back on her feet.

"I-I am."

"May I ask as to why you felt the need to propel me sideways in such a manner? Had you wanted an introduction, a simple hello would have sufficed." Nicholas had received plenty of overtures from women, but never had they thrown themselves at him, literally.

"I didn't want an introduction! I was saving your life, you fool."

The day was a bleak one, so visibility was not good, but added to that her bonnet obscured a great deal of her face, and Nicholas had no idea what the woman looked like.

"If I may?" He reached over and tugged the left side, righting it.

"Thank you."

"I'm sorry if you believed my life was in danger, madam, but I assure you it was not. Also, I am rarely if ever, a fool."

"I don't care to know if you are a fool or not, only that I have no wish to witness your demise right before my eyes."

"I beg your pardon?" Nicholas leaned closer, attempting to see her eyes. Perhaps she was addled, and if so, who looked after her?

Glancing about, he saw no one nearby.

"There," she turned and jabbed a finger behind her, "is a large hole in the ground that you were heading directly for. Had I not intervened, you would have likely broken your neck, sir."

Nicholas looked around the woman and saw the hole a few feet away.

"Good lord."

"Indeed."

"I wonder who the idiot was who left that open?"

"Some fool who should have known better is my belief."

Her voice was quite deep for a woman, almost growly like his niece Meredith, who was just starting to understand how her lungs functioned.

"It seems I owe you my gratitude, madam. I would have indeed been injured had I fallen through it."

"Yes, well, it is done. Perhaps in future you should show more awareness of your surroundings, sir. London is not a place to be distracted; there are any number of hazards about the place."

"You are right, and I shall endeavor to be more observant."

He had no idea the color of her hair, but her eyebrows were dark. Moving closer, he felt a jolt of awareness as he looked into her green eyes. He knew quite a few people with just such a color, but this was something more... a recognition. They were set in a heart-shaped face, with pale skin and a nose that may be a touch too long on her, but he couldn't be sure in this light... or lack thereof. Her lips formed a thin straight line of displeasure, no doubt for his behavior, so he had no idea of their shape either.

In short, she was an interesting-looking woman. Nicholas would even say captivating but he couldn't be certain without the benefit of more light. But what he was sure of was that he had seen her before.

"May I have your name, madam?"

"Of course you can't! I don't just give my name to anyone in such a willy-nilly fashion."

"Willy-nilly fashion?"

"You understand my meaning, sir. Good evening to you." She started to walk away.

"Wait."

"What?" She turned slightly to look at him over a shoulder.

"Surely you should not be walking about in such a place at such a time of day. Where are your attendants?"

Nicholas had a sister and would not want her in a location like this alone. Of course, her large, protective husband would not allow it either.

"About." She waved her hand in a circle but no direction. "And the hour is not overly late; darkness has not fallen completely. As you know, this horrid place loses the sun"—

she looked upward—"or what there is of it at an early hour. Now I must leave or they shall grow concerned."

"It does not usually lose the sun early in the summer months, however today is bleak and disagreeable." Nicholas wasn't sure why he was defending the weather. But he didn't want her to walk away from him. In fact, he felt a desperate need to keep her close, which was odd. Nicholas rarely felt desperate emotions any longer, at least not since he was sober. Before that he'd pretty much been desperate for a drink at most times of the day and night.

"I'm sure you're right. Now, as I stated, I must leave as they will grow concerned."

"They?"

She was a woman of good birth, he'd lay money down on that fact, but as he no longer gambled it would be figuratively.

Perhaps she was a governess? Her cloak was thick black velvet, and the bonnet the same. Her voice was not dissimilar to his sister's, the daughter of a marquis who was now married to a nobleman.

Where have I seen this woman before?

"It is not safe," he said, closing the distance between them again. He held her arm. "I shall see you to your carriage."

"That will not be necessary. I am more than capable of making my way to it myself."

He'd deliberately referred to a carriage, and she had not refuted his words. She was definitely from a noble family.

"Good day to you, sir." She pulled free and moved a few paces away from him before stopping.

Nicholas watched as she tilted her head slightly like he had seen dogs do when they heard a particular pitch. He could hear nothing. She turned back to face him, then closed the distance between them once more.

"We must hurry, some men are coming. They said they

saw you walk this way." Her words were whispered. "You are in grave danger."

"What?" Nicholas had excellent hearing. "I hear nothing."

"Trust me, sir, your life is in danger. Make haste." She followed those words with a finger poke to his chest.

"Look." He used a gentle tone. Perhaps she was addled in the head? This thought had him even more concerned that she was out here alone. "There really is no need to worry about me. I assure you I am quite able to care for myself and have been doing so for years." Perhaps not that well for a while there, but he was doing better these days. "Now let me take you to your carriage... please."

"Yes, I can see how well that was going for you as you nearly fell to your death in that hole."

"I was preoccupied."

She made a small hissing sound that Nicholas had no idea how to interpret.

"These men will rob you and likely slit your throat. Plus, I have already saved you, so you should trust me."

"I don't trust on such a brief acquaintance." He'd learned that lesson the hard way many times.

She grabbed the lapels of his jacket and tugged them hard.

"You're in danger, you fool!"

"I believe I told you I am no fool." Addled she may be, but he wasn't taking her insults.

"I implore you to put your ego aside momentarily and move your feet... quickly," she added, looking left. "These men will not care a jot if they injure you or worse whilst stealing everything you have on your person!"

"I hear nothing," he said again. "And this is not about ego, I assure you, madam."

"You owe me for saving your life, now move it." The finger jabbed him again.

She certainly didn't seem addled, and yet he knew some who hid it well.

"Oh, very well." Nicholas decided to humor her. Then he would see her safely to the home she lived in, surely under the care of someone. Taking her hand, he tugged her with him down the road until he found a small opening between buildings. "Come along, we shall stay in here until they are gone."

She was likely harmless, so a few minutes longer in her company would not hurt. It saddened him that she was out here alone, obviously lost or strayed from her caregiver.

"Oh, but they are not after me."

"You are alone, and if there are two men approaching, that sounds to me like it could present danger to you also. Now be quiet." He played along. "In here," he whispered. He'd give her a few minutes of his time. Perhaps it was a game she played often?

"Sssh," she hissed.

Nicholas nudged her into the small space and followed.

"I don't like small spaces," she whispered furiously.

"I'm not entirely fond of them myself, but as you insisted we needed to hide—"

"You, not me! Sssh, they approach."

He fell silent, aware of the woman beside him. Her breathing had increased to pants, and yet they had not been running. He wondered again at her mental state.

"I-I can't do this."

"Do what?" He leaned over to whisper the words into her ear.

"Stay in here."

"Then we shall leave at once."

"No, they are here."

He turned her to face him. Not easy in such a small, tight space, yet he managed it. She had her eyes clenched shut.

"Come now, there is no need to be scared." Perhaps she was no longer enjoying the game.

"Really scared," she muttered.

Nicholas placed a hand on her shoulder to reassure her.

"Wh-what are you doing?"

"I have no wish to hurt you, just ease your fears. My sister has this problem, and when she was younger, I used to hold her, but of course I will not do that with you. Still, a reassuring pat on the shoulder should help."

"I am not a dog," she whispered furiously.

"No, they are much more appreciative. Come, enough now, the game is over, we shall leave here."

"They are here!" Her hands grabbed his lapels again, holding them tight.

Nicholas was about to move when he heard the voice.

"He went this way, Badger. Swear it, I do."

She was right.

"You told us to wait, give him a head start, now we've lost him!"

"Maybe he's down here. Looked like he'd be plump to pick too."

She rescued me again.

The footsteps faded, and then there was silence. Nicholas became aware of two things in that moment. The first, that this woman had saved his life twice. The second, how good she felt in his arms. Her lovely body was now pressed to his chest, and he held her close, as if instinctively needing to protect her.

"'Tis all right now, they have gone," he whispered in her ear.

"Please, I wish to leave this space."

"Thank you," he said to the top of her head. "You saved my life again."

He'd thought her in need of his help, and yet the opposite was true.

She looked up, and this close he could see every feature of her lovely face. That jolt of awareness traveled through him again, but the memory was still out of his reach.

"I must go."

"Yes."

Neither of them moved. Eyes locked, bodies touching, he found it suddenly difficult to breathe. The air around them had changed; it was now charged with tension.

"Who are you?" His voice was gruff.

She raised a hand and touched his chin, a fleeting brush that had him sucking in a breath.

"Tell me your name," Nicholas breathed the words against her lips.

"A-Alice."

"I'm going to kiss you, Alice."

She didn't speak as he closed the last few inches between them. He was suddenly desperate to taste her lips. In that moment, he wanted this woman like he had no other.

Nicholas had vices. He'd managed to rid himself of a few, but his love of women was not one of them. But this was different... felt different. She tasted like sin, and in seconds he'd forgotten his own name.

"Why did you kiss me?" She pulled back slightly.

"I... ah, I have no idea. Why did you touch me?"

"I don't know, I-I just needed to."

"As I needed to kiss you," he said, lowering his head and taking her mouth beneath his again. She took his kiss, arching into him, seeking more.

He didn't know how long they stood there, only that in this moment nothing but them existed.

"Dear lord, what is wrong with me?" She wrenched her mouth from his.

"And me," he managed to rasp out.

What the hell was the matter with him, kissing a strange woman like that? He hadn't even a drop of alcohol in his body to blame for his reckless actions.

"M-move at once." She placed a hand on his chest and pushed.

"Of course." He shuffled backward, out of the opening. She followed. He felt as if he was waking from a dream... a sensual dream where this woman played the starring role.

"Tell me where you live?" He felt a desperate need to know how to locate her. He couldn't let her leave now, not after what they'd just shared.

"I cannot. Good evening."

She brushed past him and hurried away before he could stop her. Nicholas shook off his shock and followed, but she picked up her skirts and was soon running. In seconds he'd lost her, as she had clearly ducked down one of the lanes he'd passed. Retracing his steps, he looked for her, checking every alley, every object she could hide behind, but it was no good, she was gone. Why did that thought make him feel empty inside?

"What the hell just happened?" No one answered him, of course. "Exceedingly strange."

Shaking his head once more, he wondered if it was he who was losing his mind and he'd imagined the entire incident. He pinched his arm, the sting of pain assuring him he wasn't.

Walking away, he vowed silently to find her, his Alice, if it was the last thing he did.

CHAPTER 2

*N*icholas made his way along the street, attempting to work through his memory once more, now he could find some clarity in his thoughts, as to where he'd seen her face before.

"No!" It came to him in a rush.

She was in his vision. Last night, he'd had a woman come to him, that woman, and in her arms had been a babe. She'd told him to find the boy and return him to his mother.

He'd woken aroused, his body tight with need.

"Christ, what the hell did that mean?" It was her, he'd stake his life on that.

"Nicholas?"

"Max?" He looked at the large man walking toward him. At his side was another, equally as large. "What has you here?"

Pushing thoughts of the woman to one side until he had more time to formulate a plan to find her, he shook the hand Max held out to him. He was part of Nicholas's sister's family by marriage. Max Huntington, a wealthy merchant who had married a nobleman's daughter. Big, with the coloring of a tawny lion, he was not to be crossed, but if one was in his good books, as Nicholas usually was, he was a great person to have in your corner.

"Ace and I are looking at an investment into a plot of land nearby. Have you two met before?" Max waved a hand at the behemoth at his side.

Nicholas wasn't a small man, but these two made him feel that way.

"Oliver Dillinger." He held out a large, dinner-plate sized hand for Nicholas to shake. "Ace, if you wish."

"Nicholas," he replied.

He knew who Dillinger was; there were not many who didn't. He had made his fortune with his fists, then moved on to increase it through investments. He then married the Duke of Stratton's sister.

"For what purpose are you looking into purchasing the land?"

Max always had his eye on some investment or other. Nicholas was often dragged in, as was the rest of their family.

"Housing. I have a vision for a complex of houses. James has been doing some drawings for me, and Ace has the men to build the project."

"James draws?" Nicholas hadn't known this about his cousin, who was Max's brother and also the Duke of Raven.

"He's quite good, actually, but don't tell him I told you that."

"Your secret is safe with me."

Unlike the other members of the Raven and Sinclair families, Max was quiet and didn't speak unless he had something to say.

"Ace is also helping me find my siblings."

"Putting you in touch with the right people," Ace clarified. "I have contacts in France; we're hoping they can help."

The man smiled, and it changed his face completely. He

appeared almost boyish now. Big, dark, he was a man who would intimidate anyone, but not while he was smiling.

"I was unaware you had siblings, Max."

"I have a sister and a brother. I have been trying to locate them for years."

"I wish you luck then."

"I must leave you, Max. I am to meet Thea and the children. If I do not arrive, they shall be displeased and let me know about that for the remainder of the day," Ace said. "Good day to you, Nicholas."

"Good day." He nodded, watching as the two men made plans to meet again.

"And you, Nicholas. What has you here on such a gloomy day?" Max asked after Ace had left.

"I'm not entirely sure." He went for the truth. "A hunch, or a need to ease my housekeeper's misery."

He would not speak of the woman, Alice; that was his memory alone.

"I'm intrigued."

"I was playing cards last night—"

"It was my understanding you didn't do that anymore."

"With my staff. We play for splinters of wood," Nicholas said stiffly. He knew what he'd been but hoped those he called his family understood that he'd now changed.

"Forgive me, I spoke only as your friend and out of worry. Of course you are no longer gambling."

Nicholas exhaled. "No, you are right to ask, forgive me for overreacting. It is one of the two vices I no longer allow myself to indulge... well, for money anyway." Last night he'd gambled a woman's clothes off her body. They'd been in her bedroom playing poker.

"The second being alcohol?"

"Yes."

"Continue with your story."

"My housekeeper is usually a demon at cards and beats me regularly."

"I doubt that. I've heard you are something of a legend with numbers. Dorrie told me that you taught her a few card tricks, and I have not beaten her since."

Nicholas laughed.

"Mrs. Potter, my housekeeper, told me something that disturbed me greatly."

"What?"

"She said she was at the birth of her first grandchild and vows the child was alive and wailing in good health. But the midwife took it into the other room immediately after it was delivered. When she returned, she was without the babe. She said she could do nothing to save it."

"Is your housekeeper sure she heard it cry?"

"Very much so. She heard it clearly because she went to find out why the babe wasn't returned to her daughter. When she walked into the room, the door to the street outside was open and the midwife was handing the infant to a man. She then asked what she was doing, and the woman said the child was dead and severely malformed, so the man would take him away and bury him."

"But surely the parents should bury the child?" Max sounded horrified.

"The midwife said it was best the mother never saw how disfigured the child was, so she'd had someone take it away."

"Dear Christ." The words hissed from Max.

"Precisely. The mother also believed she heard the babe crying."

"But there is more to this than just the word of two emotionally drained women, isn't there, Nicholas?"

"You don't think their word is enough?"

"I do. But as someone who has stood outside the door

while his wife suffers through childbirth for many hours, believe me when I tell you it plays its hand on your sanity."

I had a vision. The words didn't leave his head.

"Will you trust me when I tell you that I feel disturbed enough about what my housekeeper told me that I am investigating the matter?"

"Of course."

"I fear that telling you more will bring my sanity into question."

"You do know who my family is, don't you?"

"I do, as my sister is part of that family."

"Sanity is a fine line, Nicholas, which we deviate from regularly. I love each and every one of them, but there is little doubting that at times even I have to question their motives."

The words had been said to make him laugh, to ease the tension that was suddenly in the air.

"I'll tell you something that happened to me before I left your brother-in-law's house earlier."

"Lilly is well?" Nicholas asked.

"Of course, fit and beautiful as she always is. Settle your fears, Nicholas, nothing is wrong with any family member."

He exhaled. His sister had become very important to him when he came to his senses and escaped the self-destruction of his soul he was undertaking on a daily basis.

"What happened?"

"Lilly said she'd been unsettled all day and felt something was off with you. She'd sent word to your house, but you had not replied. She then had a carriage drive her and Dev there, but you had left the house earlier."

Nicholas wasn't sure how to respond to that. He'd often felt his sister's pain and worry for him; that she felt his made him feel warm all over. Not that he wanted to worry her, but still it was a nice feeling.

"It is natural to worry about those you care for."

"Not that much, and not so much that you feel what they feel," Max added.

"Is this your indirect way of getting me to tell you what you want to hear, Max?"

"It could be, but I told you to strengthen the thought that we are all different, Nicholas. Some more than others, and believe me when I tell you the Sinclair and Raven family, of which you are part, are very, very different."

"I have visions," Nicholas said slowly.

"What form do they take?"

He hadn't scoffed or told him he was a fool; Max had simply asked what form they took.

"Someone is usually asking me to do something. The vision I had the other night, just before I learned of my housekeeper's misery, was of a woman holding a boy child. She asked me to help him come home. That he was alive but living with the wrong family."

Not just any woman, but one who had saved his life.

"That has to be unsettling."

"Extremely."

"How long have you had these visions?"

"For as long as I can remember. I pickled them in alcohol for a while, but now that I no longer imbibe, they are back."

"Interesting. You need to tell the others about them."

"I don't think so."

"You must, Nicholas. Trust me on this. They will understand."

"What aren't you telling me?"

"I can say no more, as it is not my story to tell. But you must speak to them."

"Very well." Nicholas doubted he would but said the words anyway.

"But now we will visit this midwife. I will stand at your back, looking menacing."

"A position you fill very well. How did you know I was going to pay a call on the midwife?"

"A hunch."

He led the way, and soon they were approaching Cobbs Lane.

"What number?" Max asked.

"17."

The lane was like a dozen others in London. Narrow, with buildings bordering each side. Tall, they were pressed together like books on a shelf.

Max was a silent, calm figure at his side, lending his support simply by being there.

A freshly painted sign with the number 17 on it told him he'd found his destination. Unlike the other buildings, this one was set back slightly. Walking up the narrow path, he found an old wooden building, another sign, this one with the word Midwife above the door.

"I shall wait here," Max said.

Nicholas had left his house at 3:30 p.m. so he estimated it was closing in on 6:00 p.m. now. Was it too late to call? He knew nothing about the hours a midwife kept, but thought they were likely nocturnal. Taking the two wobbly steps up, he left Max behind and avoided the last step, which had a crack, then rapped on the wooden door. He had only a few minutes to wait before it opened.

"Good evening." She was tall, close to his own height, and of a slender build. Nicholas put her age at approximately sixty years, but then he'd never been overly accurate judging a woman's age, and to be honest, what man would want to try?

"Good evening. Is it possible for me to speak with Mrs. Adley?"

He'd thought about what he would say if he encountered the midwife who attended Mrs. Potter's daughter's birth. If there was something sinister going on, he had no wish to alert the woman to his suspicions, and yet he needed to ask questions.

"I am she. Do you have a woman giving birth?" Noticing Max, who was still at the bottom of the stairs, she gave him a nod.

"Good day," Max replied.

"No. I wish to discuss the birth you attended three nights ago."

Something changed in her face; it was slight, but as Nicholas was looking directly at the woman, he saw it clearly.

"Which birth?"

"Shall I enter your establishment, and we can discuss the matter further?"

"I'm on my way out," she rushed to say.

She was panicking now. Eyes wide, gaze shooting from him to Max. He doubted it was his presence creating this reaction, but he would not discount that it was guilt-induced fear.

"My housekeeper is one Mrs. Potter. Her daughter recently gave birth; she is the one I wish to discuss. Mrs. Jane Budd. She gave birth to a son you declared dead soon after."

"He was dead!"

The panic had moved up a notch, and her knuckles turned white, clenched around the door. She was also shrieking at him.

"In their grief-stricken state, both Mrs. Potter and her daughter believed they heard the babe cry."

"The women were crazed with grief, they would react no other way! Now I must go."

Nicholas placed his boot in the doorway as she attempted to close it and gave it a small push.

"I have not finished asking questions, Mrs. Adley. Why

were they not allowed to bury their babe? To have nowhere to grieve is surely the cruelest of things for a parent to suffer after the loss of a child?"

"I have nothing to say to you!"

"Why did you take the child away so the parents couldn't see him, Mrs. Adley?"

"H-he was deformed. It was f-for the b-best." Her face was pale, and she was shaking now.

"Who's there, Lissy?"

He watched a man appear behind the midwife. Big and burly, he looked like someone who could be ready with his fists. But Nicholas had learned a trick or two during his gambling days, and combined with James's teachings, he was more than capable of defending himself should it be required.

"Good day to you, sir. I am Lord Braithwaite."

The man nodded. "Mr. Adley. Do you have a woman expecting?"

"I do not. I have some questions that I would like answered," Nicholas said calmly. Mrs. Adley was now looking desperate. She was pushed aside roughly by a large hand, forcing her into the wall.

"What questions?"

"Are you all right, Mrs. Adley?"

"I asked you a question," the man demanded, jutting out his jaw.

"And I will answer it as soon as you apologize to your wife for your behavior." Nicholas's anger was usually slow to rise, but he could not abide bullies. "You are twice her size, sir, and had no right to treat her in that manner."

"I can treat my wife how I want, now leave here." The man took a menacing step toward Nicholas. He stood his ground.

"It's been an observation of mine that bullies are cowards. Care to test my theory, Mr. Adley?"

Nicholas stepped back as the door was slammed in his face.

"That went well," Max said from his position at the bottom of the steps.

"I'm glad you came to watch over me," Nicholas said, joining him.

"You were never in danger. In fact, you were taunting a reaction from him."

"I don't like bullies or men who intimidate woman," Nicholas muttered.

"Agreed, even if there was something off about that entire exchange."

"She was nervous."

"Extremely. Guilty, I would add to that. Something is not right there, Max. I need to find out what."

That boy needs to go home to his parents. He is living with the wrong family. The woman had told him that in a vision. The woman with green eyes and no name. The woman who had felt like sin in his arms and tasted like heaven.

The woman named Alice.

CHAPTER 3

"*S*o how does one go about proving a babe was alive when it was taken from the mother?" Nicholas said as they retraced their steps. "And what if it wasn't alive, and the parent just felt it was and hysteria, as you alluded to, was the reason they believe it is alive?"

"You're doubting yourself now... after that conversation?"

"No... yes," Nicholas sighed. "It almost seems unbelievable that someone would do such a thing."

"What about your visions, Nicholas? Are they usually steeped in fact or fiction?"

"Fact."

"I think you have your answer then. Something is off, and for whatever reason, you have been chosen to look into the matter."

"What the hell does that mean... chosen?"

Max shot him a sideways look as they walked along the gloomy London street.

"It means that you had the vision and the housekeeper to alert you to this. It's up to you now to do something about it."

They walked as the rain started to fall.

"I loathe this weather," Max muttered.

"At least it's not cold."

"Small consolation, I assure you. Now hurry it along."

"Where are we hurrying it along to?" Nicholas asked.

"It's the twins' birthday dinner. They will love it if you are there."

Nicholas liked his family, as he called all of them now. The entire Sinclair and Raven clan. After all, he had a foot in each. He was the Duke of Raven's cousin, and brother-in-law of Lord Sinclair.

"I don't have a gift."

"We'll stop somewhere on the way."

"I really don't want to intrude." He gave a half-hearted protest, when really the prospect of not going home to his empty house was a pleasing one.

"You're family, how is that intruding?" Max waved down a hackney as they reached the main road.

"I had plans," he said, because he did, but not until later... much later.

"She'll wait, I'm sure."

"How do you know it's a she?"

Max raised a brow as he settled in the seat beside Nicholas.

"I like women."

"Did I suggest otherwise?"

"Oh, very well." Nicholas gave in. "I can come for an hour."

He made the hackney stop at a sweet shop, where he purchased toffee wrapped in large bows. Then a smaller bag for him and Max to eat on the journey.

Minutes later, they were traveling down the street to Dev's house. The same street the rest of the family all lived on. It was a complicated family structure, but one that worked for all concerned.

"Lord Braithwaite, Mr. Huntington, good evening," the Sinclair butler greeted them as they entered the house.

"Good evening, Tatters," Max said. "It is a trifle damp out there. Are the family all present?"

The butler did not blink at the name the family had shortened his surname to. He'd been born Hildebrand Tattersly, but the children had decided on Tatters.

"They are, Mr. Huntington, and I shall bring something for you to dry yourselves with."

"And set another place, please, as Lord Braithwaite is to going to eat with us."

"Of course."

"Hello, Max. Nicholas?"

Warwickshire Sinclair now stood before them. Tall, with the look of his brothers, there were glimpses of the man he would become.

"I have no wish to intrude, but Max insisted I join your sisters' celebrations."

The boy rocked back on his heels like his eldest brother often did and studied Nicholas with a frank gaze. It didn't unsettle him; he sat in the House of Lords and dealt with people every day in some capacity or other, but still, there was no doubting who his brothers were.

"You are family, therefore you are always welcome anytime."

"Well said." Max ruffled Warwick's hair.

And it really was that simple to the boy, as he'd known no different. But Nicholas had. For a while he'd been rudderless and without family or friends... by choice, but when he reflected back on that period of his life, he did not like what he saw.

The changes he'd undertaken would not be reversed, he knew that, but sometimes when he was with his family, he felt vulnerable. As if one day all this would be taken from him in punishment for his past sins.

Foolish, he knew, but there it was.

"Come, it is always good to have another man about, considering the number of females in this family. Isn't that right, Warwick?" Max said.

"Yes."

They followed the butler up the stairs and through the grand house that his sister shared with her husband, his three siblings, plus Lilly and Dev's children.

Loud voices greeted him as Tatters opened the door.

"Lord Braithwaite, Mr. Huntington, and Master Warwickshire," the butler said. No one heard, as they were doing what they did best: speaking over the top of each other.

"I hate that name," Warwick muttered.

"I think it an excellent name. Mine is common, yours is not," Nicholas said to the boy, who stood at his side.

"Really?" Warwick looked at Nicholas, hope in his eyes.

"Nick, Nicholas, Nicky." He shuddered for effect. "Hardly inspiring when there are at any given time at least a dozen of us walking about the streets of London."

"I never thought of it that way."

"Shall we trade names?"

"I don't think so," the boy said, then walked away with a small smile on his face.

"Uncle Nicholas is here!"

This shriek came from his niece Hannah. A combination of her parents, she had her father's dark hair and mother's smile. Nicholas placed his gifts on a side table and then bent to greet the child. At five, she was showing signs of her mother's beauty. It always surprised him how much his nieces and nephew loved him. There was Mathew, who was serious like his father at seven, and Hannah, then the baby, Meredith, at three years.

He didn't delve into why their love of him was surprising too much, as he was sure it was because he didn't believe himself loveable. All Nicholas knew was that he would sell his soul to the devil to keep them safe. They were part of him now, and he loved them fiercely.

"Nicholas, I am relieved to see you. What has you here tonight, and with Max?"

Turning with Hannah in his arms, he looked at his sister. Elegant, happy, and extremely beautiful, Lilliana was his younger sibling, and someone he owed much to. It had been his job in life when their father passed to care for and love her. He'd failed miserably. He now made sure she never had reason to doubt her big brother's love and support.

"That's a fierce look." She came forward and kissed him, then her daughter, who was settled against his shoulder. "Is all well with you?"

"It is. I met Max while attending to some business. He told me you felt something was wrong and that you called, but I was not home."

"It's true I was worried, but now I am not, as I can see you are well."

"What alerted you to the fact you believed something was wrong with me? I don't think that's happened before," Nicholas asked her.

"It has, but I ignored it before. Now I don't have to." She kissed his cheek again.

"If I say sorry once more, will that help?" The guilt was never too far away.

"I need no more apologies for past sins, Nicholas. We've been over this multiple times. Now tell me what has happened, as I can see in your eyes something has."

"Nothing that you need worry over. We will talk more

later. I hope you don't mind, but Max insisted I come for the celebration."

"As long as there is enough food for me, Braithwaite, you can stay."

These words were said by Cambridge Sinclair. He was one of the middle Sinclair siblings, of which there were seven. Tall, of a build like Nicholas where they did not carry any extra weight, he was a man with a wicked sense of humor who had also forgiven him for his actions many years ago. Married to the gentle Emily, the Duke of Raven's sister, he was not always a comfortable man due to his openness, but an honorable one. If Cambridge felt something needed saying, he said it.

"Cambridge." Nicholas shook the hand he held out. "I shall not eat too much, I promise."

"Cam."

"Of course."

The Sinclair green eyes studied him, reminding him of the ones he'd looked into earlier that evening.

"If I have moved on, then perhaps you should also?"

That was another thing these people had that was not a comfortable trait. Directness.

"Pardon?" Nicholas played for time, and yet he knew exactly what Cambridge alluded to. He and this man had history, dark, ugly history. One of them had put that behind them. It wasn't Nicholas.

"Leave the past there, Nicholas." Cambridge slapped his shoulder, then moved away. "I have and give you permission to do so."

Excellent. He'd been in the house no more than a handful of minutes and had experienced more discomfort than he had in the past month.

Not exactly true, he thought, remembering a pair of lovely green eyes again. *Alice.*

"Nicholas." His brother-in-law, Devonshire, Lord Sinclair, head of his family, greeted him next. Looking into his vibrant green eyes, Nicholas hoped Alice had made it home safely.

"Good evening, Devon."

"Nicholas." Eden, Duchess of Raven, another Sinclair, and the only one with gray eyes, was next to greet him.

"Good evening, Duchess, you look beautiful as always."

"Does she, I hadn't noticed." The Duke of Raven arrived at his wife's side.

He was Nicholas's cousin and had been part of the reason for his change. Part of the reason his eyes were opened to the man he had become. Nicholas would be forever grateful to the duke for that.

"We are waiting on Wolf and his family before we begin the meal," Eden said. "And can I just say, thank you for what you said to Warwick when you arrived."

"What did he say?" Dev asked.

"He said Warwick should be pleased with his name as it is original. Our youngest brother seemed extremely happy after that."

"Did he? Well done, Nicholas," Dev said.

"'Tis nothing." He brushed the words aside. "Are Wolf's sisters enjoying the season? I have yet to meet them."

"I'm not entirely sure enjoyment is the term," James drawled. Quiet, powerful, the man, along with Dev, was the foundation to which these families were tethered. "I believe Wolf is looking a little strained as of late with Alice's antics."

Alice was a common name; no need at all for his heart to start thudding hard inside his chest. Surely there were any number of green-eyed Alices trotting about London each day?

Dear God, he hoped so.

"Antics?"

"Alice is... *was* quiet, studious, and bookish. But she keeps slipping out of the house without telling him where she is going. Simply put, it is not pleasing her brother."

His necktie was suddenly strangling him.

"I think Alice is just unused to the way of things in London," Essie said, coming to greet him. She was after Dev and Cam in the Sinclair pecking order. The gentle Sinclair, he'd always classed her. The healer, she had an ability that he had never understood, but was grateful for the few times she'd healed his ailments.

"Where does she slip out to?" he made himself ask.

"Bookstores, lending libraries, and I think she went to a lecture."

Essie's words made him relax. Alice Sinclair would not have been in that part of London today. Absolutely not.

"London is not a place to walk about unescorted, no matter what part you are in," James said. "My sympathies lie with Wolf. Having three sisters and a wife, I feel his agony."

"A pooh to that," the duchess said. "We cause you no trouble but are merely high-spirited."

"Best day of my life when I handed her over to you," Dev added, which earned him an elbow in the ribs from Eden.

"I'm hoping Miss Penny has made a large cake for the twins' birthday," Nicholas heard Cambridge say.

"Hello." Two Sinclairs and one Raven were next to greet him. The surprise when he looked at them was that they were no longer children. Just as Warwick had changed, so had they. When had that happened?

Dorrie and Somer Sinclair were twins, and James's sister Samantha was at their side as she usually was.

"Happy birthday. I hope you both don't mind that I've invited myself to your party?"

"No!"

He'd noticed they often talked as one.

"Can I ask how old you are, or is that rude?"

"Fifteen."

"Are you really? I'm not sure when that happened."

"Neither are we," Dev drawled.

"I have something for you both." Nicholas retrieved the boxes of toffee and handed them one each.

They were extremely happy with the gifts.

"You will eat those after your meal," Dev said.

"He has eyes everywhere," Dorrie muttered, clutching her box to her chest and then walking sideways past Cambridge so he didn't see it.

"I seem to have blinked and they've become young adults," he said to Lilly as they headed to the dining room.

"Indeed, and Dev and James's headaches are just starting."

"It seems Wolf and his family have arrived. Prepare yourself, all is not well in his world by the sound of the argument taking place," Eden said, and Nicholas wondered how she'd heard anything above the noise the families were making. For that matter, how had she heard the conversation he'd had with Warwick?

There had always been something a little odd about this family; he'd just never been able to pinpoint what exactly that was. They heard and saw things long before anyone else. And Cam often sniffed the air like a dog. Nicholas had gotten used to their odd ways, but he did wonder about them.

"Brace yourselves, they are close," Eden said dramatically. "Everyone take a seat and talk, make it look like we haven't been listening to their conversation."

"*We* haven't, my love. You have."

Eden poked out her tongue at the duke in a very unduchessy way. Then they walked into the dining room and began to seat themselves.

Nicholas wasn't sure why he felt suddenly tense, but he did.

CHAPTER 4

"Oh dear, it seems Alice has been testing Wolf again," Eden said from down the table next to her husband.

"Perhaps he should send her back to the country until she understands how to behave in London?"

"She is not a dog, Nicholas, in need of training."

"I understand that, Lilly, but if she does not grasp the dangers of walking about London unescorted, then she is a danger to herself."

This Alice was definitely not his Alice, he was sure of it.

"She is used to her freedom in Briarwood, the village they were raised in."

"Which is vastly different from London," Nicholas pointed out.

"Alice is a wonderful, determined young lady who has been well received in society, with many young men enamored by her. It's my belief that soon she will not have time to be bored," Eden added.

Nicholas hid his shudder. Debutantes were a frightening

group of young women, eager and controlled by their mothers. He often felt like a rare and hunted species around them.

"Wolf just said he's thinking of putting another lock on her door... the outside."

How did Eden hear this? Nicholas hadn't heard a word.

"I'm sure given time they will work things out," James said.

Suddenly he heard the voices approaching, the rumble of Wolf and the lighter tone of a woman.

Rose Sinclair, the duke's other sister and Wolf's wife, was first to enter the dining room. Pretty, with red-gold hair, she was the most recent addition to the Sinclair/Raven clan. Next came a woman he had not met before—a sister—then Wolf.

It was the last person to enter the room who caught and held Nicholas's gaze.

It's her.

The breath he'd just taken seemed to lodge in his throat as he studied the woman.

Alice Sinclair was his Alice. The thought made him want to get to his feet and run from the house. He took the few seconds before she looked his way to compose himself. She didn't have the same luxury.

Shock had her eyes widening. Color flooded her cheeks, and Nicholas wondered if her reaction would alert others to the fact something wasn't right. She rallied, her mouth snapping shut as the green eyes narrowed. Shooting a look left and right, she mouthed something to him.

Not one word.

Had she actually just dared to threaten him? Her face suggested that was the case.

Disturbed that she was here, in the room with him, and far more disturbed that she was family in a roundabout way, he took a large, fortifying mouthful of his wine.

32

What the hell did this mean? She was in his vision, and then his arms, and now here she was again. Had he been a man with a delicate constitution, this would put him in bed for weeks.

Their eyes caught and held, and Nicholas felt the pull of attraction they'd shared earlier. His face remained composed. If his gambling days had taught him nothing else, they had taught him to hide what he felt.

"The point is, Alice, it's dangerous out there. You cannot simply wander about the streets of London as you did in Briarwood. I wonder how many times I must say this before you understand it," Wolf Sinclair said.

Big like Dev, Wolf was a quieter and yet no less determined Sinclair male. Pressed to his ankle was the shaggy Sinclair dog, Myrtle.

That was another odd occurrence about the Sinclair family. Animals seemed to be overly fond of Wolf. Nicholas's horse was no different. If they were riding together, he was jostling with others to get close to the man.

"I merely slipped out to visit the lending library, Wolf. I am here, safe. Stop fretting."

She shot Nicholas a look on that lie. He kept his gaze impassive.

Her hair was as black as midnight, like the rest of her family's, and if he had to use only one word to describe her, it would be "disturbing."

He'd known hers was a delicate beauty today in that street, even though he couldn't see her as clearly as he could now. In his dreams she had been beautiful too. Like an angel, actually.

He also now knew what she tasted like, and the feel of her pressed to his chest. Neither of these were comforting thoughts.

Christ, she's Wolf's sister.

He of all men had no right to touch such an innocent.

Lush lips and hair, and a sweetly curved body. Her dress was lemon with a satin ribbon beneath her breasts. The perfect dress for a sweet, innocent young lady. Nicholas dragged his eyes away. Her nose was definitely not overlong as he'd first thought.

She was not for the likes of him. Nicholas had to forget about his visions and what had happened today. Nothing would come of it, and he did not want her family alerted to any part of it.

"I am not fretting," her brother gritted out. "I am attempting to explain to you that London is not a safe place. Even your sainted Barty would not like to hear his future wife is gadding about London in such a manner."

She was to be married to someone else! The thought made Nicholas feel slightly queasy, which in turn made him angry. He did not know the woman. Yes, he'd kissed her, and yes, she had a lovely mouth, but that did not mean he wanted anything further to do with her.

"He is not sainted, and I always take care."

Wolf had a strained look around his eyes as he glared at his sister. A captain in the army, now retired, he'd been wounded, and it had taken many months and loving care from his family for him to recover.

"You were my sensible, studious sister. God's blood, you will be the death of me," Wolf growled. "I will again attempt to explain the right way to behave in London—"

"Again?" Alice looked pained. "I could recount this lecture word perfect already. And I *am* studious and sensible, I just wished to visit the lending library."

She lied without blushing. It was a trait her future husband, the sainted Barty, should be aware of, or the woman would make his life a misery.

Nicholas told himself he was relieved she was to marry. That would put her completely from his reach.

"And yet still you have not grasped the concept," her brother growled, sounding like distant thunder.

He was not as well acquainted with Wolf as he was with the others, but he did know that it took a great deal to ruffle his feathers. His sister seemed to have done just that.

Why had Alice Sinclair been in that street today?

"That will do, Wolf. Alice will promise not to go out in the future without informing you of her destination."

Rose was Scottish, and her gruff little burr had not changed in the years she'd resided in London.

"Will she... really?" Wolf glared at his sister. "I'm considering hiring someone to watch her every move, because only then can I really be sure she won't take any more risks."

"You would not dare." The words snapped from Alice's lips in a furious volley. "I don't remember you being this dramatic before leaving Briarwood. Perhaps if you return, your vile humors will be cleansed!" Her hands clenched on her hips as she glared at her brother.

"We are not in Briarwood!" Wolf thundered.

Nicholas had once asked Dev why his family did not wait for privacy to argue rather than air everything in public. The answer had been that there was no privacy in this family, and they only spoke openly with people they trusted. That comment had suggested he was considered family and trusted, which had made Nicholas feel ridiculously pleased.

"You," Wolf jabbed a finger rudely in his sister's face, "will do as you are told. It's hardly surprising Mother said it was like taking off a tight and ill-fitting pair of shoes, arriving in London where I could help her care for you and your sister. The both of you are hoydens."

"Are we?" And just like that, the scowl fell from Alice's lips. "How wonderful. Did you hear that, Kate?"

Her smile transformed her face into a thing of beauty. Nicholas searched hard for a defect... there had to be one. A missing tooth or ill-placed mole? Perhaps she had shocking eating habits? Did she snort when she laughed... no, that wouldn't bother him, his sister did that. There had to be something ugly about her. No one was flawless.

Lord, I hope so.

"I did, and it's something I've always aspired to be," Kate, the younger sister, said. She was fussing with the youngest member of the clan, baby number three for the Duke and Duchess of Raven.

"Do you know, I've only been called bookish and reliable, Wolf. It pleases me that in coming to London it seems I am changing."

Alice's smile made something inside Nicholas's chest tighten. As he had yet to eat, he could not blame it on the food.

"I want your word that you will behave and not leave the house again without someone accompanying you," Wolf demanded. "Or I will tell your beloved of your behavior."

"I wish you would not call him that—"

"You and he have been declaring your love for each other since you were infants." Wolf cut her off, further increasing her discomfort. "What other term should I use?"

"Did Alice tell you Barty is here in London?" The words came from Kate.

Nicholas looked around the room. No one seemed to be paying attention to the discussion between Wolf and his sisters except him. So used to multiple conversations occur-ring at once, they were milling around the table sorting out seats.

"Barty is here? Why has he not called to see you?" Wolf looked confused.

"He is busy." Alice brushed the words aside, but Nicholas

had a feeling there was more to the sainted Barty's absence than she was letting on. And why he knew that, he had no idea. What's more, he didn't care, he reminded himself.

"Too busy to see the woman he professes to love madly?"

"We made that declaration as children, Wolf. Please move on."

"Yes, but you are to wed, so one would hope it still stands."

She was to wed. Nicholas should be extremely happy about that.

"Perhaps we are, but then perhaps not. But I have no wish to continue this discussion, as I am hungry."

"Yes, you're not very pleasant when you need to eat," her brother said in that way siblings did just to be annoying.

"Be quiet, Wolf."

"Very well, shall we continue to address the other matter at hand?"

"I don't want to discuss that anymore either. Now please leave it, brother. I have done nothing wrong, nor have I been anywhere that would concern you." Alice shot Nicholas another look.

He could cause a great deal of trouble right then for Miss Alice Sinclair. He had the power at his fingertips, and the look she shot him suggested she knew that. Those green depths were filled with panic, but she was trying hard not to show it.

"But you will not leave the house unattended again, Alice." Rose nudged her sister-in-law in the side. "Will you?"

The siblings glared at each other, neither ready to yield.

"Will you just say the words, please, Alice. I'm hungry," Kate said.

"Oh, all right," she said with little grace. "Yes, I will tell you in future when I leave the house."

"And you will take someone with you."

"Oh, for pity's sake, all right."

"Uncross your fingers, and I may just believe you," Wolf drawled.

She shot her brother another smile. It was wide and genuine, and Nicholas could imagine that if she flashed that about in society she would have a great many men falling at her feet.

She raised her hands to show her brother her fingers.

"Which does nothing to reassure me."

The standoff was interesting to watch. She wasn't intimidated by the scowl on Wolf's face. Alice Sinclair simply stood inches away from him and folded her arms. He did the same.

Why was she in my vision? Why was she in that street today?

"They've done this often," Kate Sinclair said, drawing his eyes. She was a replica of her sister and had taken the seat to Nicholas's right. "They can stand there like that for hours. Both are as stubborn as the other. Once, I was able to eat all my plum pudding and Alice's and she didn't move, no matter how much I taunted her. I then ate Wolf's."

"You do not challenge your brother, Miss—"

"Kate," she said before he could finish her name. "Oh, I do, just in other ways."

"And I am Nicholas, Lilliana's brother."

"Oh, I know who you are, Nicholas." She had a sweet smile, not quite like her sister's, but pretty nonetheless. "We have heard all about you."

Nicholas wasn't entirely comfortable with hearing that, as his past and present exploits were not fit for a young lady's ears. He hoped whoever had told her had kept his less than stellar traits out of the conversation.

"I should imagine you and Lilly have had your challenging encounters, Nicholas, as all siblings do."

He shot his sister a look. As if sensing him, she turned and smiled. He felt the sharp tug inside his chest he always felt remembering how badly he'd treated her for so many years. He wondered if the shame would ever ease.

"We had our moments" was all he said after acknowledging Lilly.

"Oh, all right," Alice Sinclair said, drawing his gaze once more.

"The words, Alice," Wolf said, unmoving.

"I will also not leave the house without an escort of the human kind."

"Excellent." Wolf grabbed his sister in a hug. She in turn laughed and threw her arms around his neck, hugging him back.

"She's actually the serious one of the three of us."

"Pardon?" Nicholas turned to Kate again.

"Alice. She's usually very serious-minded."

"Surely she is not more serious-minded than your brother?"

"Hard to believe, I know, but it's actually true. She loves books and spends hours scribbling away in her diary and notebooks. The problem usually arises when she wants to do something that Wolf disapproves of."

Nicholas tensed as Alice took the seat across from him, the only free one, which did not please her... or him.

"Which happens a great deal?"

"She likes to learn, so the lending library is a lure for her."

"Surely between all the Raven and Sinclair houses in this street, there is an extensive library?"

"There is, however, she also likes to attend lectures."

"That will do, thank you, Kate, as I am sitting right here and can hear every word you speak. Plus, I'm sure Lord Braithwaite has no wish to hear any more."

Nicholas looked at Alice. "Good evening, Miss Sinclair."

"Call her Alice," Kate said. "And this is Nicholas, Alice."

"Good evening," she said with a tight smile on her face.

39

"And now that matter has been gnawed to death, we shall have the first course," Devonshire Sinclair said.

"Apologies," Wolf told his cousin.

Dev waved a hand down the table. "Think nothing of it. I have four sisters, Wolf; you have my sympathies."

This produced howls of outrage from the Sinclair sisters.

Sinclairs and Ravens didn't do things quietly, it just wasn't in their natures.

"That's a fierce scowl, Nicholas. Care to share your worries?"

"No, thank you, Cambridge, I was just thinking on a matter."

"Clearly it was taxing you."

He was sharp-witted and equally sharp-tongued. Cambridge liked to verbally spar with people constantly.

"I could outthink you in my sleep."

"Come now, we all know that I'm the intelligent Sinclair."

This was followed with more howls of protest.

"Only because they do not want to hurt your feelings," Nicholas drawled.

"Oh, that was a great comeback, Nicholas," Warwick said.

He raised his glass.

"You'll keep, Braithwaite." Cambridge smiled. The man was not easily insulted.

The meal progressed in that vein. Alice didn't contribute much but focused on her food with a great deal of concentration. She had elegant table manners and didn't talk with food in her mouth.

"Are you enjoying your first season, Alice?" He made himself address her. Perhaps with familiarity, they could move past that kiss. Move past that moment today when he'd felt like everything but this woman had ceased to exist.

Damn.

The green eyes were cool as they looked his way.

"I am, thank you."

"No, you are not," Kate said. Nicholas thought he quite liked her at that moment, especially as her sister shot forks of fire at her. "You told me last night it was boring."

"I'm sure Lord Braithwaite has no wish to hear your opinion, or mine for that matter."

"Nicholas, please. And of course I wish to hear them. I asked the question, after all."

"But it was just a polite query," she said, glaring at him.

He wasn't sure why he was the recipient of such a look; after all, he was keeping his silence for her.

"Social conversation," she added.

"We are all family, Alice. Social conversation does not matter here," Kate persisted.

"Exactly." Nicholas smiled at Alice, which he was sure would annoy her further. "We are all family here."

Her eyes narrowed.

His smile widened. "I would like to know why you are finding this season boring, Alice."

She exhaled through her teeth.

"I am suffering through the season as it is my brother's and mother's wish that I do so. Is that enough honesty for you, Nicholas?" She spoke his name deliberately in three syllables.

They were both unsettled and were dealing with that by antagonizing each other.

"You have a great many more events to suffer through," Nicholas pointed out. "As the season has yet to start in earnest."

"I know." That thought did not make her happy.

"But perhaps things will get better as you meet more people?"

"And it's only because your family want what is best for you, dear," Eden said from the end of the table.

"But as she has already set her heart on a man, she believes there is no need for all this."

Kate's words made the food he'd just swallowed settle uncomfortably in his stomach.

This has to stop.

CHAPTER 5

*H*ow was it possible that the man who had held her as if she was made of spun glass was Nicholas Braithwaite, Lilly's brother? For those few brief moments today she'd experienced what some women spoke of. The feeling of belonging to another. The rightness of being in that small space with this man had shocked her.

She'd never experienced that with Barty.

Of all the luck, it had to be him that she'd saved tonight, a bloody Raven by blood. The curse struck again... not that she was telling anyone about it. They would make entirely too much of the incident, considering the history between their families.

"Is something the matter with your soup, Alice?"

"It is excellent, thank you, Lilly."

"You wrinkled your nose."

"Sorry, just thinking."

"Yes, I can see how that would be taxing on you," Wolf added.

No one could annoy her quite like a sibling. But she had one thing over them that made them gnash their teeth, as they could not better her at this particular skill. Alice used it whenever she needed to prove a point. Now was an excellent time to regain her footing and perhaps show the man across from her she was not disturbed by his presence at the dinner table.

"Calculate 9,658 + 4,596 - 254, Wolf." She waited two seconds, then said, "14,000," at the exact time Nicholas Braithwaite gave the same answer.

Shock had her gripping the spoon in her hand. She felt off-balance, as if the floor had tilted slightly without her knowledge. Looking into those dark eyes, she knew he felt the same.

They'd shared a connection today, no matter how much both of them wanted to deny it... and now this. She grappled to regain her composure.

"Oh, the day just improved drastically," Kate declared. "At last someone who can do computations as swiftly as you, sister!"

Wolf laughed, and Alice quickly spooned soup into her mouth to stop from commenting.

"I did not realize your mind worked in such a way, Nicholas," Wolf said.

"Yes, he was extremely vexing to be around whilst we were growing up," Lilly added. "Constantly trotting out numbers that I could not calculate as fast as him."

"Alice does that," Kate said. "It's always annoyed me."

Of course she'd heard snippets about the Marquis of Braithwaite. Overheard Lilliana telling Eden that she was pleased her brother had come into the light after so long in darkness. She'd added that it wouldn't harm him to adjust some of his other rakish ways, but those she could cope with, considering his past. What she hadn't realized at the time was that he would be the man to turn her life on its head.

They'd shared a kiss. And he could calculate numbers in his head like she could!

And lord, what a kiss. In that moment when panic held her in its grip as they'd squeezed into that small space, he had stripped her fear with his touch.

She'd never experienced an emotion like that before. Her body seemed to melt into his as their lips met, and all else was forgotten.

He'd looked at her as if he really saw her, saw deep inside to the yearning and longing she experienced but kept hidden.

When Barty kissed her, which he had done a total of three times, she'd liked it, but there had been none of the emotion she'd experienced today. It had not been uncomfortable, magnificent, and all the other words Alice attached to the kiss she'd shared with Nicholas Braithwaite on her journey home. A journey where she'd been gripped with sadness that she would never see this man again.

As it happened, she'd been wrong. How was she to act like today had not happened?

Looking at his handsome face, composed once again, she wondered if today meant something to him as it had to her? It certainly seemed so at the time, but then she was naive, and he a man of the world. A powerful marquis with a long lineage seeping from his pores.

It was there in the tilt of his head and the large emerald sparkling on his finger. The gold band was old and wide, and the gem set deep. It twinkled as the candlelight caught it.

"I can spell better than Alice," she heard Kate say.

"Spelling is such a handy ability," Cam added.

Alice had been hurrying down that lane to the carriage when she felt the tension inside her climb. She'd seen him then and the hole he was close to stepping in. Alice had to come to his aid, as he would have been seriously injured had she not.

The tension inside her had not eased, but instead gained momentum after she'd saved him; minutes later she'd known why as those men's voices had reached her.

And then he kissed the thoughts from my usually sensible head.

When finally she'd reached Wolf's home, her brother had been waiting. They'd still been arguing when they arrived at Dev's house.

She hadn't told him the truth as to why she'd gone out today, or the previous days, as she'd promised, but she'd wanted to and had still not ruled it out if her search continued to be fruitless.

"Shall we test them to see who is best at calculations?" Eden asked.

"I think not, as it will make us feel woefully inadequate," Cam said, winking at her.

"When did you realize you could calculate large numbers inside your head, Alice?"

His voice was deep and smooth like aged whisky, and as he'd spoken to her she must answer.

"I have been able to do so for as long as I can remember. And you, my lord?"

"Nicholas, and like you, for as long as I can remember."

His hair was a dark chestnut brown, thick with a slight curl that she was sure could be hard to tame. The lines of his face were perfectly formed. Chiseled cheekbones, arrogant nose. But around his eyes were laughter lines that softened the severity of the angles and planes.

"Wolf hates lies," Kate chirped across the table, and Alice realized she'd missed the beginning of that conversation. She needed to stop thinking about Nicholas Braithwaite; nothing could come from her contemplations. He would be in her life now, and she must get used to that until he left it once more.

"As do I," Nicholas said.

"But sometimes lying is the only way to stop people from getting hurt," Alice said before she could stop herself.

"True. And yet surely if it is a lie, then you are hurting people more by not speaking the truth?"

He was talking about what she'd done tonight. But Alice could not speak the truth—she'd promised. She thought about her reply while the plates were cleared and the next course placed before them.

"That is true... in part."

"Which part?" He gave her a small smile. It was nothing special, and nothing like the ones the others in this family used, and yet it made something heavy settle in her chest. Warmth, she realized. Like his kiss, his smile had stirred something inside her.

Stop this!

"Well." Alice rallied her thoughts. "If someone who is dear to you would be upset about hearing the truth, then surely it is better to keep it from them?"

"It would of course depend on the truth. If it is harmless and has no impact on their lives, then yes, I think you could be right. But if not speaking the truth could impact on them in the future, then no."

Alice slowly cut into her beef as she prepared an answer.

"The left one is bigger."

"No, it's is the exact same size as the others," Alice said to Kate, who she knew was deliberately needling her.

"It is not. That one there," Kate leaned over the table and jabbed her fork on the beef, "is smaller."

"Your table manners leave a lot to be desired, sister."

"We are among family, they don't matter," Kate replied.

"Am I missing something?"

Alice looked at Nicholas; his dark brow was raised.

"My sister likes things uniform in her life. Sometimes she will spend a great deal of time cutting her meat into

47

matching shapes and sizes. Things on her dresser are placed in perfect symmetry also."

"Must you share all my faults, Kate?" Alice sighed.

"Of course."

"I do not spend a great deal of time doing it, in fact it barely concerns me—"

"Unless you're tired, then it concerns you greatly. Remember, I have lived with you my entire life. You are perhaps the most practical, sane person I know who has touches of madness," Kate said as if they were discussing the weather instead of her character... or lack thereof.

Nicholas's loud bark of laughter had all eyes focusing on him.

"I'm glad my sisters are entertaining you."

Wolf gave her one of his gentle smiles to take the sting from the argument they had recently had. Her big brother was a wonderful man, and Alice knew she shouldn't worry him as much as she did.

"I was just telling him about Alice's faults, Wolf," Kate said.

"And you managed to get all those out before the meal has ended?"

"Extremely amusing, Cam." Alice poked her tongue out.

When Alice and Kate had arrived in London for her first season, it was to find a large family awaiting them, filled with wonderful people they had never met before. Her mother had exhaled, relieved to hand her daughters into her son's care. She had then gone to visit friends and as yet had not returned.

The sisters had stepped into the family, and it was as if they'd been here their entire lives. Alice loved being part of this... she just wasn't entirely sure that society was the right fit for her. A country girl, she felt awkward and out of place at the few gatherings she attended.

"Nicholas, do you have any words for us?" Dorrie called, drawing everyone's eyes and Alice from her thoughts.

"I do. Spell jargoyle. I want an explanation of the word also."

He hadn't raised his voice but it carried to all corners of the room.

Alice looked to the twins, Warwick, and Samantha. No longer children, but young adults, they were extremely intelligent like the rest of their family and loved to be challenged. Their heads were now pressed together as they conferred.

"You may have them there," Dev said. "It's not a word used in daily conversation, and one I doubt they'd found in books."

"I read an old book on words not often used anymore. I knew it would come in handy with your siblings."

His eyes were as black as midnight. Deep and fathomless.

"Jargoyle, and it means to confuse or jumble, and I believe goes back to the seventh century," Warwick said before his sisters or Samantha could utter a word.

"Believe? Come now, Warwick, that is not good enough," Cam taunted his youngest brother.

"I would rather you did not jargoyle my thoughts, Cam," Warwick said, winking.

"Excellent, I had thought that one may be harder. How about ludibrious?"

He picked up his wine, and the large emerald winked at her. Had many Lord Braithwaites worn it before him?

"Cam would understand this word."

Nicholas snorted as Dorrie spoke.

"Ludibrious is to be the focus of everyone's jokes," she added.

"Why, you little—" Cam's next words were drowned out by a shriek as he lunged at his little sister. She was soon being tickled mercilessly.

"'Tis their way," she said to Nicholas.

"I know that, thank you, Alice."

Of course he did, he'd known these people longer than she had.

Alice watched the antics as the other siblings joined in. "They are quite wonderful."

He didn't agree or disagree.

"I call Jack Straws, in Spanish!" Warwick Sinclair suddenly cried.

It was a testament to how much time she'd spent with these people that Alice didn't flinch. At home in the country, it had been just the three Sinclair women, and they'd lived a quiet life for the most part. Here there were many more, and these games were a daily occurrence.

She looked at the man seated across from her, but he didn't seem confused as to what was happening.

"Only because it's your favorite game," Max said.

"I'll take Jack," Alice said.

"I'll take Straws," Lord Braithwaite added.

"Mine will be in German," she said, for some reason needing to best him. Needing to gain control of the entire situation. Alice liked to have control.

She'd kissed this man, and that was playing havoc with her peace of mind.

"Wonderful," he replied, as if everyone spoke German as a daily occurrence. "I shall state mine in Russian."

"Excellent." There was a snap to her word. Damn, Alice had never learned Russian. She would be sure to change that.

She flicked each finger slowly. His eyes, which had been focused on Warwick, turned back to look at her fingers, and the breath lodged in her throat.

"I believe finger flicking is the sign of a troubled mind, Miss Sinclair, or so I've been led to believe. Care to share your worries?"

Bloody hell.

"I have nothing troubling me, thank you, Lord Braithwaite, it is merely a habit." Alice was proud of how calm she sounded.

"Stop delaying and play the game, Alice!" Warwick shouted down the table.

"Julius acknowledges Caesar's kindness," Alice said slowly, wishing she hadn't chosen German, as it was definitely not her strong language.

"Well done." Kate clapped, as did the others. Alice nodded, and waited. She had no doubt this man was intelligent and the challenge would present him no problem, but the small, mean part inside her wished it did.

"Shakespeare talks rambling anecdotal words sweetly."

His Russian was flawless and rolled off the tongue. Cad! "That made no sense," Alice said. "Shakespeare is never anecdotal."

"Oh, it's meant to make sense, I hadn't realized." The look he sent her made heat color her cheeks.

"That was brilliant, Nicholas."

"Thank you, Warwick."

"I think he got the better of you there, Alice," James said.

"I can accept defeat." She even managed a smile, but it didn't meet her eyes.

"But it is not comfortable on you, as you are flicking your fingers again, Alice."

Damn.

CHAPTER 6

"*I* often flick my fingers. A simple habit, and one I have done my entire life whilst thinking. Apologies if it is upsetting you, my lord."

"It does not upset me, I assure you."

"You lived with Lilly after all," Dev added. "She has many peculiar habits."

"I do not!"

"Of course you do, my love."

"Everyone has faults, Lord Braithwaite," Alice said, drawing his eyes again.

"I did not suggest finger flicking was a fault, Miss Sinclair, please forgive me if you believe I did." Nicholas knew they were antagonizing each other because of that kiss.

Both were still off-balance and trying not to show it.

"Are you always stuffy?" She asked.

"I beg your pardon?"

"A simple question, I thought."

"On the basis of a few minutes in my company, you've ascertained I'm stuffy?"

He hadn't been stuffy when he'd held her lovely body pressed to his earlier.

"I'm intuitive."

"Loosely interpreted, I understand that means nosey?" His smile was insincere.

"He has you there, Alice," Kate crowed.

"I am not nosey!"

"Says who?" Wolf scoffed. "You have to know everything that everyone is doing from the minute you open your eyes."

"We're not talking about me." Her frown was fierce, black brows almost in a line now. "I asked you a question. Have you always been stuffy?"

"Have you always been impetuous?" Nicholas shot back. Did she not realize that with a few words he could ruin her evening by informing her brother where he'd found her?

"I asked first."

He hesitated... just long enough for Cambridge to join the conversation.

"Actually, he is not stuffy at all. In fact, he's something of a legend in society for his gilded words and flattering speech, especially among the ladies. I should imagine he is merely on his best behavior now."

"You make me sound like a glib-tongued popinjay, Cambridge." Nicholas was uncomfortable with this description of his character.

Yes, he liked women and was polite to everyone he met— especially those he had once treated abysmally—but he was never overtly effusive.

"A legend is rarely a popinjay, Nicholas. My words were flattery, I assure you, considering how unpleasant you once were."

"Thank you, I believe that will do," Nicholas said, hoping Cambridge listened, but it was a faint hope at best.

"Unpleasant how?" Kate asked.

Looking across the table, he encountered Alice's eyes. She must have seen something in his, and suddenly there was a smile that made warmth spread through his chest.

"I don't want to know about boring Lord Braithwaite anyway. I was just teasing him. Now tell me instead what happened at *The Trumpeter* today, Cam. I'm thinking I will write an article for your unusual happenings section."

"Are you really? If it is good enough, we shall certainly publish it."

"Of course it will be good enough," she bragged.

She'd drawn Cambridge's fire as they discussed the newspaper he owned.

He gave her a small nod. She smiled again.

Nicholas watched as she played with the stem of her glass. Her fingers were long and slender, the nails rounded.

What had put her in that street today? Why would she take that risk when Wolf had forbidden her to do so?

Any one of these people would care for this woman in whatever capacity she needed. Her brother would move heaven and earth to see her safe... so why then was she there alone?

Nicholas had no wish to expose her, and yet he also could not turn his back. If anything should happen to her, he would not be blameless. Therefore, he needed to ensure she did not walk about alone in such a place again. But what he needed to do first was to find her reasons for being there.

Is she in some kind of trouble?

Nicholas ate and talked and thought about how he would approach her. So much lay between them now. They must move past that.

When the meal was finished, they made for a parlor where the twins, Samantha, and Warwick would entertain them with music.

"Talk to them about today, Nicholas." Max moved to his

side. "They know people and could help with this. I doubt it is something you can deal with alone."

Two somethings, actually.

He could not discuss Alice, but he could discuss what he had been told by his housekeeper.

"A problem shared is a problem halved," Max added.

"So I've heard."

"Do you have a problem, Nicholas?" Cam asked.

"I believe I may, but as yet do not have absolute proof."

"Good enough for us. We work on gut feeling constantly in this family."

"Whereas I work on facts."

"And yet?" Dev said.

"And yet I have a feeling something is wrong," Nicholas said slowly as he thought through what he wanted to say.

"I tend to agree with him," Max said. "After seeing that woman and her clear discomfort, I think Nicholas may have a point. I'm just not sure to what degree yet either."

"What woman?" Dev asked.

Nicholas told them about his housekeeper and her daughter then. About his meeting with Mr. and Mrs. Adley.

"And you believe she was nervous?" Dev questioned.

"I do. Her knuckles turned white where they gripped the door."

"Which could simply be that you are a peer and she was intimidated by your magnificence," Cam added.

"Unlikely."

"He intimidated me when he dealt with her husband," Max drawled.

"Did he, by jove? I have not seen this side of him as yet, but I did hear a rumor."

"From who?" Nicholas demanded, glaring at Cam.

"Lady Belinda told Eden that she had heard from the Countess of Ripley that you threatened her husband if he laid a hand on her again in anything but reverence, he would be answering to you."

He had said those words when he'd found her weeping the day he visited her husband to discuss purchasing a piece of land he owned. She'd had a vivid bruise on her cheek.

"He deserved it."

"Undoubtedly. It's my hope you scared him witless. Man's a bully and a fool, a lethal combination, and not in a good way," James said, joining the conversation.

"But what purpose would a midwife have to tell a woman her child is born dead when he's not?" Cam asked. "That is surely a heinous crime?"

"You of all people know what some are capable of when motivated by greed, Cam," Nicholas said. "I was one of them."

"Was, but no longer are. We see that, Nicholas; perhaps it is time for you to also."

Perhaps one day he would.

"There are those who want an heir and can't have them," Dev added. "Some people will go to great lengths to have a son."

"But to break the heart of a mother—"

"Many are governed by greed and status, Cam."

"I realize that, Dev, but what I want to know is why you believe there is truth behind your housekeeper's words, Nicholas. Surely she was emotional, having just lost a grandchild," Cam added.

What did he tell them? *I had a dream about the baby*. They would think he was mad.

"My housekeeper is a sensible woman with a sturdy soul. She is not the type to become emotional for no reason."

"How is it you know this about her? She is, after all, your housekeeper?" James asked.

Max started laughing softly. He knew the answer.

"What?" Cam asked.

"I play cards with my staff for splinters of wood. I have learned much about them in this time."

"Do you really? My, how you have changed." Cam smiled. "For the better."

Nicholas remained silent.

"Tell them the rest," Max said.

"I don't think—"

"I do, and they will understand, trust me."

"What are you not telling us?" Dev asked.

"It is a little complicated." Nicholas went for honesty.

"Nicholas," Cam sighed. "Complicated is the Sinclair/Raven motto. We thrive on it."

"I would really rather not—"

"Does it cast you in a bad light?"

"It could."

"Excellent. You've been a bloody saint for years now, it's time you did something to tarnish your reputation once more."

"I am hardly that, Cambridge."

"A rake, yes, but a good one for all that."

"I have much to atone for," Nicholas said, sounding stuffy.

"As do we all, but as we have forgiven you," Dev said, "and your sister loves you, then perhaps it is time to forgive yourself."

Could he?

"Yes. Holding on to all that poison cannot be healthy for a person," Cam said.

"Enough on that, let's hear about what else is bothering you," Wolf said.

"I have these dreams... more like visions, actually."

Suddenly Wolf, James, Dev, and Cam were alert. Eyes focused entirely on Nicholas.

"They tell me things."

"What kinds of things?" Cam fired the words at him,

having lost all of his usual jocularity. He was now deadly serious.

"Truths, things that are about to happen or have happened. Do any of you have dreams like this?"

They shook their heads.

"Then we shall leave the matter there." He felt foolish for raising it now.

"Good lord, is it possible, Dev?"

"I don't know... I mean, that's not the same, and yet it would suggest he is in his own way. And considering Lilly...."

"Tell us about the dream you had that led you to believe the child is alive," Dev asked him after he and Cam had confused him with their words.

"I did not say I believed the child is alive, Cam."

"You would not have gone to see that woman if you did not believe there was a grain of truth in what your house-keeper said, Nicholas."

True.

"Let's hear it." Dev waved a hand at him.

"I saw a baby swaddled. It was being held by a woman." He swallowed, not wanting to disclose exactly who that was. "Ah... the thing is...." There was no way he could say this without sounding a fool, so he simply said it. "The baby conveyed to me that it wasn't dead, and that I should find it."

"Conveyed to you how?" Cam asked. He did not look as if he was about to bundle Nicholas off to the nearest asylum; in fact, he looked deadly serious.

"Through the woman who held it."

Dev's eyes had suddenly changed, they were so bright it was almost hard to look at them, and his pupils were dilated.

"Dev?"

"His color is normal."

"Pardon?"

"I don't smell anything on him, no alcohol or any other substance."

"I beg your pardon?" Nicholas glared at Cam after these words. "I no longer drink to excess, nor do I inhale anything."

He had once however, and Cambridge Sinclair had been caught up in Nicholas's web of greed and self-destruction. It was still a miracle to him that the man had forgiven him.

Cam shot him a small smile. "Apologies, I had to check."

"What?"

A look passed between Cam and Dev.

"He would never tell; besides, no one would believe him," Wolf said.

James and Max simply stood, silently listening to the Sinclairs.

"We will need to discuss it with the others, but Lilly has been wanting to tell him for years."

"Tell me what?" Nicholas was getting angry now. "You are talking in circles, and I have no idea why."

"They constantly speak like that," James said. "Have you ever thought there was something different about them, Nicholas?"

"Other than you're entirely addled and have no idea how to conform to society's rules, do you mean?"

"Other than that." Dev smiled.

"There are one or two things that I find odd," Nicholas conceded.

"Excellent. We shall discuss this no further tonight, but soon. For now we will think on this matter you have broached. If it is true, then a heinous and grave crime has been committed and it must be rectified," Dev added. "My fear is that it is not the first child to have been taken from its mother."

"What have you been whispering furtively about?"

"All will be revealed, Lilly, my love." Dev dropped down beside her on the sofa.

Nicholas sat, unsure what had just happened, and around him others gathered like hens settling in to roost. Cam on the arm of Emily's chair. Dev lowered his arm around Lilly, and Wolf sat with Rose at his side.

Connected, Nicholas thought. They always made those they loved aware they were close. Aware that they were loved. *Did he ever want that feeling?* He refrained from looking at Alice Sinclair.

CHAPTER 7

"Come, we are ready for our performance." Alice looked to the doorway where Samantha had appeared. "It will be brilliant."

"So modest, sister." James laughed.

Alice listened as Dev spoke with Nicholas as they once again regained their feet to walk to the music room.

"We will discuss this more later, especially the visions, as your sister will want to speak on the matter." Dev clapped Nicholas on the shoulder. "Fear not, we shall get to the bottom of this other matter."

"It is for me to investigate, but I would appreciate any input."

"Why is it for you to investigate? Do you believe you alone have been chosen to do so?"

"No... yes." Nicholas sighed. "I'm not sure what I believe— or understand, for that matter. Only that I must do something with what has been presented to me."

"And you will, and we will assist you as best we can."

Alice watched Nicholas look around the room after the

conversation with Dev. She tried not to stiffen when he elected to take the seat next to her on the sofa.

She decided to speak first. "Did you speak with the midwife after we met earlier?" The words were spoken out the side of her mouth so only he could hear.

"I did, but I'm not sure how you heard that conversation from across the room."

"I have excellent hearing. I'm pleased your housekeeper had someone to speak to. Will you tell me about your visions?"

"No. Will you tell me why you were in that lane tonight?"

"No."

"Let me rephrase that. Tell me why you were in that lane tonight."

"No."

His eyes were facing forward, watching her family perform. Dorrie and Samantha playing violins, Warwick the cello. Somer playing the piano.

"Your brother quite clearly has no idea where you were, or it's my belief his reaction would have been a great deal more severe. The lending library, I believe was your falsehood."

"This is none of your concern, my lord."

She couldn't tell him about Barty. Couldn't tell him, as she had yet to tell her family.

"I have no wish to alert him of course, but if something were to happen to you while you were in such a place, I would be a guilty party as I had knowledge of your location—"

"Are you threatening me with exposure if I do not tell you why I was in that lane... saving you from certain death, this evening?"

Alice's words were now a furious whisper.

"Come now, certain death? I'll have you know I'm agile as a cat. I would have survived that fall."

"And what of those men? Would you have survived that attack also?"

"Very likely."

"How conceited of you to think—"

"Just tell me why you were there, Alice. Are you in some kind of trouble? Perhaps I can help if you feel you cannot approach your family."

"No."

"Then I must speak with your brother, as I owe this family a great deal and would never harbor a secret of such magnitude from them."

She turned and looked at him. He did the same, his dark eyes steady on her face. This was a disconcerting man. A man who could easily make a woman forget a rational thought, as he had today. His eyes went to her mouth, and her lips tingled. She knew what his kiss felt like.

"What do you owe them?" Alice asked, hoping the change in subject would stop him asking her questions. It didn't work.

"That is neither here nor there. The matter at hand is why you were in that lane at such an hour."

"It was not late."

"Late enough to be dark, and you were alone, which you should not have been at any time of the day. Anyone could have come upon you and...." His words fell away.

"Taken advantage of me?"

"Forgive me for what transpired in that lane today, Alice."

"Forgive me also," she said quietly.

"No, it was my fault alone." His face looked grave.

"Because you are experienced in... in areas of life and I am not, what happened must therefore be your fault? How magnanimous of you to take the entire blame."

"Are you mocking me?" He looked down his noble nose at her, and Alice knew it was the look he used to quell those he believed needed subduing. She was immune. Her brother tried that look on her regularly.

"Yes."

"I am apologizing." The words were clipped and said under his breath.

"By taking the blame for what happened, yes, I understand that. But I was equally to blame for what took place today."

"It can never happen again."

She nodded, yet inside, the part of her that had been awoken today wept.

"Please tell me why you were in that lane today, Alice?"

"Will you tell Wolf?"

He was silent for too long, which told Alice all she needed to know. He would tell Wolf. The man clearly had an annoying sense of honor.

"You cannot expect me to hold something from him if you are recklessly throwing yourself into danger."

"I am not recklessly throwing myself into danger. Do I look like the sort of person to do such a thing? Good lord, I cut my meat into matching squares and calculate large numbers for enjoyment."

"I'm not sure what that has to do with anything? Do people who like symmetry and calculations not take risks then?"

"My point is that I'm not reckless."

"Your brother clearly thinks so."

"I wish you would be quiet and let the matter alone."

Her words surprised him.

"Clearly you are not used to people speaking in such a manner to you, Lord Braithwaite."

"You live in this family, Miss Sinclair. Surely you know they would and do speak that way regularly to me."

"And yet my words surprised you, which would suggest you are not used to women such as I speaking that way, then."

"You cannot know that about me." He looked annoyed.

"Cam said you are glib-tongued and women worship you but rarely censure you."

"What has that to do with anything?" His brows were drawn together now. "We are straying from the point, which is your behavior."

"Will you sing for us, Alice, with Eden... please?"

"Gladly!" Alice leapt out of her seat and away from the disturbing Lord Braithwaite and his demand to know why she had been in that lane today. She would not tell him and doubted he would speak with Wolf. For now, she was safe.

Looking at the large, dark male, she didn't know for how long, however.

"I shall play, and Eden will stand and look beautiful," Alice said, taking a seat at the piano.

"Thank you, darling, but you are the beautiful one. I've had children, can you not see the gray hairs and lines?" the duchess drawled, moving to stand beside Alice.

"There is little doubting her beauty has dimmed, it's true," Cambridge said.

"Positively whey-faced," Essex Huntington, Eden's sister said.

"Don't listen to them, darling. You're as stunning as the day I first saw you," the duke assured.

Alice fussed with the music as she thought about what he'd said to her. *It can never happen again.* He was right, of course. She was no trollop to carry on as she had with a man who was not her husband, but there was also little doubt she felt drawn to Nicholas Braithwaite in some way.

Distance, Alice realized. From now on, she would need to keep away from him.

"We shall begin," Samantha declared grandly, interrupting Alice's thoughts. "Ready?"

She nodded.

With her hearing, she could detect each note clearly, and knew if an instrument needed tuning or if a person hit the wrong key.

Her eyes shot to Nicholas Braithwaite; he was looking at her, his dark eyes focused intently on her face. She could read nothing in his expression.

"You sing too," Eden whispered, and of course Alice heard.

Alice knew that together they sounded good, possibly better than good, and the faces of her family and Nicholas Braithwaite told her that was the case. The applause at the end confirmed it.

"And now I must depart, but thank you for a lovely evening."

Alice exhaled slowly as Nicholas got to his feet to say his goodbyes.

"Good evening, Miss Sinclair, and thank you, I enjoyed the musical interlude."

"Good evening, my lord." She acknowledged his bow with a curtsey.

"I will expect an answer when next we meet." He whispered the words, and then he was gone, leaving the room in a purposeful stride not dissimilar to her brother's. They weren't men who strolled or dallied, they went from A to Z, and never stopped at B on the way. Alice sometimes wished she had a purpose.

She listened as Nicholas spoke to Dev outside the room.

"Any investigating you undertake, I would suggest you do so quietly, Nicholas, so as not to rouse anyone's interest. If there is something nefarious afoot, then it is the worst kind of depravity to do such thing to a woman who has carried that child for nine months."

"Aye, and they must be found and dealt with."

"Agreed. Good evening, brother."

Dev returned.

"I have something to discuss with you all. Alice and Eden likely know what that is, so they'll have to sit through me explaining it to the others," he said, taking the tea Lilly handed him as the family settled around him.

"I saw you deep in discussion," Essex said.

"Lilly, my love, has your brother ever exhibited any signs like yours? Anything unusual that would suggest he has a gift of some kind as we do?"

"I don't think so. Why do you ask, Dev?" She looked perplexed.

"Nothing at all? I need you to think about this, love."

Everyone was silent while Lilly thought.

"In later years, as most of you know, Nicholas and I had a tense and unloving relationship. I spent no time with him, but as children we were close. There were a few times when he would say something to me and I would wonder how he knew." Lilly frowned. "But I have not thought about those moments again until now."

What had kept the siblings apart?

"Why are you asking me this, Dev? Is it possible you believe he has some kind of gift? Surely I would have realized?"

"And yet he is not aware of yours, love."

Lilly could heal with the touch of her hands. It was a rare and amazing thing to see, but she did not do it often, as it took a toll on her strength.

"You're right, of course, but Nicholas...." Her words fell away, and Alice could see she'd remembered something.

"Nicholas would have been about eleven when our father told us one of the daughters of a tenant was found dead in the stream. Her father blamed a nobleman who lived in the village, stating he'd drowned the girl after he'd abused her. Apparently he was quite fixated with her. Father said the nobleman refuted that claim vehemently. Being of noble birth himself, he believed the man, as they had been acquaintances for some time."

"Noblemen always stick together," Cam said.

"The following day," Lilly continued, "Nicholas told our father that he wanted him to question the farmer who owned the land the river was on, as he believed the nobleman was guilty."

"And was he?" Dev asked.

"At first Father wanted to know why, but Nicholas simply said it must be done and that if he did not then he was doing the dead girl and her family a grave injustice. Eventually Father gave in and spoke to the farmer."

"It was brave of Nicholas to speak up and your father to do as he asked," James said.

"Our father was a good man, and he said later that Nicholas had no reason to lie about the matter. It turned out the farmer who owned the land had been too scared to speak up for fear of retribution from the noble families in the area. Father said he would ensure that didn't happen, and the man bore witness that he'd seen the nobleman drown the girl."

"Did you ask Nicholas how he knew, Lilly?" Wolf asked.

"I did, he simply said he just did."

More silence while everyone digested this piece of information.

"Good lord, he's one of us. It hardly seems possible." Eden broke the silence.

"I think visions come to him in his sleep, visions that are the truth," Dev said. "What has been, or what is to be."

"Good lord." Lilly fell back into her chair, stunned. "That must be disconcerting. I wonder how he has coped with that all these years?"

"Perhaps they could be part of the reason for what he became?" Cam said, frowning.

"Good lord," Lilly said again, looking stunned.

"And he is of my blood and yours," James said. "Another one." He sighed. "We shall keep him away from Kate and Alice going forward, as tradition would suggest he'll wed one of you!"

Everyone laughed; Alice's was forced. They would never know what had happened between her and Nicholas Braithwaite in that lane today. She would make sure of it, as would he.

It can never happen again.

CHAPTER 8

"My lord, if you have a moment?"

Looking up from his morning paper, Nicholas watched his housekeeper approach. Her face appeared to have aged in the last week. Sadness and anxiety were etched in every line.

"Of course, Mrs. Potter." Lowering the paper, he nodded for her to continue.

"I talked to my Jane again as you suggested. She is adamant she heard her child crying."

"Could you describe the man who took the child away, Mrs. Potter?"

"I only got a glimpse of him, as I wanted to get back to my Jane. But he was big, bullish I would say if I was describing him. And mean... it upset me that he was holding the b-babe."

He gave her a moment to compose herself.

"And you say the midwife said the baby was badly deformed, Mrs. Potter?"

"Yes."

"And your family believed her?"

"You have to understand they were distraught with grief,

my lord, after the midwife delivered the news. They were not thinking clearly. It all happened so fast."

Which Nicholas just bet whoever had taken that child was relying on.

"Of course, your family have my deepest sympathies, Mrs. Potter. If there is anything I can do for them, then please let me know."

The worn face seemed to crumple.

"It's very g-good of you."

"There is something you wish for?" Nicholas did not like tears. They made him feel helpless, a very uncomfortable emotion as far as he was concerned.

"I-I cannot ask, but thank you."

Nicholas was out of his chair as she turned to go.

"What is it? Tell me, please?"

He had played cards with Mrs. Potter for the last two years, and she had a lively wit and shrewd mind. But now her shoulders were bowed and her face lined with grief; he did not like to see her this way.

"Come, Mrs. Potter, you must tell me what else is distressing you."

"It's my son-in-law, Bill. He was late to work yesterday as he was comforting my Jane, as she's n-not recovering as quickly as she ought. Today he lost his job because of it."

People, Nicholas realized, were extremely cruel. He knew that, as he'd once been one of them.

"Because he missed an hour or two at work?"

She nodded.

"What does he do?"

"Works with horses, my lord."

"Have him come here when he can. I shall speak with him and see if there is a place for him in my stables."

She cried then, pressing the back of her hand to her mouth.

"I-I cannot thank you enough."

"If he is a hard worker, then it will be me who is grateful to you."

His butler chose that moment to appear.

"Mrs. Potter is unwell and needs to see to her family. She will not be here for the remainder of the day. I assume the household will cope?"

"Of course, my lord."

"Look after her, Hopkins. And when she returns tomorrow, she will have her son-in-law with her. I wish to meet with him," Nicholas said softly, so only his butler heard.

"I will ensure it happens, my lord. Come, Mrs. Potter, we shall see you home."

After they'd gone, Nicholas sat and stared at his plate.

Was it possible someone was stealing children? Nicholas knew most things were possible, but something as depraved as this... had human nature sunk so low?

Deciding that he needed to do something, he called for his horse and left the house minutes later. He would go to the watch and speak with someone about his concerns. It would be a start.

The journey to the watch house was not overly long. He nodded to several people as he rode through the busy streets.

As he approached one of the more popular roads for shopping, Nicholas saw a pretty pink ribbon fluttering under the chin of a lady. She appeared to be watching two young men swagger by. At her side was another woman, who he thought was her maid.

Nothing unusual in that, this was, after all, Bond Street, the place to be seen. However, a trickle of awareness told him to take a closer look. She turned, as if sensing him, and he saw it was Kate Sinclair.

Nicholas pulled his horse to a halt.

"Good morning, Kate."

"Hello, Nicholas." She tipped her head back to look at him.

"Are you here alone?"

Nicholas dismounted and moved to stand before her.

"Did you see those men prancing down the street, Nicholas? Quite a sight, don't you think?"

Definitely nervous.

"I did, and they looked foolish, but then you are standing on Bond Street, and it is the place to be seen."

"Is it really?" Her eyes shot right to a men's fashion establishment.

"Are you here with Wolf?"

"No. Good lord, look at that bonnet!"

He didn't, instead keeping his eyes on her.

"Surely you are not here alone, Kate?"

"Not exactly."

"Then who, exactly, is with you?"

"Alice."

"And where is she?"

She exhaled loudly.

"Kate."

"Oh, very well. In there." She pointed to the right.

"She's in a men's fashion establishment? Is she perhaps purchasing a gift?"

"No."

"Wanting to take up wearing breeches?"

"No again."

Looking around him, Nicholas found a young boy milling nearby. Waving him over, he handed out a few coins and asked him to hold his horse.

"I shall return shortly."

"Where are you going?" Kate looked worried.

"Inside the shop."

"I am her lookout. She will not be happy if you do."

"Why is she in there?"

"Barty. We came upon him while we were out strolling."

"Why do I not believe you were out strolling without a reason?"

Her sigh was loud. "How is it you know us so well on such a short acquaintance?"

"Behave while I retrieve your sister."

"I always behave."

"The sensible sister, then?"

Her smile was sly. "I wouldn't go that far."

Snorting, Nicholas left her to enter Tetley's, a place he often frequented.

Why he was concerning himself with the Sinclair sisters' activities when his intent had been to avoid one of them, he wasn't sure, but he was, and especially after finding Alice in that lane... alone.

"Good day to you, Lord Braithwaite."

Nicholas nodded to the proprietor, who stood behind a counter.

"How may I help you today?"

"There is a woman in here. I wish to speak with her."

"It's most unusual, you understand, to have them in here." The man didn't look pleased.

"Perhaps she is purchasing a gift?"

"Perhaps." The man looked doubtful.

"I will do my best to remove her for you."

He nodded, then pointed to a room off this one. Nicholas headed that way, and as he approached, he heard Alice's raised voice.

"She is concerned, Barty, and surely has every right to be."

He found her behind a cabinet. Her back was to him, which allowed him to study the man she spoke to without her realizing it.

Sweating, red eyes, and there was a faint odor of alcohol

coming from him. If Nicholas was not mistaken, the man was in the grip of a ripping hangover, or was ill. He went for the former, as he had personal experience of the condition.

Not overly tall, the sainted Barty was of a solid build and had a pleasant face. Nicholas disliked him immediately and had no wish to delve into the reasons why. Especially as they all likely centered on the woman before him.

"I am a man and can do as I wish, Alice. My actions are of no concern to you or my sister. I shall return to Briarwood when I am ready, just as I will wed you when I am ready!"

Her gloved hands were clenched into fists at her sides, and anger held her rigid. Nicholas wished he could see the fire in those green eyes.

"Don't you dare dismiss me in such a way. You are behaving in a selfish manner, Bartholomew. And let me assure you of this: I will never wed a man with so little respect for himself and his family!"

"I will not be dictated to by you... a woman."

"A friend," Alice ground out. "A friend who is worried because you are draining your family's coffers dry." Her voice was a low, angry growl now.

"How dare you discuss such a thing with me, Alice Sinclair, and in public. Your brother needs to teach you some manners, and were I to wed you—"

"Which you never will," Alice interrupted him.

Nicholas acknowledged the words made him happy but had no right to.

"Then there is nothing further to be said between us. Good day, Miss Sinclair."

Nicholas stepped to one side as the no longer sainted Barty stormed around Alice and by him, then out the door. She didn't move or watch.

"Brainless, addlepated fool."

"Very possibly, but more importantly, why are you

standing in a men's fashion establishment with a man and no companion?"

She'd spun to face him as he began to talk, and Nicholas could see she was upset. Her face was tight, eyes bright with unshed tears, and her fingers were now flicking furiously.

"I'm sorry if he upset you, Alice."

Sweet, innocent, and far too disturbing for Nicholas's peace of mind, she looked as any proper young lady should, in a cream dress with lavender ribbons.

"What are you doing in here, Nicholas?"

"Shopping."

She looked around her.

"Oh well... yes, well I shall leave you to that then." She bobbed a curtsey and prepared to walk around him. Nicholas had other ideas, stepping in front of her.

"Are you and your beloved having a tiff?"

"That is none of your concern, my lord." She had herself under control once more.

She was close, so close he could watch the rapid rise and fall of her chest. Perhaps not in total control, Nicholas realized.

"Step aside, please. My sister and maid await me outside."

"And yet you were in here with a man. Did you think that a wise thing to do, Alice?"

"Very likely not, but it was a necessity, and again I would like you to keep this... this incident to yourself."

"It seems I am to keep a great many things concerning you from your brother's ears. What do I get in return?"

"I don't think two things is a great many." She raised her chin. This woman would never admit to anything. She had backbone, and he had no doubt that sometimes that was to her detriment.

"This would be a good color on you." She pointed to a bolt of fabric. The color was a hideous mustard. "Mud brown and horse excrement green are the rage this season, I believe."

Before he could answer her, she'd picked up the bolt of fabric and slapped it into his chest, then stormed past him and out the door. Replacing the fabric, he followed, catching up with her outside on the street.

"Again, you are behaving in a reckless manner, Alice. One wonders when you will learn from your mistakes."

"I was not being reckless. My sister was keeping watch. Furthermore, my actions are no concern of yours, my lord."

"Yet it was I who found you... again."

"Again?" Kate said as they reached her side.

"I have no idea what he's talking about. And why did you tell him where I was, Kate?" Alice gave her sister a fiery look now.

"He's persistent."

"I'm not sure why." Alice glared at him. "But it doesn't matter, as we are going to *The Trumpeter* now."

A carriage pulled up beside them. Nicholas opened the door.

"Good day, Nicholas."

"Good day, Kate."

The maid followed her inside, and then he was left standing with Alice. She made him feel like a cat with his hair brushed the wrong way.

"Show more caution, Alice, I beg of you. I ask this of you as a friend of your family."

Could they be friends when all he could think about was ravishing her? Friends were all they could ever be, Nicholas reminded himself.

He took her hand to help her into the carriage.

"I do not do this deliberately, my lord. It is something I must do... to help an old friend."

"You speak of Bartholomew?"

She nodded.

His fingers tightened around hers as she moved closer to take the step up into the carriage.

"Ask for help then. If not of your brother, one of the others, or me."

Her eyes caught and held his.

"I cannot, as I have promised another."

"Promised another what?"

Before he could question her further, she was inside. Short of following or lifting her back out, there was little Nicholas could do but shut the door behind her.

He stepped back to watch the carriage drive away.

Retrieving his horse, he headed to the watch house, thinking about the dilemma that was Alice Sinclair. He didn't want to spend time in her company, but he didn't want her in danger. Did he dare speak with Wolf on the matter?

Twice now he'd found her alone in places she should not be. Granted, this was not as bad as the last one, but still, she could not keep blithely ignoring society's rules, or eventually someone would realize, and her reputation would be in tatters.

He would leave it for now, but if he heard she had left the house alone again, he would no longer stay silent.

He directed his horse to the watch house, where hopefully he would find someone who did not have him feeling like one minute he was standing on his head and the next his feet.

CHAPTER 9

$\mathcal{A}$ lice sat on her bed and read the letter that had just arrived from her friend Verity. It was the third such one, but this more desperate than the last two.

Verity was Barty's sister, and Alice had been close with the Stillwater siblings since her adolescence.

My dearest friend, I write to you with my worries again as there is no one else, and I know you love Barty as I do. I must implore you again to keep the contents of this letter a secret. It has been almost three months now without word from my brother, and our mother is distraught. Our fears have deepened upon the arrival on our doorstep of Barty's old school friend. He encountered him in London and said he feared he is gambling excessively and knows Barty has lost a great deal of money. As you understand our circumstances, dear Alice, you know our situation cannot afford him to do that.

"Oh, Barty." Alice sighed.

He would never leave us so long unless he has been led astray. I fear the worst now. Drinking, gambling, and spending his money on things that he shouldn't, Alice. What is to be done?

Alice knew that Verity wasn't prone to exaggeration. The

siblings were quiet, serious-minded individuals, so this behavior from Bartholomew Stillwater was out of character. Just as his behavior to her in that men's fashion establishment had been. He was a man who loved his family and would never want them to worry over him.

She read the last few lines of the letter.

Our suppliers have not been paid, Alice. They have told me they cannot go on in this vein unless some kind of recompense is made.

Barty had professed his love for Alice years ago, and at the time she thought she reciprocated. Alice had always feared that marriage would expose her heightened senses and see her shunned or worse. Barty did not know about her differences, but she doubted he would notice them either, and perhaps that was why she had felt comfortable enough to one day be his wife.

Alice hadn't believed herself one of those women who would find love. She'd want companionship and a friend who would eventually one day be an excellent father.

A memory of a searing kiss slipped into her head. That, she knew, was passion. But it was not for her. A comfortable life was a better option, but now she wondered if that was even a possibility.

"I want to box your ears, Barty," Alice muttered, looked down at Verity's desperate words again. How dared he put his family through this.

After Verity's first letter, Alice had sent word to Barty's lodgings, but there had been no reply. She then asked her brother's driver to stop outside and listened. Leaving the carriage when she'd thought she had heard his voice a short distance away, Alice had walked in that direction, and instead run into Lord Braithwaite, and forgotten about Barty in her haste to return to her brother's house.

Alice got off the bed and paced around the room. It was fast becoming obvious to her that she would need to solicit

Wolf's help, no matter how much Verity had asked her not to.

Verity did not want anyone aware of Barty's shame but Alice. Which was all very well if she could talk sense into him, but as was proved the other day, he did not want to listen.

Leaving her room, Alice thought a cup of tea was just what she needed before planning her next move.

"Good morning, you hideous little creature." Alice bent to pat the dog running toward her.

Hep was an ugly little black dog with bulbous eyes who worshipped the ground Wolf walked on. Her brother appeared a few seconds later. Behind him trotted Hep's best friend and Rose's dog, Zeus.

"What he loses in personality he makes up for in character, Alice."

Large and handsome, Wolf had not always been as happy as he appeared today. In fact, after the war Alice knew he'd suffered, even though he'd not told her as much through their correspondence.

"Like you then?"

"Exactly like me."

His smile alone could melt a thousand hearts, as it was not something he used readily. Wolf was the strong, silent type, a man those close to him could rely on. Alice was lucky to be one of those, even if she taxed him continually.

"I do not mean to upset you with my actions, Wolf. And I would never put myself in danger." *Well, almost never.* "I am just taking a while to adjust to living in London. I had so much more freedom in Briarwood."

"I know that, but what I don't know is why you still insist on leaving the house without notifying me."

"My destinations are harmless. The library and lectures. Nothing dangerous," she said, because she had been to one lecture, so it was not an outright evasion of the truth. Her visits to find Barty had not been for that purpose, obviously, but they had to be done for Verity's sake.

"This I know also. But you cannot continue these solo adventures going forward, Alice, or I shall be saddled with you forever, as no man will have a woman with a ruined reputation, not even Barty." His smile told her he was being silly, but she knew better. Wolf rarely spoke without purpose.

Alice fought to remain as controlled as he.

"I took Kate with me last time, and my maid."

"And yet I know you slipped out yesterday with no one accompanying you."

Drat.

"From this day forth, you will take someone with you, and as it turns out, I have found just the person for that position."

He smiled down at her, and Alice wanted to climb to her toes and slap him because she knew that look. He believed he had the better of her.

"Rose is calling for you."

"No, she's not, and lying is beneath you."

"She has tripped and stubbed her toe."

Wolf folded his arms and stood there, as immoveable as the building they currently resided in.

"Who?" Alice snapped.

"Two whos, actually. A maid and a driver."

"I do not need people watching over me!"

"Unfortunately, that is what will be happening from this day forth, so you had better get used to the idea."

"No." Alice folded her arms.

"Yes. You will like Bids, he is a wonderful man—"

"Bids, Dev's driver?" Horror was slowly dawning on Alice. He meant every word.

"The very one." Wolf bent to pick up Hep, and Zeus whined to receive the same attention. Her brother scooped the little dog into his arms also.

He should look ridiculous, and yet he simply looked more handsome. At that moment, she loathed him for the power he had over her. A man, and therefore he did not answer to anyone, but could make her do so.

"Bids, according to Dorrie, is a worrier. He questions their every move and tells Dev should they so much as step a toe out of line. Surely you do not wish that for me, Wolf?"

"You have brought this on yourself."

"I will hate you if you enforce this!"

"No, you won't. You'll love me as you always do."

Battling the urge to flounce away, she simply gritted out a smile.

"Of course you are the one with all the control. Therefore I must do as you say, but I shall state here and now that I think your actions exceedingly shabby, and I am hurt by them."

"I'm sorry you feel that way, sister." His words were spoken in a solemn tone. "But you leave me no choice."

She didn't speak, just walked around him to the breakfast parlor. Her sister and Rose were there when she arrived.

"Mother has extended her stay with Aunt Trinity," Kate said, waving about the letter in her hand. "Apparently now we are under Wolf's care, she is relinquishing the reins of responsibility."

"Wonderful, at least someone is happy."

"You are not happy, Alice? What has happened?" Rose asked.

"I happened." Wolf walked in behind her. "My sister would see me in Hades." He dropped a kiss on Rose's cheek, then handed her Zeus.

"Ah, so you told her about Bids and Kitty Trent?"

"Who is Kitty Trent?" Alice disliked her instantly, which was unfair, but her bother had forced the feeling upon her. She felt cornered, as if her life was not her own as it once had been. How would she see Barty now? Reason with him and get him to go home? She would have to speak with Wolf, and that would embarrass Barty and Verity, who had secretly adored him from afar for years.

"Kitty is a dear friend I lived with when I arrived from Scotland. She and I shared a room, and she taught me the art of survival in London," Rose said.

Alice liked her sister-in-law. She may be a duke's daughter, but she did not have the heirs and graces of one, as she'd been raised away from that wealth and status.

"I'm sure she's quite lovely, but that doesn't mean I want her as my companion."

"Which you would not need—"

"That will do, Wolf," Rose said, giving her husband a gentle smile.

He subsided, which he would never have done had Alice or Kate asked him to.

"You will like Kitty, and as she is bored due to her husband being away on business, she leapt at the chance to spend time with you."

"Rose—"

"Trust me, Alice. You will like her."

"She's certainly different," Wolf said. "In fact, when Rose suggested her I wasn't comfortable with the prospect. However, apparently now Kitty is a pillar of respectability, so she persuaded me to let her be your companion.

"I don't need one, I have my sister."

"Who will let you do anything you want," Wolf added.

"He has a point," Kate said.

Alice didn't say anything further, simply picked up her toast and began to eat while ignoring her brother. With her other hand, she rearranged the condiments into an orderly line.

"Why has Barty not come to see you, Alice?"

"He is busy."

She felt Wolf's eyes on her.

"Too busy to see us, his friends, and the woman he cares for?"

Alice heard a different voice in the house. Raised and pitched above the butler's, it carried clearly through the earplugs she wore, and whoever it belonged to was approaching the parlor they occupied.

"Someone approaches."

"Wonderful. I should imagine it is Kitty," Rose said.

"I don't think so. She just cursed loudly after kicking a side table."

"That sounds like her," Wolf drawled. "She was raised a vicar's daughter and curses louder than a sailor. In fact, I'm having second thoughts again about putting you and her together. You already know how to annoy me; I fear Kitty could compound that."

The door burst open, and in walked a vision in lilac. Her hair was the color of wheat, and her eyes vivid sapphires. The clothes were demure, but seemed anything but on the voluptuous figure of Kitty Trent. Behind her came a flustered-looking Milton, Wolf's butler.

"Mrs. Trent has arrived, Mr. Sinclair."

"I can see that, thank you, Milton."

"Rose!" The woman hurried to greet her friend, scooping her into her arms and hugging her close. "It has been an age!"

"Four days, Kitty, and no more, as you are very well aware." Rose laughed and hugged her friend back.

"They are always like this," Wolf said to Alice and Kate. "Sisters in every way but blood."

"She is beautiful," Kate whispered. "Such style."

"Kitty makes all her own clothes," Rose said, taking her seat and waving her friend into a spare one.

"Kitty, my dear, this is Kate and Alice."

Alice was subjected to a thorough inspection.

"Well, she is a beauty, but that's to be expected considering her beautiful brother."

Wolf smiled, clearly used to such compliments.

"Both of you are beautiful," Kitty added, moving on to Kate.

"As are you," Kate said, getting to her feet. "But I now must leave you as I am due to help Mr. Linus with lessons today."

"Those Sinclairs have a thirst for knowledge," Rose said. "The twins are fifteen and still insist on studying each day with Warwick and Samantha."

"It is wonderful," Kate said. "I wish I had a teacher like Mr. Linus."

"And now you do," Wolf added. "As you are there most days."

The color that filled her sister's cheeks was interesting. Alice wondered what had prompted that reaction.

"Yes, well, I must be off." Kate raised a hand and was gone.

"And is she to be accompanied by a companion and a driver?"

"She is walking with her maid along this street, and has, as yet, caused me no anxiety. I foresee no trouble in her immediate future. I have no doubt that will change over time," Wolf said.

"Don't be stuffy, Wolf," Kitty said, and Alice wondered if in fact she had misjudged the woman. Anyone who would take her brother to task in such a manner could not be all bad, surely?

CHAPTER 10

"*H*ello. You look peaky."

"How does one look peaky?" Nicholas opened the door for Lilly, who had Meredith in her arms, and helped her into his carriage.

"It's the eyes. Yours have smudges beneath, and your face is lined."

"Charming." Nicholas joined her, closing the door behind him.

"Are you not sleeping?"

Lilly and he were going to inspect another property to purchase for the children. Both houses were full most days, and they needed another now.

"Yes, I am sleeping."

"You don't look like you are sleeping," Lilly said with that persistence younger sisters tended to have. "I'll have Essie make something for you."

"Hello, Merry, come to Uncle as Mummy is in one of those bossy moods."

He took the little bundle of sweetness as she held out her arms to him and cuddled her close.

"I am not in one of those moods, I am concerned for you. It is clear something is not right."

"I am well, Lilly, relax. Now, tell me how Mathew's fencing lesson with Cam went yesterday. Has he my prowess?"

The diversion worked, and Lilly talked about her favorite subject, her children and Dev, for the next fifteen minutes.

"Cam said he even scored a point off him."

"Did you believe him?"

"Of course not, but Mathew did, and that is all that matters. Warwick has also been practicing with him. He is so like Dev."

And off she went again. Lilly loved her family, but she did not play favorites. She loved the twins and Warwick equally.

Beautiful in a long ivory jacket and matching bonnet, his sister looked as she always did, happy and content.

Meredith started rearranging his necktie.

"I spent some time on that this morning, brat."

"Well, tell her to stop then."

"Stop," he drawled.

"She is spoiled by everyone, but you are the worst."

"I love her," he said, and it was that simple.

"I know you do, and she loves you back... as do we all."

Why today those words made something catch in the back of his throat, he had no idea, but he looked out the window until it had cleared.

"Nicholas."

"Lilly."

"Nicholas, I wonder if you have had more visions and this is why you are tired?"

"Peaky, you mean?" he teased her.

"Yes, that. Have you?"

"A few, but I am also tired as I had a late night."

"What were they about, these visions?"

Nicholas ran a hand slowly down Meredith's head, enjoying the feel of her soft curls.

"Lately, they are about the child who is missing."

"Are they more regular at the moment?"

Nicholas nodded. Last night Alice had come to him with her hair flowing around her shoulders, in a white dress, looking like a bloody angel. She'd demanded he do something about the child.

"You believe it for the truth now, don't you?"

"I don't know—"

"Yes, you do, but the practical side to your nature demands solid proof."

"You know me so well."

"I do. We may have been estranged for a few years, Nicholas, but I knew you well before then, and since."

He studied her face and saw nothing but love for him, and it humbled him.

"You're not going to apologize again, are you? That's getting tiring, and frankly boring, Nicholas. Now, I need you to listen to me."

He nodded.

"You are the very best of brothers to me and a wonderful uncle to my children. I know that you love me, as do they. I watch you with our families and know they respect and care for you also. Why can you not see what you've become when we can?"

"Had I known today was going to be so uncomfortable, Merry, I would have just brought you along."

Lilly grabbed his hand and shook it hard.

"Nicholas. See the man you have become, please."

"I will try," he said solemnly.

But it is not easy.

"Excellent, that is all I can ask for. Now I want to discuss that horrid Lady Ratchet."

"What? Why?"

"Because she is boasting that you are one of her conquests."

Nicholas literally choked on air.

"Lilly! You cannot speak like that in front of the child."

"She doesn't understand," his sister said with the ruthless determination to stay on task that he knew so well. "That woman is a poisonous harpy, Nicholas. You will not do that," she waved a hand about, "with her again."

"I cannot believe we are having this conversation."

"I have been thinking this over, and I discussed it with Eden and Rose the other day, and they agree."

"I hardly dare to ask."

"It is time for you to find a wife."

"Am I to be involved in the choice?"

"We have been discussing prospects," Lilly added as if he had not spoken, "and think Miss Lindfox would be an excellent prospect, and Miss Briar."

He made a choking sound that had Meredith patting his chest.

"Thank you, sweetie."

"There is also Miss Rattle, but to be honest, she is a bit insipid."

"Lilly."

"Also, Miss Bromley. Her father is a crashing windbag, but you will not be living with him."

"Lilly," Nicholas said a bit louder.

"What?"

"No."

"No to Miss Bromley? Oh, very well, I guess the father would be annoying when he came to visit."

"No to all of them, and no to you and those other meddling women in the family helping find me a wife."

"You need a wife, Nicholas."

"No, I don't, and if and when I do, I shall see to the task myself."

"But it should not be a task, Nicholas."

"Forgive me, that was the wrong word to use. Perhaps I am slightly off-balance." He laced his words heavily with sarcasm.

"I want only what is best for you."

"I understand that, but a wife is not what I need at the moment."

"Dev said that." Lilly frowned.

"A man of great sense, that husband of yours."

"Cam said you can lead a horse to water but you can't make it drink."

"While I am not sure I wish to be likened to a horse, I like his meaning. I cannot believe you discussed this with them."

"I love you and want only happiness for you, Nicholas."

"Which I have with you and the family. Now, enough, Lilly; when I want a wife, I shall discuss prospects with you, but for now, I beg of you, do not raise the subject again."

She huffed. "Oh, very well, if you insist."

Nicholas knew it would only be a temporary reprieve. Lilly had clearly decided it was time for him to wed. He had no doubt eligible women would be fired into his path regularly from now on.

"Alice needs a husband also."

If he'd been uncomfortable before, that just made things twice as bad. Alice Sinclair, with her intelligent green eyes and lovely smile. The woman was spending far too much time in his thoughts at the moment. And his visions, he added silently.

"I thought she had the sainted Barty lined up to wed one day?"

"Wolf said he's a bit of a slow top, but for all that a good man. But we think she could do a great deal better."

"We?"

"Rose, Emily, Eden, and Essie."

"Do you form your coven weekly to discuss which family member needs your interventions next?"

"Alice has a sharp intellect and lively wit," Lilly continued not, at all put out by his reference to her and the others being witches. "I think she needs a man who will challenge her."

I would challenge her.

Where the hell had that come from?

"She'd actually make you the perfect wife, Nicholas."

As luck would have it, he had his face in his niece's neck making disgusting noises, so Lilly could not see the horror on it.

"But, as I doubt that is likely, with all the family connections and other things, we won't pursue that."

"Other things?"

"Eden thought you did not seem very taken with each other when you first met. Her words were that you were like two bristling cats circling each other."

They hadn't been earlier that day. In fact, they'd been closer than he'd even felt with a woman before.

"I was polite" was all he could come up with as he scrambled to not show what was going on inside his head.

"You're always polite. But you had that tight look about your eyes you get when you are tolerating someone."

"Since when have I got this tight look?"

The day was full of revelations and it was only 11:00 a.m. It did not bode well for what was to come, surely?

"Since always."

"I'm sure, like me, Alice will decide when and whom she wishes to marry. Stop meddling, Lilly."

"I never meddle."

He scoffed... loudly. Meredith thought it hilarious and started giggling, so he did it again.

"Merry, my love, let this be a lesson to you. When you are happily married and content, women get bored, so they meddle in other people's lives. That is good for no one, especially not the recipient of said meddling."

"It is called love, Meredith. It's what you do for family," Lilly added piously.

"And now as we are here, this entire ridiculous conversation can cease." Nicholas was relived as the carriage rolled to a halt. It had been one of the most uncomfortable journeys he'd endured for some time.

"Very well, we will speak no more on the matter now, but I want your word you will not take that heinous Lady Ratchet to your bed again."

"Lord have mercy, I promise, all right?"

"Wonderful." Lilly patted his cheek as she left the carriage. "Such a good brother I have."

Nicholas followed feeling like he'd been in a fight with a swarm of butterflies.

The house was narrow, squashed between two similar ones. It was close to Fleet Street, where Cam's newspaper *The Trumpeter* was located.

One Mr. Smith showed them through the property. Two stories, it had two long, narrow rooms upstairs that would house beds. Downstairs would be for the kitchen and living space, where they could put in some chairs and sofas.

Nicholas liked to have a place for the children to just sit together. He would fill it with blankets, and stock the fire with wood, and the small shed at the rear of the property.

"Mr. and Mrs. Davey would be more than happy to help run this, but I think we need another to come in daily also. If they wished to live on the property, they could have that small room at the rear down here," Lilly said, waving in that direction.

"I agree. But finding someone is the problem. I won't have anyone taking advantage of these children."

"I know. We shall think on it, Nicholas."

They told Mr. Smith they would take the lease, then decided to go and visit Cam.

"Shall we walk?"

"If you carry Meredith, yes."

"You poor old lady, Lilliana. How has it come to this? Is your life too indulgent, do you think? Have you become pathetic in your twilight years?" Nicholas wasn't averse to getting a few jabs in when the opportunity presented itself. Especially considering how uncomfortable his sister had made him on the journey here. "Come to Uncle, Merry. Your mother can take my arm, and we shall keep our steps small so she does not tire easily."

"Extremely amusing. But you try carrying that weight around for hours. Plus, I have had two others, if you will remember. Unlike you, I have more than myself to think about."

"There is that. Come, I have a hankering for one of those sugar buns from the baker next door. We shall purchase enough for Cam."

"It really is amazing how much that man can eat."

"And not gain weight."

Lilly tucked her arm into his, and Nicholas held Merry in the other one.

They chatted as they walked, and he thought that perhaps he could marry one day if he got to have a little bundle in his arms like this one and a wife who understood him like his sister.

Right in that moment, if he had to examine what he felt, he would say happiness.

"Clicky clacky."

"Pardon?" He looked at Meredith.

"Pass her to me and you can purchase the buns. My daughter loves the noise of the printing press."

"Really? Shouldn't that terrify her?" He handed the child to her mother and immediately missed her soft weight in his arms.

"She is Dev's child. What can I tell you but that she likes different things?"

"I'm telling him you said that."

Lilly laughed as she headed through the doors of *The Trumpeter*. Nicholas purchased sugar-coated buns. He then followed her, but he took the stairs up rather than entering the "clicky clacky" area.

Something like contentment settled over Nicholas in that moment. He and Lilly were friends again, and he had family that seemed to care for him. Perhaps it was time to forget the past and move forward.

Smiling, he reached the top step and felt as if someone had punched him hard in the stomach.

CHAPTER 11

"*A*re you all right, Miss Sinclair? Forgive me, I did not see you coming."

"Quite all right, thank you, Captain Young." Alice stepped back out of his arms, and it was then she saw Nicholas.

"I was looking for Cam," he said in a cold, flat voice. "Forgive my intrusion."

"Intrusion?" She looked first to the captain and then to the angry lord. "What intrusion? I did not see Captain Young, and we collided."

"Good day to you, Lord Braithwaite."

She'd met Captain Young one night at a small dinner party; he seemed a nice enough man and easy to converse with.

"Captain Young." Nicholas reluctantly shook the hand held out to him. "What has you at *The Trumpeter* today?"

"I had business to discuss with Mr. Sinclair and was lucky enough to run, quite literally, into Miss Sinclair also."

The smile he gave Alice was sweet, and she wondered why she felt none of the excitement she did having Nicholas near, even if he did look like a storm cloud.

"Good day to you then, Captain Young." Nicholas stood to one side for the man to pass. Instead, he looked at Alice.

"Will you be attending the Mueller masquerade, Miss Sinclair?"

"I will, Captain."

His smile grew. "Excellent. I shall look forward to seeing you there, and perhaps you will save a dance for me?" He took her hand and bowed over it.

"I would like that, thank you, Captain Young."

"Good day to you then, Lord Braithwaite and Miss Sinclair."

"Captain." Nicholas nodded but nothing more.

The silence that settled around them after Captain Young left was uncomfortable.

"Are you visiting Cam?"

He nodded, his eyes steady on her face.

"As am I." Deciding she wasn't going to get anywhere with him in his current mood, she turned away to walk to Cam's office.

"If you were caught doing that by anyone but me, there would have been consequences to your actions."

"I beg your pardon?" Alice spun on her heel to face him. "I have no idea what it is you allude to, Lord Braithwaite."

"That," he waved the hand that was not clutching sugar buns at her, "is a dangerous game. A man will take advantage of such behavior."

Alice was shocked at his words. "How dare you suggest that was anything but an accident!"

"I know men, and Captain Young is interested in you, and that did not look like an accident."

"He was apologizing when you arrived. How could you not have heard that?" Alice demanded.

"All I am saying is you don't know anything about him, and—"

"He is a very nice gentleman," she cut him off, "whom I have met once. Should I be lucky enough to do so again, I will not be disappointed."

"His eyes are too close together. That makes him shifty, in my opinion."

"They are not too close together, and he is an honorable man, unlike some."

"I hope you are not suggesting I am not honorable?" He stepped closer to her.

"And shifty, do not forget that also."

"I am not shifty!" He looked offended.

"Your past would suggest you are."

"You know nothing of my past."

"No. But I have heard rumors."

"What kind of rumors?" He was close enough she could smell the buns in his hand, and that mixed with his scent was a heady combination.

"I do not tell tales. But I will add that the only person who has taken advantage of me is you!"

Turning away, she stormed to Cam's office before he could stop her. Banging on the door, she entered.

"Cousin, how wonderful to see you," Cam said from his chair. "What's wrong?" he added, noting her glare.

"Nothing. I have the article for you."

"Nicholas." Cam's eyes moved to the doorway behind Alice. "What did you say to upset my cousin?"

"Nothing," they both said at the same time, in the same tone.

Cam sat back, watching them.

"Clearly it is something. Let's hear it."

"I have no wish to discuss the matter further. Some men are simply fools, and I have no need to elaborate on that," Alice said.

"And some women are naive," Nicholas added.

Cam's eyes went from Nicholas to Alice. He shrugged.

"Very well, keep your secrets, but only if you hand over one of those buns."

Alice moved behind Cam's desk and opened her reticule to pull out the paper she'd written.

"Read this. If you wish for me to make changes then I shall, or if you don't like it—"

"Stop talking down the article. You are a Sinclair, we are an intelligent family, it will be brilliant."

Nicholas snorted at Cam's words, which had Alice's fingers twitching to swing her reticule at his head.

"Why was Captain Young here, Cam?"

Nicholas moved to take the seat across the desk from where she stood instead of leaving as she'd hoped.

"He wishes to invest in my next acquisition. Apparently, Wolf told him about it." Cam was reading her article as he talked. The man could do any number of things at once.

"What acquisition?"

"More an investment," Cam muttered.

"What investment?"

"In the steam locomotives that will one day thunder across this country. Benjamin Hetherington and his brother are involved, and lured us in. Captain Young wishes to invest also."

"Do you really believe they will run everywhere one day?" Alice asked.

"Indeed. The first passenger-carrying locomotive is not too far away, or so Ben led me to believe."

"I should love to one day travel on that," Alice said.

"Perhaps you shall, cousin."

"I would be interested in investing. But we can discuss that later," Nicholas said, clearly not wishing to talk on the matter with her nearby, which made Alice want to say something rude.

Lowering her article, Cam took the bun Nicholas held out and a large bite.

"Would you care for one also, Alice?"

She would love one, in fact she could almost taste the sugary goodness, but she shook her head wanting nothing from this man.

"No, thank you."

"How are your investments going, Alice?" Cam said with a small smile that told her he had said the words deliberately. "After all, you are a Sinclair with that fiendish ability you have with numbers."

"You invest?"

The shock on Nicholas's face would have made her laugh if she'd had one in her. His words after her encounter with Captain Young had left her feeling angry and unsettled.

"Yes, it's a strange occurrence really. Even considering I had the disadvantage of being born a woman, I can think for myself, and with some clarity." Her words came out coated in ice.

"I did not mean to imply otherwise."

His face changed suddenly, and she could see he was fighting to hide his smile.

"I'm quite sure you did," she muttered.

"Children." Cam lifted a hand. "You surely understand why she is good with investments, Nicholas, considering you have the same freakish ability Alice does with numbers."

"As I stated, I did not intend to insult you, but even you must agree, Alice, that not many women have investment portfolios."

"I don't agree. How would any of us know if they did or didn't?" She wasn't conceding anything to him. "Women are not openly going to share such knowledge, as they are meant to be painting watercolors!"

"Hello!" In sailed Lilly, much to Alice's relief.

She'd never known a man who could pull so much emotion out of her. Those sensations the other day in that lane, the hurt and anger today. How dared he suggest she was some kind of... of woman capable of fast behavior, just because she'd walked into Captain Young accidentally.

You let him kiss you... more than once.

"Hold this child, Nicholas, she's been chanting your name in her garbled language since you left us."

"Hello, Merry."

The smile he bestowed on his niece was so gentle it made Alice's insides quiver, which in turn made her angrier.

"I just met Captain Young on the stairs," Lilly said, taking a bun. "He's a very nice young man, Alice."

"Yes, he is. I met him also."

"I know that look," Cam said.

"What look?"

"The Lilliana meddling look. Eden has one, as do the other married women in this family."

"I have no idea what you mean. All I'm saying is he's a fine gentleman and it would not hurt Alice to understand that."

"Understand what?"

"That Captain Young is a nice man."

"I already agreed with you, Lilly, that he is."

"Surely you are not that slow." Cam looked over his shoulder at Alice. "Lilly thinks Captain Young will make you an excellent husband."

Shock held Alice still. Her eyes found Nicholas's, and something passed between them. She thought maybe it was sympathy.

"Stop meddling, Lilliana."

"I am not meddling, Nicholas. Just stating facts. Captain Young is a good man."

"She itemized a list of prospective wives for me on the

journey here. You'll be pleased to know I crossed you off, Alice."

He said the words to make them all laugh.

It can never happen again. She remembered him saying this to her the night of the twins' birthday. Well, if he would not kiss her again, he certainly would have no wish to wed her. She felt no different. The man was too much of everything for her. Too experienced. Too jaded. Too handsome. Not entirely logical, yet she didn't want people looking at her husband in sympathy as he was saddled with her. Too secretive. Nicholas Braithwaite had a past, and she knew it was dark, and Alice would need to know every detail but doubted he'd be willing to share.

After she'd catalogued the reasons they should not marry, she felt better. Not that he'd asked her, but at least now she could be happy that he wouldn't

You are clearly losing your mind, Alice Sinclair.

"It really is an excellent piece, Alice," Cam said. "I shall let you know when we print it."

"Really? That's exciting. I have many others that I could write."

"Write them."

"May I read it?"

She didn't want to look at him, because he was disturbing enough without a small pink-cheeked child in his arms. Plus, she was still angry with him.

"No."

"Yes," Cam said, handing her paper to Nicholas. "For goodness sakes, the man reads *The Trumpeter*, Alice. You will need to develop a thicker skin if you are to publish in my paper."

"Why do you not wish him to read it, Alice?" Lilly asked her. It was curiosity and nothing more in her expression, which pleased Alice. After all, Nicholas was her brother, she would not like it if Alice spoke harshly about him.

"They were angry with each other when they arrived," Cam said. "As yet, I have no idea why."

"Really? Tell me what you said to upset Alice, Nicholas."

Meredith was seated in his lap, playing with the large ring on his finger.

"How do you know I said anything?" He did not lift his eyes from her article.

"Alice, what did you say to upset Nicholas?" Lilly asked.

"Are you ready, Alice, dear? I have drunk a pot of tea and eaten two of those delicious little sugar buns!"

Alice exhaled with relief as Kitty Trent wandered in looking like she'd stepped out of the pages of the latest *La Belle Assemblée*. Her eyes went from Lilly to Cam and then to Nicholas.

"Another one." She clutched her heart. "I cannot take much more of the handsome noblemen this family associates with. And this one is holding a darling little girl."

Nicholas had regained his feet with Meredith in his arms as Kitty entered.

"Kitty Trent, this is my brother, Lord Braithwaite."

As Lilly made the introductions, Nicholas dipped into a bow with Meredith, making the girl giggle.

"It's is a pleasure to meet you, Mrs. Trent."

Kitty sighed, then kissed Meredith's cheek.

"Come, Alice. I have left you alone long enough. If your handsome brother finds out, I shall be in trouble."

"She was with me the entire time," Cam said. "I promise," he added solemnly. The expression did not reach his eyes.

"Wicked man" was all Kitty said.

She then held out a hand to Alice, who made hurried goodbyes and took it.

Bids pulled up with the carriage as they left *The Trumpeter*. Alice exhaled as they rolled away with her inside.

"That man is far too good-looking," Kitty said.

"Who? Cam?"

"The other one, Lord Braithwaite. Now he has broken a few hearts. You mark my words and stay away from the likes of him, Alice."

After today, she thought that was sage advice. But one thing she knew for sure was that Alice would never allow him to break her heart.

Going forward, it was important she showed restraint and control when that man was nearby. Both things that she'd never really mastered.

CHAPTER 12

The Mueller masquerade was a genteel affair, unlike some masked occasions he'd attended. A mask often let some lose their inhibitions, he'd certainly enjoyed many a flirtation at such events.

Nicholas wandered in through the front doors.

Torches flickered outside the door, and the liveried servants lined the paths, bowing and directing.

"As if we can't find our way in a front door," the Earl of Grant muttered.

"There are fools who walk among us," Nicholas replied, as something was expected of him.

"Too true. One to your left, Braithwaite."

He turned at Grant's direction and saw Lord and Lady Nibley.

"Who dresses like their wife, Braithwaite?"

"Apparently Lord Nibley."

"I always question a man in puce."

"Not a color I would choose," Nicholas agreed.

It was not a subtle shade and therefore easy on the eyes.

No. Lord and Lady Nibley wore a violent shade of puce. Their dominos were the same color.

"Idiots," Grant muttered before stomping away.

"Agreed." Nicholas followed.

"Hello, my lord."

"Lady Mueller." He took her hand and bowed deeply. Beside her was her husband, who was elderly and deaf.

"My husband is leaving Friday on parliament business, Lord Braithwaite."

The words were whispered for his ears alone.

She fluttered her lashes through the small holes in her mask and plumped out her breasts.

"Is he? How lonely you will be."

"Very." She pouted. "Perhaps you could help alleviate that boredom?"

He made the appropriate reply, but strangely had no wish to share her bed.

"Duke," she then added, looking over Nicholas's shoulder.

He turned to see James, Dev, and the rest of the Raven and Sinclair clans. He found the green eyes of Alice Sinclair watching him. She couldn't have heard the words he'd spoken with Lady Mueller, but something in her gaze told him she was angry.

"My lady."

Nicholas moved on to allow them to acknowledge their hostess.

He'd made a fool of himself at *The Trumpeter*; it had taken her leaving Cam's office for him to realize that. Seeing her in the arms of Captain Young had produced a nasty and immediate reaction inside him. He'd struck out at the nearest available target. Unfortunately, it had been Alice.

"Black, silver, or pink, my lord?"

A footman stood behind a table of dominos. These were

for those guests who'd hoped to sneak in without wearing a mask. He was one of them.

"Oh, pink," Cam said from behind him.

"Black," Nicholas corrected, taking it from the man. "I loathe these things," he added.

"But for a man such as you they offer so much fun." Lilly joined him.

"I don't think that statement was complimentary, sister."

"It wasn't." She patted his cheek. "But I love you anyway."

He kissed her cheek.

"As you are not escorting anyone, Nicholas, will you take Alice's hand for the walk down to the ballroom?" Wolf whispered the words to him. "I fear she is nervous and trying hard not to show it, and I will have Rose on my arm."

"Of course." He could hardly refuse. And did not point out that Wolf had another arm.

She was lurking at the rear of their family group, eyes going from left to right. Her dress was the softest blue, almost white. Demure, hinting at the body beneath, it showcased her beauty. All that black Sinclair hair was piled high and held in place with at least a dozen small pins with sparkling gems on the ends.

Nicholas liked experienced women, he reminded himself. Women who had no expectations of commitment from him.

He was sure that with exposure, his reaction to this woman would wane. After all, he had kept company with some of London's most beautiful women, and none had made his heart beat faster.

"Good evening, Alice. You look beautiful."

"Thank you." The words were uttered in a distracted manner as she wrestled with the silver domino in her hands.

"Allow me." Nicolas took it from her and lowered it gently over her eyes. "Hold it in place." She did as he asked, and he tied the ribbons together. "Now if you will take my arm, we will enter the ballroom."

"Oh... I had thought Wolf...." Her words fell away.

"Take my arm, Alice."

She did, her fingers clenching and then relaxing on his sleeve.

"Please allow me to apologize for my behavior at *The Trumpeter*. I am not usually such an idiot."

His words forced a laugh out of her.

"Thank you for apologizing."

"So can we conclude that I am no longer shifty?"

"We can."

"But am I honorable?"

"Do you want to be?"

"Very much so." Strangely, he was no longer laughing. He wanted this woman to believe that of him, at the very least.

"Then of course you are honorable."

Nicholas was far too happy with her words.

"I would much rather be in Briarwood, curled up in my bed reading," she whispered.

"No, you wouldn't." They walked along the mezzanine above the ballroom. "Look down."

"I would rather not."

"I always think of them as brightly colored peacocks, all strutting about the place waiting for someone to notice them."

She snuffled.

"If you'll look down and slightly left, by that large pillar below, you'll see the Dowager Duchess of Hope. Stay well clear of her. Once she captures your interest there is no escape for at least forty minutes, and that's on a good day. She is prone to waxing on about her ten grandchildren until you want to stab yourself with the nearest hairpin simply to escape."

"She's very large."

"Very, and wears far too much scent."

The fingers on his arm slowly relaxed as he talked.

"To the right of her is Major Trent. Another to steer clear of. He tends to have both wandering eyes and hands."

"Ah."

"Exactly."

They were soon halfway down the stairs.

"Remember, Alice, you are a Sinclair. Your uncle is an earl. You have a duke and marquis at your back also. You cower to no one."

"I really don't want to like you," she whispered. "But it seems I must. Are you the marquis at my back?"

"I am. I shall try to do something to reverse your opinion of me soon."

"I'd be grateful."

They reached the ballroom, and Nicholas kept her hand on his arm and moved slowly around the room with the others. He was reluctant to let her go, especially considering the appreciative looks she was receiving from the young men in the room.

"Remember that some will see wearing a mask as an excuse to approach you and not behave in as gentlemanly a manner as they should."

"I will not leave my family."

"Good girl."

"Thank you again, Nicholas," Alice said when he released her to them.

"It was my pleasure. I hope you will save me a dance also."

"Of course." Her smile was nervous.

He had the urge to stand at her side; instead, he bowed and walked away.

Nicholas danced with several ladies; some he enjoyed for

their conversation, others he didn't. Miss Gimlett was firmly in the latter category.

"The wainscoting, you'll understand, is second to none in this room, my lord. Lady Mueller employed the services of the renowned French designer, Lequart."

He made the proper noises as she waxed on about the mundane subject of wainscoting and furnishings and let his eyes search the room for Alice. He couldn't find her, but knew she'd be with her family somewhere. So far she'd danced with Captain Young, which he should be happy about as the man was harmless. Then Lord Sydney, who Nicholas knew was looking for a wife with money and connections. Alice certainly fitted those requirements. Next came Mr. Halladay. A nice enough man, if a little boring.

Taking Miss Gimlett back to her friends as the dance ended, he wandered the room.

"Smile, brother."

He forced his lips upward as he passed his sister dancing with Dev. Leaving the ballroom, he decided on a walk. Lord Mueller had an exquisite display of statues; he'd take a look at them.

The room was large and lined with curtains drawn against the night sky. He wandered down the first row, studying the beauty of the white marble. Turning up the next, he found Alice observing the statues alone. She'd taken off her domino and was swinging it back and forth between her fingers. His was in his pocket.

"I think you're meant to be upstairs, Miss Sinclair."

She could be one of the statues, looking at her side profile, the elegant sweep of her neck and delicate curve of her chin.

"Cam told me about these. I wasn't sure I would get another chance to see them."

"The Three Graces," he said, drawing near enough for

Alice's scent to reach him. Soft, elusive, and yet very much her.

"Aglaea, Euphrosyn, and Thaila," she said, pointing to the statues of the three women.

"Splendor, Mirth, and Good Cheer," he added.

"Well done," she congratulated him.

"I am quite well read actually."

"For a rake, do you mean?"

"Who told you I was a rake?"

"I have good hearing and worked it out myself from snippets of conversation."

"Listening to gossip, Alice, tut tut. Surely you know not to believe everything you overhear?"

"Some of those women find you irresistible. It's quite nauseating actually how they wax on about you."

He could do nothing to stop the bark of laughter.

"Some of their adoration is for my title, Alice, I assure you."

"Some, but not all."

He looked down at her. Their eyes caught and held. Something heavy settled around them. Expectation, awareness; there were plenty of words for it, and all of them should have had him walking away from her.

"Was that a compliment?"

"No, merely the truth." Her voice had lowered to that gravelly tone he liked. The one she used when she wasn't trying to be a lady. Strange how he knew this about her already.

"So, are you enjoying your evening, Alice?"

"Yes, thank you, it is interesting."

He moved closer.

"Interesting how?"

"Interesting to see that the men who wish to dance with

me do so because of my associations, not because they wish to know me better."

His hand rose before he could stop it. She closed her eyes as he touched her cheek.

"You are beautiful, and that is the reason they want to know you better."

"No—"

"Yes." He leaned closer. "Tell me to walk away, Alice."

Instead she closed the distance between them and kissed him.

The moan came from Nicholas as he slipped a hand around her waist and pulled her closer.

She drove every rational thought from his head. Every warning vanished, and all he could think about was how much more he wanted from this woman.

Pressing her to his body, Nicholas took the kiss deeper. The feel of her was exquisite, just as it had been that day in the lane. The need inside him rose higher.

"Alice." He whispered her name against her lips, then kissed her deeply. This was what he'd wanted. Another taste of her, and yet he knew it was wrong. Knew that once more would never be enough.

It was only the sound of footsteps that had him stopping. Nothing else but exposure could have done that. She slipped from his arms and walked down the row of statues.

"A note has arrived for you, my lord." A footman reached him holding a silver salver.

"How did you know I was down here?" Nicholas's voice sounded raw.

"The butler saw you come this way, my lord."

"Thank you." He took the note and the footman left.

"Is something wrong?" Alice returned.

"Other than the fact that I shouldn't have kissed you... again, do you mean?"

She remained silent.

"It can't happen anymore, Alice."

"Then stop doing it!"

She had a point. His body still simmered from the feel of her pressed to him, but he should know better than to kiss an innocent like Alice Sinclair, especially considering his connection to her family.

"There can be nothing between us, Alice, ever."

She looked away from him so he couldn't read her expression. When their eyes met again, her face was emotionless, just like his.

"Excellent. At least I have now had kissing practice for when another occasion arises."

"I beg your pardon?" He couldn't believe she'd just said that. "You will not go about kissing men for practice."

She raised her chin, eyes the cool green of a forest.

"I must learn somehow."

She was bluffing, he knew it, as did she, but it still annoyed the hell out of him. He felt a swift bite of jealousy at the thought of another man anywhere near her.

"Open the note, it could be serious." She said the words dismissively as she studied the Three Graces once more.

He threw her a last look, his eyes lingering on her lovely body wrapped in that soft dress.

Meet me in twenty minutes. I have news about the missing baby. Go to the terrace, then take the stairs down. Take the right path and walk. I will approach you soon.

Nicholas folded the note and placed it in his pocket.

"I must go."

"Where?"

"To meet someone."

"Here?"

"Yes, here."

"A liaison?"

"What do you know about such things?"

"I hear things." She shrugged, looking far more relaxed than him. Especially considering what they had been doing just minutes ago.

"Go upstairs, Alice."

"Yes, I must. I am due to dance with Captain Young shortly."

"You have already danced with him," Nicholas said, then wished he'd shut his mouth.

"Yes, and he is a nice man so I will do so again." She left. He followed.

"Be careful, you cannot be seen to show favor to one man without rumor starting." Excellent, he was turning into his mother. She would have said exactly that.

She ignored him and entered the ballroom to the left. Nicholas turned right. He encountered Cam.

Bloody Sinclairs. You couldn't walk a foot without stumbling over one.

"Who's stroked your fur the wrong way?"

"I am not a feline, Cam."

"Your eyes are narrowed like one."

Cambridge was leaning on a wall, sipping a drink.

"Why are you not dancing?" Nicholas joined him.

"I don't like to dance if Emily is not present, and as she rarely likes to go into society, I don't dance a great deal."

"Why don't you dance if she is not here?"

"I feel as if I am betraying her."

And this, Nicholas realized, was true love.

"But you're not. Married people dance with other people constantly."

"I know that. It is just the way I feel." Cam shrugged.

"Why do you come then, if she cannot?"

"Will not. She could come but chooses not to."

"My question still stands."

"She makes me. Emily thinks it's important for me to come to these affairs occasionally and continue to mix with these people. I've tried to tell her I have no wish to, but she won't listen and says that a social person like me needs this type of thing."

"I have complete faith you will wear her down."

"Thank you."

They watched the dancers in silence. He found Alice taking the floor with Captain Young. As he'd rarely experienced the emotion, the sting of jealousy hit him hard.

"That could be a good match."

"Who?"

"Alice and Captain Young. Lilly was right about them; he'd make her an excellent husband."

"He's too stuffy for her, and his eyes are shifty."

Nicholas felt Cam's eyes on the side of his face.

"Young is a good man, Nicholas. He would make sure Alice is provided for and happy. She would do well with him. I'll grant you that his eyes are too close together, but that does not make him shifty."

"As I have no say in the matter, your words are better saved for Wolf. But I had believed she was promised to the sainted Barty?"

Cam made a noise in his throat.

"What?"

"I think that was a loose arrangement, or so Wolf led me to believe, even though he teases her about it. Apparently the man's a bit vague."

"Well, she shouldn't contemplate Captain Young, is all I'm saying."

Cam made that noise again.

"What?"

"Nothing."

"That noise was something."

"Just clearing my throat."

Without punching him, Nicholas knew he would not get an honest answer from Cam.

"That's a good match." Dev wandered up with Lilly. They were looking at Alice and Captain Young.

"I agree," she added.

"I just said that, but Nicholas disagreed," Cam said.

"I was merely pointing out that she has known him only briefly. Alice cannot know if Captain Young is a good match yet or not." Nicholas's necktie felt like it was strangling him all of a sudden. "Plus, there is the sainted Barty."

"No, you said he's too stuffy and had shifty eyes," Cam said with annoying accuracy.

"I must go." Nicholas said as Alice left the dance floor. "I am to meet someone."

"Who?" Lilly asked. "Not horrid Lady Ratchet, I hope?"

Nicholas glared at his sister before walking away. No words were necessary.

He headed out the French doors and onto the deck. Once there, he took the steps down and veered right, his thoughts on Alice marrying Captain Young.

It would be a good match, he could admit that now he was alone. Unlike him, who was tainted by life's experiences and far too jaded for a sweet young lady like her, Captain Young had a pristine reputation, from what he knew of the man.

His feet crunched on the shell path as he walked. Pushing Alice aside, he focused on whoever was waiting for him up ahead.

Someone knew he was investigating the matter. Nicholas could think of only a handful of people. His family would not be sending him notes, and it was unlikely to be from the constable he had spoken with at the watch house. Which left Mr. and Mrs. Adley or someone connected to them.

I can't believe I kissed Alice Sinclair again.

"Excellent, at least I have now had kissing practice for when another occasion arises."

She was a mouthy woman to say those words to him, and he loved that about her. No, not loved... but respected. Yes, that sounded a great deal better to Nicholas.

Lord and Lady Mueller had extensive grounds. Nicholas knew he could be walking for a while before anyone approached him.

Should he have told someone where he was going? Too late for that now.

The torchlight was only for the paths closest to the house; as he advanced, darkness settled heavily around him. He'd been walking a while when he became aware he was no longer alone.

Turning, he found six men behind him and realized just how stupid he'd been to come out here alone. Alice had addled his usually rational thought process.

"You have news for me?" Nicholas said calmly.

"No."

"I received a note." He braced himself, knowing that these men were here to harm him. He was a fool for walking into this.

"Oh, we sent it, all right, and what will follow is a warning to you. Keep your nose out of business that doesn't concern you, or next time you won't recover."

The words were spoken by the man who had stepped out of the line. Not overly tall, he was solid. Had it been just him and perhaps another, Nicholas could hold his own. James had taught him tricks that they would not expect.

"You would harm a marquis... while on a nobleman's property. Tsk tsk, when they catch you, all six of you will be sent on a nice long voyage to the colonies or locked away for a very long time."

"They won't catch us!"

"How did you get in here?"

They didn't answer.

"Are there perhaps people inside who are involved in your schemes? Is that how the note was delivered?"

The man's surprise gave him away.

"How interesting. Scum comes from all levels of society, it seems."

"Shut up!"

"You are indeed foolish for thinking you can get away with whatever you are planning here."

"No one knows we're here."

"Except the nobleman who sent you to harm me, and let us not forget the people hiding out here doing things they shouldn't. Just how much of a simpleton are you, sir?"

Now his eyes had adjusted, he could see the men clearly. The leader was not happy at his taunts.

"I ain't no simpleton!"

"And whoever is behind this child-thieving business had to send six men to silence me. It seems I am far more menacing than I realized."

"They wanted to make sure you understood the warning."

"They? So there is more than one nobleman involved, how interesting."

"I did not say that!" The man was getting agitated.

Nicholas thought about running. The path behind him would lead him away and deeper into the grounds. There he could get lost. There he could also meet his maker at the hands of six men.

Settling his weight evenly on his feet, he tensed his muscles and prepared for the fight that was coming.

CHAPTER 13

"Your beauty eclipses all others, my dear Miss Sinclair."

"Thank you, Mr. Cellar."

"Your eyes are the color of a dew-drenched forest after a rainfall."

"It's very kind of you to say so," Alice said, looking over his shoulder hoping for rescue. Surely the dance was due to end.

"I had thought there could be no other in your family that eclipsed the beauty of the last, yet I was wrong."

"I have a sister," Alice felt duty bound to point out.

"Alas, I fear my heart will not survive another one."

The man was surely the silliest she had encountered, and there had been a few.

Mr. Cellar turned his head, and the points on his collar nearly took out an eye, they were so ridiculously high and... well, pointy.

Who wore a lemon jacket?

After visiting the statues and being kissed senseless by Nicholas, she'd danced with Captain Young again just to annoy him further. The captain didn't raise sparks of excitement inside her as Nicholas did, but then he'd not kissed her so perhaps he would... however, she doubted it.

Why had he kissed her again when clearly he had no wish to? Or did he wish to but knew he shouldn't. It was a perplexing thought that she had no answer for.

What Alice did know, however, was that she liked his kisses way more than she should.

Something that she labelled unease slithered suddenly down her spine. Looking about the room, she tried to locate her family. This reaction usually meant something was not right with one of them.

"I hope you will dance with me again, Miss Sinclair."

"Of course." Alice felt the tension in her climb.

"Soon."

Something was wrong. Thankfully, the dance ended. Cutting Mr. Cellar off as he began to wax on about how light she was on her feet, Alice thanked him and walked away.

She found James first. He stood talking to a gentleman she didn't know. He excused himself as she approached.

"Something is wrong."

His eyes went from her to search the room.

"I see all the others except Nicholas. Eden and Rose are just walking through that door to help that silly woman who feels faint."

"It is Nicholas then, I'm sure of it." She reached for her earplugs.

"It will be too loud for you in here."

"I must." She pulled them out. James gabbed her arm to steady her as the noise hit her from all sides.

"What is wrong?" Wolf arrived, sliding a hand around her back.

"Alice thinks something is off with Nicholas. She is listening to see if she can hear him."

"Christ, in here? She'll have a headache in seconds."

Dev, Lilly, and Cam appeared next.

"Nicholas is in trouble, I can feel it," Lilly said, looking worried.

"Alice feels it also," Dev said, taking his wife's hand. "Take a breath for me now, love."

"He's not in this room," Alice said placing her hands over her ears to dim the noise. "We need to go outside."

James didn't hesitate, just took her arm and led her out the door, and Wolf stayed at her back. Alice inhaled deeply as they stepped into the cool evening air and away from the music and voices. She felt herself steady.

They moved along the balcony away from the other guests, then stayed silent while she listened for any indication of where Nicholas was.

"He received a note."

"When?" James asked.

"I was looking at the statues and he arrived. A footman found him and handed it over."

She heard voices then. "He's in trouble. That way." She pointed to the right.

"Let's go!" James started running, and the others were soon on his heels.

"What can you hear, Alice?"

"He's fighting, but he is outnumbered! The men are saying to harm but not kill him."

"Nicholas!" The name was torn from Lilly.

Cam took the lead, running hard with the other men on his heels. Alice felt her sides start to burn as she clutched Lilly's hand in hers. With their skirts hampering them, it was not easy to run at any great speed. Stopping, both hiked them above their knees and ran on.

"Do you still hear him, Alice?"

"Y-yes, Lilly."

"Thank God! I have only recently found my b-brother again, I have no wish to lose him."

They rounded the bend in the path and stopped. Alice was confronted with a mass of men. They were all fighting, but it was hard to see a great deal in the dark even with moonlight.

The women moved sideways in a circle, keeping their distance from the men.

"Good shot, Dev!" Lilly cried as her husband knocked one of the men backward.

"I cannot see Nicholas, Lilly."

Alice shuddered as she heard a fist connect with flesh. She searched through the mass of bodies, trying desperately to find him.

"He has fallen!" Lilly cried pointing to the right.

Alice saw him then, on the ground, with a man over him. She watched as he drew back his foot and kicked Nicholas in the ribs.

"Cur!" Alice screamed, running at the man. She jumped, landing on his back. Wrapping her arms around his neck she squeezed as hard as she could.

"Get off me!" the man roared, spinning in circles, his hands trying to grab her.

"God's blood!" She heard Nicholas shout. "Get off him, you little fool!"

"Jump clear, Alice!" Lilly's words had her leaping off the man's back, and seconds later she swung a branch hard at his head. The man crumpled to a heap on the floor.

"Excellent shot, Lilly!"

Looking for Nicholas, Alice found him back on his feet, fighting, moving left and right, fists raised. A man lunged at him, and he did a kicking motion that made the man grunt in pain.

"Well done!" Alice cried.

"Move!" he roared at her.

Lilly grabbed Alice's hand, and they scurried back a few steps.

James charged his man, sending him stumbling backward. Alice moved a few feet to the left and stuck out her foot; the man tripped, fell, and hit his head. Dev landed a blow and his did the same. The last men who had attacked Nicholas, realizing they were beaten, then ran off into Hyde Park.

"Wh-what the hell were you two doing?" Nicholas stalked toward them, the breath rasping in and out of his mouth. "You are mad!"

"Helping you," Alice said, backing up a few steps, which put her at Lilly's side. The women locked arms as Dev approached.

"That was reckless and dangerous. One punch would have felled either of you!" Nicholas roared. Blood ran down his face from a cut under one eye.

"Lilly, my love. What have I told you about staying out of danger?" Dev said, grabbing his wife and hugging her close. "But you are both very brave," he added, kissing her cheek.

"Brave? It was foolish! Christ, they could have been hurt, or worse! I cannot believe you would say that was bravery. It was idiocy!"

"They are safe, Nicholas," Cam said. "All is well."

They heard the sound of running feet, and soon Eden and Rose arrived.

"Ouch." Nicholas deflated like a balloon before Alice, his legs buckling as he staggered a few paces clutching his chest.

James grabbed him.

"Where are you hurt, brother?" Lilly rushed forward.

"My ribs."

Alice watched Dev's eyes flare bright in his face. They were focused on Nicholas.

"He needs healing, love. His ribs." Dev whispered the words to his wife.

"Wolf, take his other side, please," Alice said, coming forward to stand before Nicholas. She then took a handkerchief out of her brother's pocket and pressed it to the cut on Nicholas's eyes.

"Alice—"

"Let me stop the blood now, Nicholas. Let us help you."

Alice knew that both Dev and Cam were touching Lilly as she touched Nicholas. Her spare hand gripped her brother's, and she knew Wolf would be connected to the others in some way, just as Eden would.

"What did those men say to you, Nicholas?" Alice distracted him as Lilly joined the circle, now without her gloves on.

"I'm still angry with you," Nicholas rasped, then hissed as he tried to breathe.

"Very well, but that doesn't stop you from telling us what they said, surely." Alice blotted the blood on his cheek.

"Nicholas, I'm going to touch your ribs now," Lilly said.

"Why?"

"To check they are not broken."

He nodded, as clearly talking was taking its toll on him.

"M-my ribs feel warm?"

"They don't appear to be broken," Lilly said.

"What do you know of such things?"

"A great deal, actually; Essie taught me."

It was only a matter of seconds, maybe a minute, and then Lilly stepped back. Dev reached for her.

"I am well," Alice heard her whisper.

"You need to rest and eat," Dev whispered back. "Let me help you to the carriage, my love."

"Come, let us leave. James, you and Eden get the coats, and we shall see you at the carriages," Cam said. "We shall retire to the duke's residence, where he can feed us and Essie can come and look you over, Nicholas."

"I am well."

"Undoubtedly, but that cut under your eye will need something to stave off infection."

"I will go to my house. My housekeeper can tend me."

"No, you will go to mine," the duke said. It was not a tone he often used, but one that had them all moving.

Alice wasn't sure how it happened, but she ended up in the coach alone with Nicholas. Probably as she still had her hand pressed to his cheek, blotting the blood with Wolf's handkerchief.

"Alice is alone with Nicholas!" She heard Wolf come to the same realization as the carriage started moving.

"And will be fine," Rose soothed. "No one will know, and he is family."

Wolf grumbled about it not being right, but as his carriage was now some distance ahead of the one she occupied with Nicholas, she could not hear Rose's reply. Which was odd, she could usually hear for some distance.

Lifting the handkerchief, she noted the bleeding had eased. Nicholas grabbed her hand as she pulled away.

"You should not have taken that risk tonight, Alice." His eyes were as black as midnight. She saw other bruises starting to form on his face, but it did nothing to deter from the beauty she saw in it. Or the raw emotion radiating from him.

"I would do it again," Alice said, unmoving.

He moved to the edge of his seat and pulled her closer until she was trapped between his legs.

"Why must you take risks! Damn you, woman, why can you not understand the danger you place yourself in!"

He was roaring at her now. Surprisingly his words did not make her wince, almost like her hearing was normal. He needed to do this, she realized, needed to release the emotion the fight had built up inside him.

"You were the one in danger, Nicholas. Now sit back and let me tend you."

"Alice, you must show more care." The words were desperate. "This is not your village, there are bad people—"

"I am not a fool. Now, you must calm down."

"I don't want to calm down. When I saw you jump on that man's back I... I...."

"Yes?"

"You shouldn't have done it."

"I will not stand by and watch while people I care for are harmed."

The anger left him as quick as it had come.

"You care for me?" His hand cupped her cheek. Suddenly he was no longer angry.

"M-my family."

"Me," he whispered, closing the distance between them.

The kiss was everything that the others had been and more again.

"Alice." Her name was torn from his lips. "This... we cannot."

"I know, you've already told me that, but here we are, kissing once more." She said the words against his lips.

"I am not the man for one as sweet and innocent as you."

"Why?" Alice whispered as his lips moved over her face, his hands trailing up her sides, leaving fire where they touched.

"Because I am the dark where you are light." His hand reached the underside of her breasts, and the breath lodged in her throat. "Because I would do this when I know I should not." The hand moved up and cupped her breast. He swallowed her cry, crushing her lips.

And then he released her and moved away.

126

"No more. I am not myself. Forgive me, it will not happen again."

His face was once again closed tight, each muscle clenched as if chiseled in stone.

"Why am I not for the likes of you?"

His eyes moved from the window to her.

"Because I am a sinner, Alice, and nothing and no one can change that. My life has been one of debauchery and salacious behavior. The only companion I am fit to keep company with is Lucifer himself."

Alice did not speak again, because for the first time in her life she didn't know what say. That he thought himself fit company for Lucifer was both disturbing and sad. She vowed to speak with someone about his past, and this time she would get answers.

She watched from her side of the carriage as London passed her by and tried to think about how wonderful it felt to have his hand on her breast. Surely she was indeed a loose woman.

Wolf was the first to their carriage as it stopped, running his eyes over her as he helped her down.

"I am well, Wolf. I received no injury, and it is Nicholas who needs your attention." Alice moved aside, and Wolf leaned in to help him.

"I can manage."

"You look ready to fall."

"I am not an invalid."

"Be quiet, Nicholas, and let Wolf help you," James said, joining them.

Alice followed them inside. James and Wolf were on either side of him in case he should stumble.

I am not the man for one as sweet and innocent as you.

What had he done?

They gathered in James's study, a wonderful room with

comfortable furnishings and books that she loved. This room had a soul that wrapped around a person when they entered it. Tonight, it did nothing to ease the cold that had formed inside Alice.

"I have sent a footman for Essie."

Nicholas tried to bite back a moan as they lowered him into a chair. Now that the fight had left him, he was suffering.

"Don't wake her, Dev, I am all right."

"Shut up," James said, handing him a brandy.

Soon everyone was there; even Max had come, looking rumpled, with Essie carrying her supplies.

"Don't fuss, Essie, I am well." Nicholas tried again to get them to leave him alone. "Return to your beds."

"I will be the judge of that." She dropped down beside him. "Warm water, please, James, and cloths."

Nicholas rested his head on the back of the seat and closed his eyes, knowing that he was outnumbered.

She watched Essie turn to Dev, who changed his vision and checked Nicholas over. He then motioned to Nicholas's ribs and pointed to Lilly, who was resting in a chair eating and drinking to regain her strength. Essie nodded.

She cleaned and stitched the cut on his eye. Nicholas never moved.

Alice drank the tea Rose handed her and watched. Why him? What was it about this man that was different from the others?

"Tell us what happened, Nicholas. Why you were out there alone tonight?" James said.

He opened his eyes and took the tea Essie handed him. He sipped, then gagged.

"That is revolting."

"But it will help you grow into a big, strong boy, so drink up," she said. "Plus it will help you heal."

His hair was messy, his necktie missing, and shirt and coat torn. In that moment, she could imagine him as Lucifer's companion.

"Speak, Nicholas, and I shall decide how angry I am with you!" Lilly said.

"I am all right, sister."

"You are now, but only because of Alice."

His eyes found hers.

"Why Alice?"

"I couldn't find you, and she told us about the note, so we came looking."

Of course they couldn't tell him the truth.

"Thank you." He nodded, then winced. "A footman brought me a note, as Alice told you. It directed me to meet whoever wrote it outside, as they had information about the babe that my housekeeper—"

"I thought you more intelligent than that, Nicholas. You are a bloody idiot for going out there without alerting us!"

Nicholas was shocked at Cam's anger.

"I don't see why?"

"God's blood," Cam muttered. "The man's a fool."

"I am not a fool. The note was addressed to me."

"And you walked into a trap," Lilly said. "You are a fool."

"The problem here, Nicholas," James snapped, "is that you still don't see yourself as part of this family. If you had, you would have never done such a reckless thing. You would have alerted one of us to your actions!"

They did not often see the duke angry, but he was now.

"I did what I felt was right. What was reckless was Alice leaping on that man's back!"

"This is not about me, so do not try and deflect away from your reckless actions, Nicholas." Alice's anger flared once more at the risks he'd taken. He censured her, but his actions had been worse.

She'd been so scared when she realized he was being hurt. Unsure what they would find when they reached him.

"Well, it bloody well should be about you! You need to make sure she is not so foolhardy again, Wolf. In fact, lock her in her room until she promises to behave!"

Wolf looked from Alice to Nicholas, and she had no idea what he was thinking as she could not read the expression. Looking around the room, she encountered similar expressions from her family members. It was unsettling that everyone but she and Nicholas appeared to be considering something.

It disturbed Alice enough that she got out of her seat and stormed from the room without saying good night. Of course, as she was in James's house she could not leave, but still, she'd find a room to wait in that was not near that foolish man, Nicholas Braithwaite.

CHAPTER 14

Three weeks after the Mueller Ball, Nicholas decided it was time to reenter society. Today there was to be a ride in the country with a picnic beside a lake, which sounded perfect and not overly taxing.

His body had surprisingly not taken much healing. He'd first thought his ribs broken, but they had stopped aching almost immediately. The cut to his face, black eye, and damaged nose had taken longer. But Essie's potions had aided his recovery.

What had taken longer was what was going on inside his head. He'd needed time and distance to no longer be consumed by thoughts and visions of Alice Sinclair. For days, he'd felt the soft weight of her breasts in his hand. Known the terror of seeing her on that man's back after she had leapt recklessly to his rescue, but no longer.

Nicholas now believed he was over that particular infatuation. Although she had come to him last night demanding he find that babe yet again, and the other in her arms, at least now he felt he could see her and feel nothing.

"A momentary insanity." He put it down to that.

"Pardon, my lord?"

"Nothing, Percy. The brown jacket, if you please."

"Surely not, my lord? The green is far better for such an event, and may I suggest the ivory and black waistcoat?"

Nicholas had woken today feeling different and couldn't quite put his finger on why. Lighter inside somehow, which was surely only due to the fact that he'd finally caught up on sleep and read more books than he had in a single year.

"The brown, Percy."

His valet made a small sound reminiscent of a wounded animal and exchanged the green jacket for the brown.

"I am wearing a waistcoat of bronze and cream, surely the brown goes best with that?"

The color was a hideous mustard. Mud brown and horse excrement green are not the rage this season.

Alice had said those words to him. Perhaps he hadn't quite eradicated her from his head entirely, but he would. It was vexing how he didn't seem to be able to forget anything she told him, and yet he couldn't remember what he'd done yesterday... not actually true, as he'd read whilst reclining in his favorite chair, as he had the day before that.

"And it is very nice, but surely the occasion warrants the ivory and black?"

His valet was a small man* with boundless energy and bright eyes. He had been with Nicholas for many years through many trying times.

"No," Nicholas said, holding out his arms for the brown jacket.

"Very well." Percy's lips pursed.

"Cheer up, there is after all the Stratton Ball tomorrow night. I shall wear exactly what you wish to that event and shine like the brightest beacon of sartorial elegance."

Percy did not comment but looked skeptical.

"All right, I may not, but surely I will cut an adequate

figure. Besides, had you your way, I would leave the house looking like a dandy."

Percy looked wounded. Nicholas knew better; the man had the hide of an elephant.

"Gloves, please." Nicholas held out his hand, and his valet showed restraint and placed them in his palm gently.

"My wish is for your day to improve, Percy."

"Mrs. Brown has made plum cake, my lord."

"Excellent. Have two helpings, it will restore your humors. You can moan extensively about your tiresome employer while eating it."

"I believe you may be onto something, my lord."

Nicholas was laughing as he left his room. He had spent the last few weeks alone for the most part, something he rarely did as he did not particularly like his own company, but strangely he had this time.

Of course, his family were constantly on his doorstep checking up on him. And maybe that was part of the reason he felt lighter. They were forcing him to accept he was part of them, and perhaps he finally had.

Unfortunately, with them came Alice, but he hoped she married her sainted Barty with expediency, then he could forget about her entirely. But not Captain Young of the shifty eyes. The thought of her marrying either left a vile taste in his mouth, so he swallowed and ignored it.

Today he was to ride with his family and friends and then attend a picnic that Lord and Lady Levermarch had organized. He hoped the day uneventful of anything but what it should be. Food, companionship, and exercise. All things he was ready for.

He thought about that night at the Mueller Ball often. The knowledge that had settled over him when those men had appeared to harm him. He wanted to live, but to do that he had to fight to survive. When his family had arrived, he'd been doing just that. They'd waded in without hesitation. The duke, the lord, the captain, and Cam. Giving no thought to their own welfare. He, Nicholas, had been in danger, therefore they would help.

It was a humbling thought on top of the knowledge that he now wanted to be part of their family.

He'd put distance between them because he believed himself unworthy, they had not allowed that.

At his cousin's prompting, yesterday he had employed the services of one Mr. Spriggot, a small innocuous man who James and the Sinclairs had assured him was a superb investigator. With him came Mr. Brown, a large, bullish fellow who was a Bow Street Runner.

An odd pair, but James had assured him there were none better. He had set them to investigating the matter of the missing babies and who had attacked him at the Mueller Ball.

Leaving the house, Nicholas mounted his waiting horse.

"Thank you, Joshua."

"Have a good day, my lord."

He rode through London, enjoying once again being outside doing what he loved, riding. They were to meet in the park and ride out from there. Those not riding would take carriages.

The sky wasn't exactly blue, but he saw no sign of rain clouds and hoped it stayed that way. Enjoying the sensation of harmony within his soul, he reached his destination to find several people milling about on a large stretch of grass.

"Nicholas, good to see you."

"Will." Nicholas nodded, reaching over to shake the hand of the man who rode forward. He had not been close with many noblemen for years, but the changes in him had adjusted that. This man he now counted as a friend, as he did his family.

"Come, our party is over there, join us. Your disreputable family are with us."

William Ryder was a well-respected member of society with a duke for a brother and a marquis for a brother-in-law. Nicholas had always liked him, because when he was the cad he'd been, Will had always spoken with him as if he was worthy of his time... which he certainly hadn't been, but Nicholas appreciated it all the same.

"Nice mount."

"His sire is Jezzop, from the Halton stables," Nicholas said as Will studied his horse, Ferdinand, which he'd recently found out his stable master had shortened to Freddy.

"Obedient?"

"Extremely." As the words left his mouth, Freddy stretched his neck, jerked the reins from Nicholas's hands, and charged forward.

"Stop at once!"

The horse did, coming to an abrupt halt wedged nicely between Alice Sinclair and her brother.

"Hello, Freddy." Wolf stroked a hand down his neck.

"Do that again, and you'll be put out to pasture in a paddock with no grass," Nicholas growled in his horse's ear.

"He likes Apollo."

"I don't know why; your beast is always trying to nip him."

"They have a love-hate relationship."

"Come now, surely your ego can stand what just occurred, my lord?"

Of course she would never just settle for "hello" after what they'd shared. Alice was no shy miss who would blush and stammer or avoid him.

The emerald green of her riding habit did startling things for her already amazing eyes. It had black braiding marching down the front in the military style that was currently in fashion, and a black hat sat on her head. She was beautiful, but no more so than others, so he refused to feel anything other than admiration. And would not give that kiss in his carriage another thought. Which he just did and wanted to kick himself for.

Stop now!

"Good day to you, Miss Sinclair." The use of her full name was to put distance between them.

"Why is she Miss Sinclair?" Wolf asked.

"I am being polite."

Wolf hooted with laugher, and Alice had a look on her face he couldn't read.

"Can your ego not cope with such behavior from your horse, Lord Braithwaite?"

"My ego has nothing to do with it, Miss Sinclair. I simply have no wish for my horse to disregard my orders in favor of seeking out your brother's beast."

"My brother has an affinity with animals." She tilted her head slightly to study Wolf. "I'm not entirely sure what that says about him."

"It says that animals are fine judges of character," Wolf drawled.

"Or understand when someone is at their level," Cam added from behind them. "Hello, Nicholas."

"Good morning, Cam."

"I thought we discussed you gadding about London with a groomsman from now on, or one of us."

"I have never gadded anywhere and was in no danger riding from my house through the busy streets to here."

"Just don't take any notes from footmen," Cam added.

"Unless they are on horseback, I think I am safe."

Their party was a large one, with many of society's more prominent members in attendance. All the Sinclair and

Raven clan were here, as were the Langley sisters and their husbands.

Warwick was to ride, but the twins, Samantha, and the children who were with nannies were in carriages, as were Essie, Kate, Rose, and Emily.

"We shall be off now, as I have no wish for the ices to melt," Lady Levermarch declared.

"Hello, Nicholas. I did not see you at Tattersalls yesterday."

Recently married, Benjamin Hetherington and his twin Alex were the Marquis of Levermarch's brothers. Once, they'd gambled with him, but their big brother had soon put an end to that.

"I had another appointment."

"'Tis a shame, as Linley put that black stallion of his up for sale."

Nicholas bit back a groan. He'd been after that horse for years.

"I hope you purchased it for me."

"I purchased it for myself, and if you are good I will let you come over and pat it occasionally."

Nicholas said something foul, and Benjamin rode off laughing.

"There will be other horses, my lord."

"Not like that one," Nicholas said to Alice as they left their meeting place.

She slowed her horse, and he was glad she was soon behind him somewhere so he wouldn't have to look at her the entire journey.

"I can just not get past the fact that someone is stealing babies, Nicholas."

"Good morning, sister."

"Good morning, brother."

Lilly wore blue, the skirts darker than the jacket. She looked happy and content, and he loved seeing her that way.

"And yes, it is not a comfortable thought."

"Are you feeling completely healed?"

"I am, thanks to the care of you and Essie. I thought my ribs would take longer to heal, but they gave me no pain at all."

"Strange things, ribs, but I have heard they heal fast. Now tell me what you plan to do next about these babies. Without taking any further risks, of course."

He talked as they rode out of London and headed over the hills and valleys to the location Lady Levermarch had designated for their picnic.

"They are good men, Mr. Spriggott and Mr. Brown. I'm sure in no time you will have news. Until then, do not walk anywhere alone," Eden said, joining them.

"I am now not the only one who knows about the babies, ladies. I'm sure there is no longer a threat to just me."

"You started it, so the threat is still with you as far as I am concerned," Lilly said. She then rode off to Dev's side. Clearly the conversation to her mind was concluded.

"Miss Gillett is looking lovely today, don't you think, Nicholas?"

"Is she, I hadn't noticed, Eden."

"Well, I will be sure to introduce you."

The duchess wore red, and it looked stunning on her.

"I have already met her, so there is no need to go to the trouble. Thank you."

"She plays the piano and sings also."

He turned in his saddle slightly to look at her. Clearly he needed to be blunt.

"I have no wish to marry Miss Gillett, Eden."

"I think you'll change your mind before the season is over."

"I doubt that."

She rode away looking annoyed. The conversation with Lilly in the carriage the day they went to *The Trumpeter* came back to him then. Was it possible his family was trying to marry him off this season? He would be putting a stop to that.

"I understand your horse is sired by Jezzop, from the Halton stables, Lord Braithwaite. I have a mare with the same bloodlines." Lady Levermarch took Eden's place at his side.

"Yes, he is a wonderful horse when he's behaving."

"My mare is the same, extremely strong willed."

Once he got over his surprise to be discussing bloodlines with her, he enjoyed the conversation very much. Nicholas had been guilty of placing women in two categories: those who wanted to bed him, and those who didn't. He'd rectified that now he was sober.

"You can stand on your horse's back?"

She flashed him a smile that Nicholas was sure brought her husband to his knees often.

"Indeed. I can do many tricks. Will had a groom called Moses, who used to ride tricks in a carnival, it was him who taught me."

"Good Lord. How did your brother in law and husband cope with that?"

She shot him a wicked smile. "Badly."

He laughed as she rode away.

She was considered one of the most beautiful women in London society, and with her pretty face, honey-blonde curls, and lush curves he could see why.

"If you are about to drool, I shall find someone else to ride beside."

He turned to find Alice beside him once more.

"I beg your pardon?"

She nodded to Lady Levermarch, who was now beside Lilly. "She is a beautiful woman. I have seen men trip over their own feet when she is near."

"Do I seem like a man who would trip over his own feet when an attractive woman is around? And surely if that was the case, I would have done so before now around you Sinclairs and Ravens."

She didn't blush. Nicholas knew this as he was looking at her. Instead she made a scoffing sound.

"Don't play the pretty with me, my lord. I know what I am."

"And what is that?"

Alice waved a gloved hand about.

"What does that gesture actually mean? You appear to do it a great deal when you can't find the right words."

"It means I don't have to explain, and I don't want you to add anything further, and I can always find the right words."

"All that from a hand wave? How clever at communicating you are. But getting back to the subject at hand, am I to understand you do not think you are beautiful... or more importantly, as beautiful as Lady Levermarch?"

She ignored him, turning away, which allowed him to run his eyes over the delicate curve of her jaw... the jaw he'd kissed.

"I have spent a great deal of time in the company of beautiful women, and I find it is not just the outside beauty that matters."

She turned to face him.

"I'm not sure if that is bragging or just the simple truth."

"Simple truth. I have been in society for many years."

"Not many men feel that way."

"Many men are fools, Alice. Remember that. I have first-hand knowledge of this, as I was one once."

Their eyes held, and Nicholas felt it again, the tightness in his chest.

"And how is your sainted Barty?" he made himself ask.

"Sssh, I have no wish for Wolf to overhear your words."

"Because?"

"Because I don't."

"What is wrong with Barty? You both seemed upset the other day in the men's fashion establishment."

The frown formed lines between her eyes. Nicholas had the ridiculous urge to reach over and smooth them.

"He needs to go home," she said softly.

"Alice, if you need help—"

"No, I have it under control, thank you, my lord."

"I'm sure you do." How did he convey to her that she needed to show more care? "But I would still caution you to take care."

"I am always careful."

He could do nothing to stop the snort.

"I am!"

He remained silent.

"Well, I try to be."

"As your friend, I would like you to try harder."

She looked at him.

"Are we to be friends, Nicholas?"

"Yes, as we can be nothing else, Alice."

A heavy silence settled between them.

"Very well, but as we are friends, will you now tell me about the man you were, or something I do not know about you?"

"There is nothing in my past that can be of interest to you." There was absolutely no way he was enlightening her about the man he'd been.

"The thing is, Nicholas, no one in my family will furnish me with this information, which is odd, as they are usually more than happy to gossip." She was frowning again. "However, on the matter of your past they are surprisingly tight-lipped. It is most vexing."

Excellent.

"I have no wish to discuss the matter further, thank you," he said, sounding stuffy and pompous, but when his back was against the wall, that was exactly how he reacted.

"Come now. You feel comfortable poking and prodding into my life, surely I am allowed a small window into yours?"

"I don't poke and prod into your life. Unluckily for me, I come across you when you are doing something you shouldn't."

She raised a brow.

He looked away from her and at the others who rode before him. All chatting, happy to be out enjoying the fresh air.

"Tell me something... anything."

"No."

"That's it? No?"

"Yes."

Now be quiet.

"Surely someone as lofty as you couldn't have done anything overly exciting?"

"You will not needle a reaction from me, Alice."

"Cam I know was a bit of rogue and got into trouble, and it's my belief that you are in some way involved in that—"

"Let it be, Alice."

Her sigh was forlorn.

"Very well, I will tell you one thing. My sister has a house for children who live on the streets. They go there if they need care or shelter."

"I know about Temple Street. Also that the Sinclair and Raven ladies knit for the children who sometimes shelter there."

"That's right. But did you also know that we have another house, and I look after that one, as it is above a tavern by the docks and both Dev and I forbid Lilly to go there."

"I didn't know that. It is a very noble thing to do, Nicholas. Which simply reinforces my belief you cannot have been that awful before."

"I was."

"I would like to visit this place and help the children if—"

"Absolutely not!"

She gave him a smile that told Nicholas she'd known exactly what she was doing by speaking those words.

"I walked right into that," he muttered.

"I believe friends do that to each other. It's called teasing."

He laughed as she'd wanted him to, and while he was aware of her like he had never been another woman, he thought that possibly, with distance and less exposure, he could call her friend... if an uncomfortable one.

CHAPTER 15

*A*lice had known she must simply act like nothing had transpired between her and Nicholas when he'd joined her and Wolf, for both their sakes. No awkward silences or avoidance; their families would realize if she behaved differently around him.

So she'd teased him.

He looked handsome and vital today. Dressed immaculately as always, hair slightly ruffled beneath his hat. Sitting with ease on his horse, as if he'd been born to ride.

He wanted them to be friends, and while Alice had her doubts as to whether she would ever truly feel comfortable in Nicholas Braithwaite's presence, she would try.

Over the last few weeks she had come to the realization that perhaps he was the first man she'd ever truly wanted to the point that she forgot to be sensible. He robbed her of that. Because he had vowed there could be nothing between them, Alice had spent the time apart from him shoring up her defenses.

While she'd never believed herself capable of the burning passions that some experienced, she realized after their first kiss that in fact she'd been wrong. But he had no wish to marry her, and she should have no wish to marry him. After all, he'd only kissed her, *and touched her breast;* she was naive to believe he had not done that and more with women.

No, this was for the best. Friends they could be... but nothing more.

As they crested the hill, the gleam of a lake caught Alice's eye. It was a beautiful scene spread before them. The picnic had been set up at the base of the hill, with rolling pastures to the left and right.

"It's in moments such as this I wish I could paint."

"I would rather sketch it," Nicholas said.

"Are you any good?"

He raised a haughty brow. "I rarely do things I do not excel at."

"How terribly pompous of you, Lord Braithwaite."

Perhaps they could do this... be friends and laugh with each other. After all, one day she would wed, or he would, and they would rarely see each other, so until then she would pretend being near him did not make butterflies flutter in her stomach.

"What put that look on your face?"

"I'm hungry," Alice lied, nudging her heels into the horse's side and sending it down the hill, away from him.

The guests soon settled on pillows and blankets the staff had set out for them. They filled their plates from the laden trestle tables with tea sandwiches—cucumber and cream cheese—for Alice, plus a scone with jam and clotted cream.

"That is Lady Mueller, who Lilly told me is quite taken with Nicholas." Kate whispered the words to Alice, as they were currently sharing a pillow.

Her sister was not out in society as yet, but the family said she could attend today with the children.

It was decided due to Alice's age, being twenty-three and

quite ancient for a debutante, it would be best if she was presented alone, and Kate, at twenty, next year.

"Her smile would frighten small animals and babies."

She found the woman, dressed in a pretty day dress that could do with a few more inches of material in the bodice. Clearly she had not ridden here. Lady Mueller was laughing with Nicholas, placing her hand on his sleeve and leaning forward so he could have a clear view of her ample breasts.

"She seems a shy sort," Alice said, nibbling on her scone even though it tasted sour.

"Very. Someone should teach her how to communicate better. She is doing a terrible job. Why, Nicholas has no idea at all that she would like to ravish him."

"Kate! I cannot believe you said that." Alice looked around them, but no one was listening. Except maybe Eden, whose lips had tilted up as if she was smiling about something secret.

"Yes, you can, we are always honest with each other."

"Miss Gimlet looks terrible in beige, it washes her complexion away," Alice said, studying the young woman who sat at her mother's side.

"I often wonder why mothers dress their offspring in clothes that look horrid on them."

"Because they believe it looks good on them... or should I say that they want it to look good on their daughters, as once, it looked wonderful on them. 'Tis a wonder Sir Nigel hasn't lost an eye with his shirt points. And the number of folds in that necktie make him appear as if he is wearing some kind of brace," Alice added.

Kate moved her eyes from Nicholas to Sir Nigel.

"He looks like a puppy as yet grown into his skin."

"Do you think he doesn't look in the mirror, or his valet is having a laugh at his expense?"

"There are none so blind as those who don't want to see, Kate."

"Very true, which leads me nicely to my question."

"What question?" Alice dragged her eyes from the hand Nicholas placed over Lady Mueller's.

"What is between you and Nicholas?"

As luck would have it, she had just swallowed the last mouthful of the scone, or Alice was sure it would have ended up everywhere as she coughed. Like a dutiful sister, Kate smacked her hard on the back.

"Better?"

"H-hardly," Alice gasped. "And there is nothing between us, so I will thank you to never speak that way again."

Kate made a scoffing sound that had her wanting to lob the other half of the scone at her... but it was a scone, and Alice was partial to them.

"'Lo, 'Lice."

"Hello, Meredith." Relieved to be interrupted from the disturbing conversation with Kate, she was only too happy to pull the child onto her lap.

"She just called you Lice," Kate said sounding smug. "As in bed lice."

It was a known fact that no one could annoy you quite like a sibling... ask anyone who had one, the answer would be unequivocally yes.

"And I will be asking you that question again, Alice," Kate added.

Not if I can help it.

"We shall play charades!" Lady Levermarch said, clapping her hands to get everyone's attention.

"I would rather have a tooth pulled." Kate grumbled along with several of the men.

"I'm sure that could be arranged."

"I will select the teams," Lady Levermarch added.

"Dear lord, not teams." Kate sighed. "I've never been good at team playing."

"Because you're selfish." Alice blew a raspberry into Meredith's neck. "And like all the glory."

Some sisters, or so she had heard, communicated with sweet words and gestures. Kate and Alice had never been that way.

"You are in Nicholas's team?" Alice didn't look at Kate but knew the expression she would have on her face was smug.

"Excellent, I hope he has the required skills for us to win."

Alice kept Meredith as she made her way to where her team assembled. Lady Mueller was also there, next to Nicholas, still cooing at him in a silly voice. It was nauseating.

"Never behave like that, Meredith, or you and I will be having words," she whispered to the little girl, who was now clinging to her as she looked at Lady Mueller.

"Cooee, sweet little girl." The woman smiled, but it was more a baring of her teeth as she took one of Meredith's hands. Excellent judges of character, infants. The little girl tugged her fingers away and buried her head into Alice's neck.

"She is shy, aren't you, darling," Nicholas said, leaning in to kiss his niece. Alice deliberately held her breath. The man smelled far too good.

"Is she too heavy, Alice? I could take her if so."

"No, she is fine, thank you."

"I think as Lord Braithwaite is the most intelligent and handsome among us, he should go first," Lady Mueller declared loudly, obviously not happy that Nicholas' attention was no longer focused on her.

"I don't think he's the most handsome," Alice said, simply because the woman was annoying her with her foolish behavior, and honestly, how rude to say such a thing in the presence of other men. "Both Mr. Alexander Hetherington and Lord Ryder are equally as handsome... as are many of the other men here today."

"Thank you, Miss Sinclair, that is very kind of you," Lord Ryder said solemnly. However, his eyes were twinkling.

"Oh... well, of course." Lady Mueller looked extremely annoyed at Alice. Nicholas was glaring at her now too.

Surely he did not believe the woman's compliments? Was he so shallow he did not like Alice questioning Lady Mueller's claim that he was the most handsome man in their team?

"My husband is quite good-looking also," Mrs. Primrose Hetherington said, which made Alice like her immediately.

"Of course... I never meant otherwise. I was merely pointing out that with Lord Braithwaite's intellect and appearance, he could start."

"But how have you come to the conclusion that he is the most intelligent? Have you tested that Lord Braithwaite's intellect surpasses everyone else's in the team?" Alice asked sweetly.

"Indeed," Mr. Alexander Hetherington said. "How, Lady Mueller?"

Alice liked him also, as he gave her a wink.

"I think it is quite clear that I am no more intelligent than anyone else present," Nicholas gritted out, giving Alice a look that said he would have something to say to her if she didn't shut her mouth. "But thank you for stating otherwise, Lady Mueller," Nicholas added.

She was suddenly disappointed in him, and herself for believing him a better man than he was currently displaying. His ego was obviously far more inflated than she'd earlier believed.

"If everyone has a charade in mind, then we shall begin," Lady Levermarch said. "Teams will guess their own, and the quickest time will dictate the winner. Please state if it is a book or play."

"I shall judge," Max said, and no one argued. He sat with his nieces and nephews either on his lap or around him. "With help from this lot."

Lady Mueller sniffed, looking down her nose at Max.

Alice knew many in society did not like those who were untitled or of lower birth fraternizing with them, but as society was changing and the power of those like Max growing, they could do little about it.

"Do you need a handkerchief, Lady Mueller?"

"I do not!" she snapped at Alice.

Nicholas, who was still beside Alice, leaned in and told her to shut up. She elbowed him in the ribs.

"I shall go first." Sir Nigel stepped forward. "My intellect and handsomeness suggests I am equal to Lord Braithwaite!"

Alice caught Primrose Hetherington's eyes and quickly pulled away. It would be rude to burst into hysterical laughter, even if it was justified.

"I will be performing a play."

"Dear lord," Alexander Hetherington whispered. "Someone just shoot him now and save us all."

"He believes he is accomplished at charades, clearly," Nicholas said from the side of his mouth.

"How?" Alice added. "I mean, what denotes one's prowess at charades?"

"The lack of humiliation we, the spectators, feel," Alexander Hetherington added.

"There is that," Alice said, feeling her toes curl inside her riding boots at Sir Nigel's antics. She was embarrassed. How could the man not see the fool he was making of himself.

"His ego is surpassed only by the idiocy of his dress," Nicholas said softly.

The other groups stood and watched him prance

forward. He then proceeded to romp about with his fingers on his head. People from his group called out names. He shook his head, then began to play the flute. When that failed, he danced about flapping his arms as though they were wings.

"Give it up, Nigel, clearly no one has a clue," Cam heckled him.

"A complete guide to idiotic behavior?" Alexander whispered.

Sir Nigel stopped and glared at his group. Sweat beaded his brow from his exertions.

"The foolish exploits of a brainless twit?" Lord Ryder suggested. "Midsummer nightmares?"

"That was actually quite clever, Ryder," Nicholas said.

"I frequently am. Clever, that is. Just ask my wife."

"Do you all give up?" Lady Levermarch asked, clearly over watching the display.

"Yes!"

Alice couldn't remember ever laughing as hard as she did standing there watching the performances. Lord Levermarch did a credible mime of *Arabian Nights*. Grabbing his wife's scarf and wrapping it dramatically around his head. Things got a bit sticky when Mr. Jonathan attempted *An Evening's Love* and lunged for Miss Gimlet swinging her into his arms. Lady Gimlet leapt to her feet, slapping him hard whilst shrieking for her daughter's release.

"I shall now perform," Lady Mueller said, throwing Nicholas a smoldering look.

"Dear lord, save us all," Alice whispered to Meredith.

"Perhaps you could start without us." Nicholas gripped Alice's arm. "Miss Sinclair has just informed me she is feeling faint." His eyes looked cold and angry as they glared down at her.

"What?" Alice took a step back, clutching the child close.

He started walking, and there was little she could do but follow, as she had no doubt he would drag her if required.

"Release me!"

"No."

The little girl made some sort of garbled speech to her uncle.

"I know, darling, you are in the arms of a madwoman." He then plucked her from Alice. "Stay," he ordered as if she were a dog, and then walked to where Lilly stood, handing Meredith to her mother.

Alice, who had never taken orders well, made good her escape, hurrying past the other guests and making a run for it to the water's edge. Once there, she headed left to stand behind a small grouping of trees, out of sight from the others.

Whatever Nicholas's problem was, she had no wish to hear it.

"So back to my question—"

"Kate!" Alice squealed. "When did you arrive?"

"I've been here the entire time. I hid when Lady Levermarch started putting us into groups."

"My heart is pounding. You scared the wits out of me."

"Not terribly hard, considering your limited supply of them. But we digress."

"From what?" Alice looked, but did not see Nicholas.

"On the matter of what is going on with you and Nicholas?"

"Nothing."

"I know you better than I know myself, Alice. I have seen the way you look at him. The longing—"

"I beg your pardon, I long for no man."

"He looks at you the same way. Slightly confused, almost annoyed, but there is also definitely longing in his gaze."

That did not make her feel better at all.

"He longs for Lady Mueller with her large breasts and breathy whispers."

"I don't think so."

"Enough, Kate... please." She couldn't continue to lie to her sister when clearly she was right. "Nothing can ever be between us."

"He told you that?"

"I know that," Alice said firmly. "My hearing, for one—"

"He would care nothing for that if he loved you."

"And yet he doesn't, so I beg of you not to mention it again."

"I'm sorry if I have upset you, Alice." She felt a hand on her back rubbing in small circles and felt the ridiculous urge to cry.

"We are friends, Kate, no more, and it is best that way."

"Very well, I will say no more."

Alice exhaled.

"But—"

"Must there always be a but?"

"If you wish to talk, I hope it is with me."

"Of course. Now find us some flat pebbles, I wish to skim them. If we are to hide in here until they are finished, I must do something."

"Where would I find them?" Kate looked around her at the grass.

"Start looking."

"I have a better idea. I shall sneak back and get us more food, and you start looking."

"That is a good idea," Alice said, thinking of the cherry tarts she had yet to taste. "Do not tarry."

Kate scampered off, and Alice started walking, head down, attempting to find something to skim.

How could Nicholas be so shallow?

"Is there any possibility that you could give some thought

153

before you speak, Alice? Just a small window of hope that you may show sense."

She turned to find him walking toward her.

"I am eminently sensible." She turned away and began looking for stones once more. "Go away."

"And yet you took one of society's most powerful woman to task over her claims I was the most handsome and intelligent man present."

She shrugged. "It was not true."

"I know that!"

"Excellent, I was worried about your ego briefly."

"God's blood, you are a trying woman."

By a stroke of good fortune, Alice found a stone. Bending, she retrieved it.

A hand grabbed her, turning her to face him.

"You were risking social ruin by challenging her, Alice. Could you not see that?"

"I don't like her."

"I'm sure the feeling is reciprocated, but the point here is that you cannot challenge her and not expect her to retaliate. She could have you struck off every guest list in London, were it her wish to do so."

He was worried about her.

"I know to some that is a fate worse than death, but I doubt I will live in society, and I have never been able to suffer fools."

"And what of Kate? Do you want her to follow in your footsteps? Be tarnished by your behavior?" he demanded.

"You're exaggerating." She wrenched her arm free, then moved closer to the water's edge. She skimmed the stone. It sank.

"Your technique is all wrong."

"I suppose not only are you handsome and intelligent, you can also skim stones?"

"I did not say I was handsome and intelligent, Lady Mueller did. And yes, I can skim stones exceedingly well." The words were gritted out.

"Why are you so concerned with my reputation when clearly you destroyed yours at some stage, then retrieved it."

He looked uncomfortable as he searched for a stone.

"Because you are a man," she said in a flat voice, stating what he would not. "Which is ridiculously unjust. You can do whatever you wish, and you will survive—"

"Not anything I wish. For instance, I could not ride naked down Bond Street, and nor could I prance about like Nigel and not suffer endless ridicule for it."

"That man is clearly a fool or has a considerable ego," Alice said, pushing the vision of him naked to one side.

"Both. But the point is, Alice, a woman's reputation is delicate. You need to take more care of yours. You leave the house unescorted and speak your mind—"

"As do you and any number of my relatives, male and female."

"Who are established in society. You are not."

She sighed, because really, what else was there to do? Turning to face him, Alice hadn't realized how close he was to her. She backed up quickly. Her foot caught and then she was falling.

"Alice!" He tried to reach her, but too late, she landed in the water.

CHAPTER 16

*N*icholas couldn't hide his laughter as he bent to help Alice. "Once again I must rescue you from yourself."

He lifted her out of the water, placing her on the grass once more.

"This is your fault!"

"I hardly see how when I was simply talking to you."

"I wish for you to go away." Her words were a low growl.

"The front of your dress looks dry. It is only the rear. I am sure no one will notice," he said, attempting to placate her.

She looked mad as a snake now, and he was in her firing line. Nicholas found he quite liked that. She would never stroke his ego like some.

He should walk away. His feet didn't move.

"I blame you entirely for my current predicament, Lord Braithwaite. Please keep your distance from me in future."

"That seems unfair when I did not lay a finger on you. You stepped backward into the water all by yourself."

"Hideous man. I wish nothing further to do with you," she squelched by him.

Nicholas had taken her away from Lady Mueller because the woman held grudges and her sights were clearly set on Alice for daring to question her. Of course, Alice had not accepted his criticism, as he'd known she wouldn't.

He followed, admiring the wet material of her dress clinging to her lovely bottom and shapely legs.

"I had not realized what a bad sport you were, Alice."

She spun to face him, green eyes alive. Her beauty was there in every line of her face. Every expression and gesture. How could she believe she was not the equal of those like Eden and Lady Levermarch? She was that and so much more.

"You antagonized me with your words and... and..."

"Nearness? Come now, friends should be able to speak openly with each other, surely?"

Her mouth snapped shut as she struggled to contain her anger. Surely a herculean effort for one who usually spoke the first thought that entered her head.

"Speak your mind, Alice; it is not healthy to keep all that venom inside you." Why he felt the need to antagonize her, he had no idea.

"You"—she pointed a finger at him—"are no friend of mine. Furthermore, you are spending far too much time with Cam," she then stomped away.

Nicholas stayed where he was and wondered what the hell he was supposed to do with Alice Sinclair. He'd woken believing he'd put her from his head, the infatuation had passed. Clearly that was not the case at all.

Nicholas turned and skimmed the stone in his hand.

"Four, Alice!" he called after her. She replied with something foul that made him laugh.

Following her, he watched the women in her family gather around, helping her dry off.

"Hello, Nicholas."

"Hello, Rose."

"Miss Lutton is looking lovely today, don't you think? I've heard she is well versed in running estates. Apparently her father leans heavily on her."

Nicholas looked at Miss Lutton, who was pretty but did nothing for him, and then back to Rose.

"She told me she thought you were exceedingly handsome."

"Did she? That was very nice of her. I seem to be getting all the accolades today."

Alice was now standing with Wolf, still looking spitting mad. She kept shooting him fulminating glances.

"Lady Mueller is a foolish woman with far too much money and time on her hands, unlike Miss Lutton." Rose patted his hand and walked away, leaving Nicholas shaking his head.

He was clearly being targeted by the matchmakers in the family. He mulled over what was to be done about that as he collected Freddy.

"I like her." Benjamin Hetherington said, stopping his mount beside Nicholas.

"Rose? Yes, she is a lovely lady."

"Not Mrs. Sinclair, but Miss Alice Sinclair. She's nice. Alex told me what she said to Lady Mueller. Not many women would be willing to speak up against that shrew."

"She should not have spoken to a lady of her situation in such a way." Nicholas swung himself into the saddle.

"Rubbish. She has enough titled and powerful people at her back to do so. It's refreshing. I am sick of those who bow and scrape to people like Lady Mueller."

Nicholas thought about that as he urged his mount back up the hill.

He saw her then. Alice, lying broken and bloodied on the

ground. The vision filled his head suddenly, and then it was gone.

Nicholas had never had a vision while he was awake before. It terrified him. He instantly searched for her.

"Anyone for a gallop!"

The words came from Lord Ryder, and then suddenly there was a thunder of hooves and they were off.

Alice! He had to find her; she was in danger.

Nicholas felt the blood race in his veins as he nudged Freddy's flanks, and seconds later he felt the muscles bunch and release beneath him and they were galloping.

James whooped by him in a very undukish manner, with Max on his heels before Nicholas could yell at them to stop. Lady Levermarch was not far behind. He could still not see Alice.

His heart pounded, and fear gripped him. The desperation to find her was absolute.

Up ahead was a row of trees; he saw her then. Everyone else went right. She went left. Crouching low over Freddy's neck, he soon drew level.

"Stop, Alice!"

She ignored him and crouched lower over her horse's neck. She got in front of him briefly.

"Danger!" She heard him and began to slow her horse, much to Nicholas's relief. Neither of them saw the bird until it was too late. It flew up in front of Alice's horse. Stopping suddenly, she flew over its head. Nicholas tried to control Freddy, but he bucked, and Nicholas hit the ground hard enough to make his teeth rattle.

He scrambled to his feet, desperate to reach Alice. She lay a few feet away unmoving. The exact scenario of his vision, without the blood.

"Alice!"

Running, he dropped to his knees beside her. Gently, Nicholas turned her over, so she was lying on her back. Pressing fingers to her neck, he felt a pulse.

"Thank God."

He pulled off her hat. A trickle of blood ran down her forehead.

"Just a small amount, not like the vision."

Parting the hair on her head, he found a deep gash. Pulling out his handkerchief, he pressed it to the wound to blot the blood.

"Alice, open your eyes for me now." He kept talking as he ran his hands over the rest of her head. "Come on, Alice. I need you to look at me."

Fear unlike anything he'd ever experienced gripped him as he looked over her head and saw the rock she'd landed on. His hands shook, and his heart thudded hard as he wondered if her stomach or chest had impacted with it. Could she be bleeding inside?

He'd known this was going to happen.

"Alice, please wake up."

She was pale and still unconscious. Lowering the handkerchief, he ran his hands over her body to check for any other injuries. Her wrist was sitting at an odd angle. Pulling off his necktie, he slid it around her neck then tied the ends together.

"Help, someone!" He roared the words as loudly as he could, but knew it was unlikely anyone would hear him.

Easing her wrist into the sling, he watched for any sign of movement, but her eyes stayed closed.

"It's all right, sweetheart, I am here, and your family will arrive soon."

Shrugging off his jacket, he draped it over her body. Bending over her, he kissed a cheek, then whispered in her ear that she had to wake up. The sound of hooves had him lifting his head. Someone was coming.

"Alice!" Wolf arrived first, pulling his great black beast to a halt beside them and leaping from its back.

"Birds flew up in front of her horse, she fell," Nicholas said. "She has yet to regain consciousness. She has a deep cut on her head, and her wrist, I believe, is broken."

The rest of the family arrived. Dev, James, Eden, Cam, Max, and Lilly, who immediately crouched beside Alice's head. "How is she?"

"Unconscious, Lilly. Help her."

"It's all right now, brother. We will care for her."

"Dev?"

"Here, Lilly."

"Move to her feet, Nicholas, and let the family in," Lilly told him. "They can help her."

He quickly did as directed, unsure how they could help, but willing to do whatever it took. Apollo moved closer, his lips in Alice's hair. Nicholas knew the animal meant her no harm, but he was so big and Alice so slight.

"Easy, Apollo, she will be all right," Wolf told him. The horse didn't move, just kept his lips on Alice's head, occasionally blowing a breath of air on her.

"What do you see, Dev?" Cam asked him.

They were all around Alice now. Nicholas rested his hands on her ankles, simply because he wanted to touch her. Needed to know if she twitched. He looked at each of the family, and when he reached Dev, he noted his eyes were unnaturally bright.

"Her color is weak, and I see some blood inside her, Lilly."

"Alice." The word was a ragged whisper from Wolf.

Nicholas felt a hand on his shoulder and looked up to see James above him. Max stood to his side, looking down at Nicholas with worry for Alice in his eyes.

"What you are about to see will shock you, cousin. Have faith in them and know that what you are witness to is magic of the very best kind."

Shocked at his cousin's words, all Nicholas could do was nod.

"Make a connection, everyone," Dev said.

"My hunch is that we include Nicholas, and as Essie is not here, we need his strength," Cam added.

What were they talking about?

"Christ, Alice." Wolf leaned over to kiss his sister's cheek.

"Come now, Wolf, she needs your strength," Dev said.

"Take my hand, Nicholas."

He didn't hesitate, instead gripping Cam's hand tight. Now was not the time for questions. Now was about Alice. Whatever this was, he would do as he was told and hope it was enough to help the beautiful woman who lay motionless before them.

He watched as Dev held Cam's other hand and wrapped his fingers around the back of Lilly's neck. Eden held Nicholas and Wolf, who in turn held Alice's limp hand.

James kept his hand on Nicholas's shoulder, silent in his support.

"All right, love, but only until she wakes," Dev cautioned Lilly.

A surge of power gripped Nicholas suddenly, and his hands began to tingle.

"Don't break the connection, Nicholas."

"What's happening, Cam?"

"Explanations later, now you need to focus on Alice."

He watched his sister pull off her gloves and place her hands on Alice.

"Christ, she moved," Nicholas rasped.

She kept twitching as Lilly's hands moved over her head and down to her chest, then lower to the stomach.

"Open your eyes, Alice," Dev demanded. His eyes glowed like the brightest gem as they focused on her.

"Come on, sweetheart." Wolf's words were raw. Apollo swung his large head away from Alice briefly and nudged his master before returning to her.

It was almost as if Lilly was healing with her hands. How was that possible? He couldn't be seeing this, surely? It was beyond comprehension.

Slowly color began to fill Alice's cheeks and then her lashes fluttered.

"Enough now, her color is stronger." He watched Dev break the circle and ease Lilly's hands off Alice. He then took her into his arms, and she slumped against his chest.

"Lilly!" Nicholas leapt to his feet and moved to her side.

"She will be all right, the healing just exhausts her," Dev said.

"Alice?" He looked down at her, and her eyes met and held his. Something passed between them that he couldn't identify and then she broke the bond by closing her eyes once more.

"She will be all right now also."

"Oh God, Lilly," Alice said in a raspy voice. "You healed me, didn't you?"

"Well, it seems you are indeed part of the circle, Nicholas," Cam said. "We are not all present, but I felt your power. If I was in doubt before, I no longer am. You are definitely one of us."

"I d-don't understand what just happened... any of it."

He felt shaken, as if he had woken from a disturbing dream. First the vision and now this.

"You will, but not now," James said.

Nicholas had just witnessed something he would never be able to understand. But what shocked him more were the feelings running through him as he looked down at Alice

Sinclair. Her pain had been his, and the thought of her not regaining consciousness, unbearable.

Christ, he was in trouble.

CHAPTER 17

*A*lice felt every jolt and every twitch as she rode before Wolf. Nicholas was at her side, silent, somber, and shocked.

Lilly had healed her, and he had witnessed that. How did they explain it to him? Would he be repulsed and turn from them with the realization of what they could do?

Dev had Lilly before him, in his arms, and her eyes were closed as she slept. Exhausted from the healing.

"I'm sorry."

"Why did you take the opposite route to everyone else, Alice?" Wolf questioned her.

She had no answer to that, so she simply apologized once more.

"She cannot be blamed for the bird flying in front of her horse, Wolf." Her guilt increased as Nicholas defended her.

What had gone through his head when he'd found her lying unconscious on the ground? He'd yelled at her to stop; she'd ignored him. Then he'd roared that there was danger. Had he not done so, the damage to her could have been irreparable. She had hurt him too. The guilt intensified.

"But the point is, she was where she should not have been yet again. I went one way, so she went the other. It was reckless and irresponsible."

She let Wolf say what he needed to. Understood his words were motivated by worry.

"You say to me constantly you are the steady one of the three of us. Lately, I would dispute that fact."

"She is hurting, Wolf. Enough now."

Her brother's mouth formed a thin, angry line at Nicholas's words but he said nothing further, which she was grateful for.

Guilt settled its heavy weight like a cloak around her shoulders.

She looked at Nicholas, watched him flinch as he rotated his shoulder.

"Are you hurt, Nicholas?"

"What... pardon?" His eyes found hers.

"Were you not thrown from your horse?"

"Are you hurt, cousin?"

"I am well."

"Yet the pallor in your cheeks and those clipped words would suggest otherwise," James persisted.

Dev slowed his horse to draw alongside Nicholas. His eyes flashed green. "Your color is also weaker. Where is your pain?"

"I am well, don't fuss. I have just aggravated my shoulder slightly."

Alice saw a carriage up ahead, and beside it stood Essie.

"I had felt you needed me, so sent the others on."

"We do. Alice had a fall. Lilly healed her," Dev said.

"Get them inside," Essie ordered. "I have some food from the picnic, and blankets."

"Nicholas is injured, Essie. But he won't tell us where," James said, dismounting.

"I am not badly hurt," he protested.

Alice was lowered into Max's arms and placed inside the carriage. She bit back the moan as he put her onto the seat and the pains in her body intensified. Dev helped Lilly inside. He pulled out a blanket and tucked it around her.

"Here." Essie thrust him a bundle wrapped in a napkin and a flask.

He opened it and handed Lilly two sandwiches.

"Eat it, love, and then sip the brandy."

Lilly nodded, but didn't speak. Exhaustion radiated off her.

I did this to her.

Dev's love was there in the way he smoothed Lilly's hair off her face and kissed her cheek. Each gesture increased her guilt. She tried to never harm anyone but she had done so with her reckless behavior.

"I must ride home, Lilly, but Essie will care for you, my love."

"I will be fine, Dev."

His face was filled with worry, but he nodded.

"How are you feeling, Alice?"

Dev tucked a blanket around her shoulders next, then took the brandy flask and uncapped it. He lifted it to her lips.

"Just a few sips, cousin."

She did as he said, and the fiery warmth traveled through her body.

"Good girl."

She was kissed also, and then Dev backed out of the carriage.

Alice was aware what her risks had cost her family. Until today, they had affected no one but her. Yes, Wolf was worried, but she hadn't until that moment harmed anyone.

"In you get, Nicholas."

"I can ride."

"No, you cannot," James stated calmly.

"I can. My shoulder is a bit stiff, nothing more."

Essie took charge and got him into the carriage. Alice had noticed the gentle Sinclair sibling could be the toughest when required.

"Is the pain only in your shoulder? And don't lie to me."

"Yes," he grunted.

Essie slipped her hand under his jacket and touched his shoulder.

"I don't think it's dislocated, just bruised or strained. You have possibly disturbed the last injury. But I shall know more when we return and examine it. Excuse me while I speak to my siblings. We shall leave soon."

He nodded, then looked across the carriage to Alice.

"How do you feel?"

"All right, thank you."

"Now that's a lie. Your body must hurt like the devil from that fall." His eyes moved from Alice to Lilly.

"Lilly, are you all right?"

"Better now I've had food, Nicholas. I'm just tired." As she finished speaking, her eyes started to close.

Alice watched as Nicholas took the food out of his sister's hands. He then got off the seat with a grunt of pain.

"Your shoulder—"

"Is fine," he replied to Alice. "My sister needs to sleep in comfort."

He bundled a blanket into a pillow and lowered Lilly onto it, then sat next to Alice.

"Essie will ride with Max to give you more comfort," Dev said from the doorway, his eyes resting on Lilly. "Excellent, she is sleeping. I know you have questions, Nicholas, and we will get to them, I promise."

Nicholas nodded.

"If any of you need us, simply wave out the window. One of us will see and be with you in seconds."

"Thank you, Dev," Nicholas said.

The carriage was soon rolling away, and the silence inside was strained.

"I'm sorry, Nicholas. My rash actions have caused you and those I love pain."

"The accident could have happened at any time, Alice."

"No, it happened because I was reckless. Thank you for telling me there was danger, had you not, I would not have slowed."

He wanted to say something but stopped.

"I'm sorry, Nicholas, really."

"Kate told me you were the sensible Sinclair of the three of you."

Alice sighed, and even that hurt her. "I think she may be wrong."

"Alice—"

"I'm sorry you learned about us in such a way."

"Us?"

He turned his body slightly to face her. He took up a great deal of the space on the seat, his long legs stretched out before him.

"There is so much more to tell you but not now."

"I don't know what I saw, or why I experienced what I did before you fell."

"What did you experience?"

"I had a vision. You were lying on the ground covered in blood."

She saw the memory in his eyes. The fear it had caused him.

"Oh, Nicholas, that must have been awful for you."

"All I could think about was reaching you, but I couldn't find you, and when I did you wouldn't listen to me."

"I did not want you beating me. I'm fiercely competitive."

"I already knew that about you."

"I don't like myself very much at the moment, Nicholas." Her words sounded small and pathetic, but it was how she felt. "I need to grow up and become responsible."

"I think you've likely done your growing, and I quite like your spirit. If I may suggest a little more thought before you leap in future, however?"

His smile was far too gentle considering what she had put him through.

"I shall try." Alice yawned. "I feel extremely weary suddenly."

"Strong emotions can make you weary."

She felt strangely comforted to have him close. Yes, there was the awareness of him, but right at that moment she wanted no one else sitting there talking to her.

"Have you noticed anything odd about the women in this family, Alice?"

"Other than the myriad of obvious things, do you mean?"

He smiled. "Yes, other than those. I've been approached by several of them who then take great pains to point out some woman to me and extol her virtues. My sister, I understand, as she's been at me for years to marry, but I now suspect she is not the only one."

They both looked at the slumbering Lilly.

"Today both Rose and Eden spoke to me."

"Ahhh" was all Alice said before yawning again.

"Ahhh?"

"Well, I really shouldn't say."

"But you will, as you owe me."

His hair stood off his head, and once again his clothes were dirtied and mussed. She did owe him for today.

"If I tell you, you must promise not to say anything."

He placed his hand over his heart. "I promise."

"To anyone."

"To anyone."

"I would be run out of my family if you did."

"Just say the words, Alice."

"I really can't, it would be disloyal to them."

"And yet you will."

"If you go into James's study searching for a book—"

"Which I never do but will make sure of it at my earliest convenience."

"On the third shelf from the bottom on the right, there is a large blue book. The title has gold lettering and is *House-keeping for Those in Need.*"

"And that is in James's library?"

"Eden put it there, assured he'd never open it."

"Clever."

"If you were in there browsing for a book and opened that one, you may have more of an understanding as to what is going on."

"That is all you are willing to say?"

Alice nodded.

"How cryptic."

"I will not be disloyal to them."

"Them being all the women in this family?"

She nodded again, then yawned so loudly her jaw cracked. The aches in her body were now making themselves known. Every inch of her seemed to throb.

"For pity's sake, woman, sleep. You will displace your jaw if you keep that up."

"I can't sleep in carriages. Besides, I am more comfortable sitting upright."

"Because you are in pain?"

"No more than you, I am sure."

"Perhaps I can offer you my shoulder... the good one?"

"No. I don't think that would be appropriate."

"We are family, and friends also. Of course it's appropriate. Come." He reached for her gently. Angling his body more, he then pulled her onto his chest. "Forgive me," he said as she hissed in pain. "But I am not in that much discomfort I cannot hold a beautiful woman while she sleeps."

The gesture surprised her so much she didn't argue, and instead felt her eyelids grow heavy.

"I'm sorry."

"I know." She felt a hand in her hair.

"For everything."

"I'm fairly sure you weren't responsible for Nigel's horrendous portrayal of A Midsummer Night's Dream."

"It was bad, but I'm sure he thinks it quite wonderful."

"I believe it is called an inflated ego."

"I believe so." Alice yawned again. "But I am sorry for everything else." He was stroking her hair; it felt wonderful on her sore head. Highly inappropriate, but wonderful.

"Did you tell my valet to argue with me over my clothing choices today?"

"I like your choice today." Her words were slurred.

"Mud brown and horse excrement green are all the rage this season, I believe?"

"I believe it is time I grew up," Alice said again, her words sounding slurred.

"Sssh now, you sound drunk."

As the waves of slumber began to pull her under, Alice said what she now knew to be the absolute truth.

"You are a very good man, Lord Braithwaite."

"I'm not, but I thank you just the same for saying otherwise. Now sleep, Alice Sinclair, and I will keep you safe for the journey back to London."

And just like that, she did.

CHAPTER 18

*N*icholas looked up as his butler appeared in the doorway of his breakfast room.

"The Duke of Raven, Lord and Lady Sinclair, and Mr. Sinclair have called, my lord."

"All of them?"

"Yes, my lord."

"Well then, have a fresh pot heated and more food prepared, thank you, Hopkins, as Mr. Sinclair is usually hungry."

"Very well, my lord."

"And what of Mrs. Potter, Hopkins. How is she?"

His butler's face creased in worry.

"Well enough, my lord, but is still believing what she stated happened."

"Have you or any of the other staff heard any rumor about such things, Hopkins?"

"Toby, the stable lad, told me he believed it does happen and blames the nobles for it... if you'll beg my pardon, my lord."

"Of course. What did he see or hear to make him believe what he said?"

"Toby said his cousin had a child and it was taken away by a man. He had been outside awaiting news of the baby's arrival, you see, my lord. He saw a man arrive, then take the child away."

"Just like in Mrs. Potter's case?"

"Yes. Toby is also sure he heard the baby crying."

"Thank you, Hopkins, please show our guests up, and tell Mrs. Potter I will alert her when I receive any news from the investigative service I have employed."

"Very well, my lord."

It was four days after the picnic. Four days of contemplation as Nicholas tried to grapple with what had happened that day. He was no closer today than he was yesterday with finding an answer.

He'd traveled back to London with Alice in his arms. She'd slumbered deeply, her face turned and resting on his chest, and he'd had a ball of warmth lodged inside his chest the entire time. Not lust, not awareness; all that was there between them but not at that moment, what he'd felt was more than that. Luckily, he too had fallen asleep before he'd identified it.

"Good morning, Nicholas." Lilly entered the room first, looking nothing like the pale, exhausted woman of four days ago.

"Good morning, sister. What has you here at such an hour?"

"I think you know why we are visiting, brother. We gave you a few days of contemplation and recovery, now we have come to explain what you saw."

He did know but was strangely reluctant to delve any deeper into what had occurred, even though it had been occupying his thoughts. When Alice wasn't.

"We wish to discuss what took place the other day and thought to catch you before you left the house," Cam said, sniffing the air as he made for the sideboard. "Which I add yet again, you should not be doing without one of us or a footman."

"I have asked for the food to be replenished, please sit, and I am more than capable of looking after myself."

"Excellent." Cam slapped his hands together.

"You just ate at my place after eating at yours." James looked disgusted.

"I'm a growing lad."

"You're a fully grown man."

"I like to think of myself as a racehorse. Sleek lines, with endless energy that needs fuel."

"And who brays like an ass?" Dev added.

"Please, all of you, sit," Nicholas said before the argument escalated.

Lilly pulled out a chair and sat beside him, her hand covering the one he held in front of him on the table. Suddenly he could feel her tension.

"Is Alice all right?" He took her fingers in his.

"She is fine. Quiet, staying in her room, but she will recover given time," Dev said, sitting in the empty seat beside his wife. "I would like to discuss the matter of your visions, Nicholas."

"Dreams," Nicholas found himself saying, even though he called them visions.

"And yet your dreams are always steeped in fact?" James asked him.

"I told them about the incident when you were young, where you knew a local girl had been murdered by a nobleman."

"Why?"

"Because I believe it is relevant to what we are about to

discuss, and I also believe there have been other visions but you kept those to yourself," Lilly said.

He'd seen Alice lying in a pool of blood; the image still chilled him.

"We are your family, and this is something I think we need to discuss further, Nicholas. Just as we're sure you have questions about what took place the other day."

"I do have visions," Nicholas made himself say. "I saw Alice that day, just before she fell. Lying in a pool of blood."

Silence greeted his words.

"I tried to get to her, stop her, but only managed in slowing her as she heard me roar 'Danger.'"

Cam whistled softly.

"I thought you only had them in your sleep?" Lilly asked.

"I do. This is the first one I've had while awake. I have no wish to experience it again."

"With Alice," Dev said slowly. "That's interesting, don't you think?" He was looking at Lilly.

"Very," she agreed.

"And now we shall explain what you saw the other day," Dev added.

"I'm not entirely sure I want to know."

"You want to know; it just scares you because it doesn't seem possible... but let me assure you that it is."

"We are going to tell you something now, Nicholas, and it will sound incredulous to you. But as you saw what Lilly did, you will begin to understand quicker than I. In fact, you will think them mad... more mad than they are, I mean," James added with a small smile. "When first I heard I didn't believe them, but I need you to believe them, Nicholas. Because every word they speak is true."

Lilly must have felt his tension, as her grip tightened on his fingers. Something told him his life was about to take another turn, but as yet he did not know in which direction.

"Go on."

"First of all, we'll start with us, my siblings and me," Cam said, lowering his fork with reluctance. "We have heightened senses. Dev has the gift of sight, Eden hearing, Essex taste, and I can smell."

Nicholas felt the hair on the back of his neck rise as he looked from Dev to Cam, then lastly James.

"You can't expect me to believe—"

"Pick up the newspaper folded beside you and walk down the room to the end wall," James said to him. "Now, Nicholas. Trust me and do this."

"Do it, brother, and trust us... me, that I would never lie to you, as they would not. You saw what I did the other day?"

Nicholas nodded.

"Then try to understand this also."

He saw only honesty in her eyes.

Nicholas did as he was told, carrying the newspaper to the end of the room with his mind reeling. These men were not the type to lie... nor make a fool of him for no apparent reason.

What the hell is going on?

"You know that we cannot read the small print on the page from here, don't you?"

"Yes."

"Open the paper and face it to us," James directed him. "The small print on the bottom of the page, Dev. Read it out loud."

At James's words, Dev put down his cup and looked to where Nicholas stood. Suddenly tension filled the room, so thick he could almost taste it. Looking at his brother-in-law he noted his eyes were once again brilliant green, like sparkling jewels. He appeared to be focusing on the newspaper Nicholas held open with both hands.

"Really, there is no need…." Nicholas's words fell away as Dev started talking.

"An invigorating tonic is now available for men who are experiencing bouts of lethargy. For a small price, you can procure a bottle and feel its benefits in days." Dev spoke in short, clipped words. When he was done, his eyes seemed to lose their brightness and return to their normal color.

"Your turn now, Nicholas, read the words out loud," James said.

Nicholas looked at the four people seated in his breakfast parlor, his eyes passing from one to the other. All were solemn, even Cam, which was a rare thing. He felt a strange reluctance to turn the paper around, almost as if he knew deep down inside that today he was about to learn something about himself that would change everything.

"Do it, Nicholas," Cam said.

As if in slow motion, Nicholas turned the paper and stared at the words there in small black script

"Read them," James urged.

"An invigorating tonic is now available for men who are experiencing bouts of lethargy. For a small price you can procure a bottle and feel its benefits in days." Nicholas's voice shook as he repeated what Dev had said word for word.

"I don't understand."

Cam's laugh held no humor. "Neither do we, but come and sit down now, Nicholas, and we shall at least attempt to explain things."

His feet weren't working properly as he staggered back to the breakfast table and fell into his seat. He held out his hand, and Lilly gripped it once more, her gloved fingers anchoring him to her. He needed that.

"Cam has a heightened sense of smell," Dev said.

"The soap you bathed with this morning has lemon along

with all the other ingredients, which I won't outline. Your cologne has sandalwood," Cam said.

"Take a mouthful of your tea, Nicholas," James said. "Because the shock you are feeling is only going to grow as we continue on with the other members of our family."

"There are others?"

"Your sister for one, as you saw she can heal with her hands."

"Dear lord." Nicholas looked at her. "How could I not have known?"

"Did you ever wonder why I wore gloves all the time?"

He nodded.

"I'll take it from here, love, as you are far too modest," Dev said. "Her gift is perhaps the most powerful of us all and is the most precious."

"Lilly." He rasped her name.

"Yes," Dev said calmly. "As I have explained already, Eden and Alice have the heightened sense of hearing. Essex and Kate taste; these are the basic elements to our senses. Warwick, Dorrie and Somer are gifted also."

He opened his mouth, but no words came out.

"Essie also has this ability with herbs and healing, which Kate is learning. Wolf has a connection to animals. Surely you've seen them with him?" Dev asked.

"I thought he carried sugar or something in his pockets."

The laughter was small, but it eased some of the tension in the room... but only slightly.

"We all feel each other's pain and fear. Our strength is at its most powerful when we are together and connected as we were that day Alice fell from her horse."

Nicholas knew and respected these people greatly, but what they asked him to believe was almost beyond reasoning.

"Lilly." Her name was torn from him. "How you must have suffered. How you must have loathed me."

"We will not start that, Nicholas," she said in a sharp tone. "No further recriminations are required, and I want no hand wringing—"

"I was... am your big brother. You deserved more from me."

"Yes, I likely did, and now I am getting it. You still have a few things to make up for, but I shall extract those from you when required."

Dev barked out a laugh.

"I'm sorry."

"I know." She patted his hand.

"Surely you've wondered about them sometimes, Nicholas."

He nodded at James. "I did, but never in my wildest dreams did I imagine this."

"So, like me, you just thought them odd?" James said.

"But how is it possible that Lilly has a heightened sense? She is not a Sinclair." Nicholas said when the realization came to him.

"This gets a bit complicated."

"I doubt it could be more so."

"One of our ancestors and one of yours had an affair, and as far as we can determine, that is how Lilly came to be gifted, and now you with the visions. There is a scroll somewhere, or something that tells us the history. As yet we've never been able to find it anywhere. Raven Castle has been turned upside down."

"Tell me about these senses then." He looked at Dev. "They must have taken some getting used to."

"You believe us, excellent."

"I doubt someone could make such a story up, so I fear I must."

Lilly patted his hand, then rose to walk to the sideboard.

"Wolf and I can see great distances and at night. We also see people in colors."

"Colors?"

"Have you never noticed him looking at you oddly. Kind of fixed and glazed, his pupils dilated?" Cam asked. "He appears a simpleminded fool."

"Yes, thank you, Cam."

"I have, actually."

"Well, that's him checking your colors. He does it to all of us, it's his way of making sure we're not ill or upset."

"You should be married to him," Lilly muttered. "He is constantly checking me and our children."

"Such is my love and adoration for you all," Dev drawled. "Your color is yellow, but it can get weaker or darker depending on your health."

"If it's white, then you're likely going to die soon," Cam said cheerfully.

"Good lord."

"You're the same color as Alice, actually," Dev said in a neutral tone. James and Cam were both suddenly alert and focused on Nicholas.

"What?"

"Dev doesn't think you should marry anyone who is not your color," James added. "Add to that the Sinclair and Raven thing—"

"What thing?" Nicholas's throat was suddenly dry.

"I think he's probably heard enough," Dev said.

"No, tell him. It's like lancing a festering sore; get it all out at one time," Cam said.

"Charming."

"Tell me what?"

"I'll tell this part because it still annoys me," James said. "Many years ago—"

"1335, to be precise," Cam added.

"—a lowly Sinclair, they were not always noblemen—"

"But we were always noble," Dev drawled.

"—saved the then Duke of Raven," James said, ignoring him. "King Edward III bequeathed the Sinclairs the land at the bottom of Raven mountain in gratitude."

"And why is that, James?" Cam asked innocently... far too innocently.

"Because they are our bloody protectors," James growled.

"I beg your pardon?" Nicholas shook his head.

"Eden saved me from drowning, and Dev saved me when we were away fighting for our country. He then saved Lilly from being thrown from a carriage." James wasn't pleased by the revelations. "Lilly then brought Dev back from the dead."

"What?" Nicholas stood suddenly.

"You could have worded that better." Lilly wandered back with her plate of food. "Dev was shot; I healed him."

"It takes a great deal out of her," Dev added. "Saps her strength when the injury is severe, as you saw the other day when she healed Alice."

"You healed me that night at the Mueller masquerade!" Nicholas said suddenly. My ribs hurt and then they didn't."

"I did, yes," his sister said calmly.

"Christ." The word hissed from his mouth. "I can't take this in."

"I saved Emily. Wolf saved Rose, and Essie, Max. There have been many more incidents in our past," Cam continued.

"Yes, thank you, Cambridge, I believe Nicholas gets the point now."

Cam smiled widely. "We're always here for you, James, you know that."

"God's blood, Nicholas, it is the one aspect of this entire situation that boils my spleen," the duke said. The Sinclair brothers simply smiled.

"It's almost unbelievable."

"Yes, well, it takes time. I've been married for many years and still can't quite take it in."

"And now it appears you have something of us in you after all," Dev said. "And if you are now experiencing your visions during daylight hours, there is every chance that your strength is growing."

"You make me sound like a Warlock... if indeed they exist," Nicholas said, feeling like the ground was moving beneath his feet.

"Makes you wonder though, doesn't it, brother?" Lilly said.

"I felt your power that day in the field. Felt it course through me," Cam said.

Nicholas wondered, if he ran from the room and mounted his horse, could he simply keep riding and outrun whatever madness this was. Suddenly his life was spiraling out of control, and strangely, all that had started since Alice Sinclair had stormed into it... after saving him. Looking around the room, he decided to keep that piece of news to himself after what he had just learned.

Sinclairs marry Ravens.

There was always an exception to every rule, and he was it.

CHAPTER 19

"*A*nd you say the man who arrived said he was directed by the midwife to take the baby?"

Nicholas looked at the woman seated across from him at the small table. Toby, his stable hand, to her right. He had both hands wrapped around a mug of tea.

He'd asked the boy to bring him here today to speak with his cousin.

"And this happened fourteen months ago?"

"It did."

"I'm sorry for your loss."

She nodded but said nothing further.

Do you remember the name of the midwife, Mrs. Ham?"

Her face screwed up as she thought about that.

"Mrs. Adley," Toby said.

"That's the name," Toby's cousin agreed.

Another one. He wondered if Alice would visit him tonight with a third child in her arms.

"Very well, I shall leave you now. And thank you for your time. You stay and visit with your cousin, Toby."

"Mr. Marsh won't be happy," the boy said.

"I will speak with my stablemaster."

Letting himself out, he mounted and headed to his next address. Mrs. Potter's daughter, Jane.

He knew Mr. Spriggot and Mr. Brown were investigating also, but Nicholas felt he needed to do something. Alice had yelled at him last night in his vision, demanding he take action. So today he was.

When he knocked on another door ten minutes later, it was answered by a pale-faced woman.

"Mrs. Budd, I am Lord Braithwaite. Your mother is my housekeeper—"

"You employed my Bill."

"I did, and he is a fine worker."

"We are grateful to you for taking him on. What is it that has you here today, my lord?"

"I merely wish to ask you a couple of questions about the night you lost the babe."

As soon as the words left his mouth, she started to weep, and he cursed himself for his insensitivity. The woman was clearly grieving.

"I shall leave you."

"No! I want to answer your questions if it helps get my babe back."

"And you are sure, like your mother, that you heard the baby cry?"

"My babe was alive when she took him from me, but it wasn't until I'd come to my senses that I realized it for certain."

"Did you see the man who took him away?"

She shook her head.

He asked a few more questions, gently.

"Thank you, Mrs. Budd, for speaking with me about that night. I understand it must be painful for you."

He didn't understand at all, how could he? But he had to

say the words before leaving. He couldn't remember a time when he'd felt this helpless before.

"And will you find my boy, Lord Braithwaite, and bring him back to me?" Jane Budd begged him.

"I will investigate the matter entirely, I promise you that. I also have several others looking into it."

She nodded and began to rise.

"I'll see myself out."

"It's her, I'm sure of it. Mrs. Adley."

"If the midwife is at fault, she will be brought to justice, I assure you of that."

Nicholas left then, letting himself out into the dismal day that had descended on London since he'd woken many hours earlier. It was one of the days that couldn't make up its mind if it wanted to be light or dark, so it was halfway between.

The hour was not late, 3:00 p.m., and yet it felt more advanced. Jamming his gloved hands in the pockets of his jacket, Nicholas walked down the narrow lane.

Alice's visions were more disturbing with each night she visited. Perhaps because... well she was Alice, and she disturbed him, but there was also the absolute belief he felt when she talked that he would be the one to find the babies.

At least he'd had no more while he was awake. For that, Nicholas was extremely grateful. Seeing Alice bloody and lying there on the ground had shattered him.

Was it true? Could his visions be attributed to the affair many years ago between a Raven and a Sinclair? He could still not take in what he'd learned. Lilly could heal, and Alice had the heightened sense of hearing.

He couldn't imagine it would be pleasant overhearing everything that was said around you. Dev told him that both she and Eden wore earplugs to dull the noise, but he doubted that blocked out everything.

Strangely, knowing about his family and what they could

do and the fact he was one of them now had simply added to the feeling of belonging growing inside him. He liked that he was now connected to them by more than just blood and marriage.

Collecting his horse, he mounted. His next stop was to visit the midwife again. Mr. Spriggot had spoken with her, but the woman had told him nothing, simply shutting the door in the man's face. Nicholas would not be allowing that to happen this time. He wanted answers and was getting them.

He headed back down the street, and up the next. The shortest route to Mrs. Adley's house would take him past an establishment he had no wish to see, and yet if he did not take this direction, he could add twenty minutes to his journey.

"Just ride by," he muttered as he turned into the street Bastil's, one of the worst gambling hells, was on. He had not been a coward in many years and was not about to start now.

It was as he approached the building that had almost been a residence to him that he saw the carriage. Something made him look at the driver. Call it intuition, but he knew he'd been right to do so as he looked in the worried eyes of Bids, Dev and Lilly's driver.

"Good day, Bids, what has you here? Is Lord Sinclair in the vicinity?"

Turning his horse slightly so he could not see the building behind him, he focused on the man seated above him.

"Lord Braithwaite, 'tis mighty pleased I am to see you."

"Where is your employer, Bids?"

"I am not here with Lord Sinclair, my lord. He'd never be seen outside such an establishment."

Nicholas heard a small squeak coming from inside the carriage, then a loud shushing sound. His curiosity climbed.

"I'm driving for Miss Alice Sinclair, my lord. Her and that woman. They conned me, they did."

"If Miss Alice Sinclair is inside the carriage, I can fully believe that."

It was clear that even after all her talk of needing to grow up and become responsible, Alice was still taking risks. His anger started to simmer.

"They said they wanted to drop off something, and we ended up here."

"Why did you not simply keep driving, Bids?"

"They threatened to leap out if I did. Lord Sinclair loaned me to Captain Sinclair because he trusted me to watch over his cousins. But they are trouble, especially Miss Alice and that Kitty Trent."

"Watch your mouth, Bids!" The door was thrown open and a woman stepped down from the carriage. "I'll have you know I'm looking after Miss Alice so she doesn't step into trouble alone! Would you rather that was the case?"

Like the last time he'd seen her, Kitty Trent was bristling with energy. Today she wore a long coat of peacock-feather blue, with matching bonnet.

"Good evening, Mrs. Trent," Nicholas said, drawing her fire away from the trembling Bids. The man may look like he could hold his own, but not when faced with a determined woman.

She spun to face Nicholas.

"Good afternoon, Lord Braithwaite." Her curtsey was elegant. "We met at *The Trumpeter*. I've heard a great deal about you."

"Have you? I hope at least some of it was good?"

"Indeed, some of it was," she said, making Nicholas snort.

"Excellent, and now will you tell me why you and Alice Sinclair are outside an establishment as disreputable as Bastil's?"

"I would of course tell you, my lord, and yet I'm afraid it is not my story, and I will not break Alice's confidence by doing so."

Dismounting, Nicholas handed Bids his reins.

"Then I shall get the full story myself."

Nicholas had not seen Alice in over three weeks because she was healing, and because when he did see her again he wanted his defenses rebuilt and sturdy. Holding her while she'd slept had caused them to crack.

Opening the carriage door, he stepped inside and closed it behind him.

"Hello, Alice. I thought the last time we saw each other you promised to become responsible?"

She sat on the seat, not cowering as he'd thought she may be—after all, she had to have heard him talking to Bids—looking far too pretty for his peace of mind.

"Why are you here, Lord Braithwaite?"

He'd missed her, just one look told him that.

Her coat was pale rose, and her bonnet chipped with a matching rose satin ribbon that she'd tied under her chin in a large, floppy bow. Her scent was instantly recognizable and took him back to that day he'd held her.

"I think more to the point is, why are you here when I know for a fact your brother would be horrified should he learn of it, as, coincidentally, am I."

"I'm hoping you won't tell him, my lord?"

"My name is Nicholas, Alice. And did I tell him last time I found you in a place you should not be?"

She shook her head, Sinclair green eyes wide in her face.

"Kitty should not be outside Bastil's."

"She is at present arguing with Bids, and it would take a brave man indeed to interrupt either of them, I assure you."

"She's wonderful."

"I'm sure she is, but I doubt accompanying you here would endear her to your brother and sister-in-law."

Alice sighed, and it shook her entire body.

"What's going on, Alice?"

"I promised not to tell."

"Then you leave me no choice but to tell Wolf where you have been, because I would be remiss as his friend and Lilly's brother were I to ignore this as I did the last time."

"Oh please—"

"Tell me what's going on, Alice."

"Botheration."

"Indeed."

She huffed out another breath.

"I have a friend."

"Congratulations, we all need those." Nicholas let some of his anger slip into the tone.

"A very good friend."

Nicholas nodded.

"The thing is, Nicholas, after what happened in the field and how I hurt my family with my actions, I have tried very hard not to do so again."

"You've been the model sister, have you?"

"I wouldn't go that far. But I have done little to annoy my brother, and then the letter arrived."

"What letter?"

"Here, just read this." He watched as she pulled a note from her reticule and thrust it at him. "I am endeavoring to find out if Barty has fallen prey to scurrilous scoundrels in a gambling hell. It is my duty as his friend to do so, and I will not be dissuaded."

"The same Barty I encountered in that men's fashion store, for whom you have professed your love?"

"I was a child when we did so, but yes, he is that Barty, and a friend.'

Nicholas moved his eyes from her to the note in his hands. He read it twice before handing it back to her.

"Scurrilous scoundrels?"

"I like alliteration." She shrugged.

"Who doesn't, but the point here is that you should not be in such a place, in fact—"

"That note states he has now used up his family's money completely and they are no longer being allowed credit. Their situation is dire indeed, as next they will be forced from their home, Nicholas."

"I have read the note, Alice; there is no need for you to reiterate each word."

"Bastil's is the place he is frequenting. Barty's friend said that when he visited a few weeks ago. Verity implores me to do something but doubly implores me not to tell anyone. My hands were tied, surely you can see that?"

"Which does not speak well of your friend, I'm afraid. What did she expect you to do? A young woman in London. It is reckless and irresponsible of her to put this on you."

"She wants me to save her brother and yet keep his reputation intact. She asked me as a friend to do this!"

"I had not realized how dramatic you were, Alice." Nicholas ran his eyes over the note once more.

"My friend is bereft!"

"Would you have asked this of her were your situations reversed?"

Her teeth snapped together.

"Your brother could have helped you, and it is reckless of you to have come here today. This is not a place for a woman of noble birth... in fact, any woman."

"There is no need to speak to me that way. I know what you say is correct, and yet something must be done. I merely came here to listen and hope that I can hear Barty. If I did, then I was going to speak with Wolf. My brother works on facts, if I had sent him into that place and there was no sign of Barty"—she pointed over Nicholas's shoulder—"he would have thought me a fool and Verity a hysterical woman."

"There is every reason to speak to you in this way! God's blood, woman, you are at present outside one of the most notorious gaming hells in the United Kingdom. Reputations, lives, and fortunes have been won and lost inside Bastil's regularly. Were anyone to see you here, your reputation would be beyond saving. For the love of God, Alice, stop this naive belief you can simply carry on with these foolish risks and to hell with anyone and anything."

Color drained from her cheeks at his words, and Nicholas knew she was close to tears. But someone had to shock some sense into her.

"I will not stand by when a friend is in need of my assistance."

"Your brother will forgive you eventually, Alice. Just tell Wolf." Nicholas sighed. "If Barty is inside Bastil's, you alone cannot save him."

"I thought I heard him inside there," she whispered. "And I know you know what I mean."

Alice, Warwick, and Eden have the heightened sense of hearing.

"Are you wearing your earplugs?"

"Yes, I put them back as soon as I heard Barty," she said, and all the fire had gone from her voice. She was subdued, as he'd wanted her to be. Why then did he feel bad? "I have no wish to continue hearing those noises."

"Those noises?"

"Nasty sounds of other forms of enjoyment."

She wasn't even blushing, which was quite something for a woman who had been kissed by only him... at least, he thought that was the case. Had Barty kissed her? Nicholas did not like that thought.

"I was raised in the country, my lord. I know what those noises mean."

"Right." It was Nicholas's turn to feel uncomfortable. "You need to leave here at once."

"I know. I had just hoped...." Her words fell away, and Nicholas wondered if finally, she'd come to the realization that she could not save her friend. "But you are right in what you said. I was naive to believe I could help Verity by making Barty see sense."

No matter how much he fought against it, Nicholas had to admit she fascinated him. She was a woman of conviction, clearly, and a loyal friend.

He'd come to loyalty and conviction late in life, but he liked to think he was better at both now. He'd always been determined, however not in a good way.

There was also the fact that she had the softest lips and tasted like sin. Even though he was angry with her, he wanted to kiss her.

"Alice, please go home. You may just make it before Wolf realizes and locks you in your room for the next ten years."

"I am not a fool, Lord Braithwaite, no matter what you believe, I know how Wolf will react. I also know you are a man of noble intentions and will never tell anyone what you have learned."

He ignored her blatant flattery. "I never said you were a fool."

"Yes, you did, quite clearly in your decimation of my character."

"I did not decimate your character."

"This is getting us nowhere." She cut a hand through the air. "If you could just go inside and see if Barty is there, then I could leave and get Wolf."

"Pardon?" Nicholas could feel the sweat forming on his body at the thought of entering that pit of hell called a gambling establishment. His palms itched at what awaited him.

Gambling was an addiction for him. The rush of winning had kept him returning to the tables over and over again with the belief that his next foray would see him showered in wealth. That, and the alcohol he'd poured down his throat. He had not returned for many years and had no wish to. He even avoided the tamer gambling tables people set up at society events.

No, he could not go into Bastil's, of all places.

"I cannot enter that place."

"Why?"

CHAPTER 20

*E*very word Nicholas had spoken to her since entering the carriage was as accurate as the tip of an arrow. Shame had washed over her when he'd called her naive. Fear for Verity had been the catalyst for her actions. Actions she'd taken again without careful consideration. Her dear friend was suffering, and she wanted to help. Silly fool that she was.

Once she'd shown caution, but since arriving in London this side of her nature seemed to have dissipated.

"I will not go in to Bastil's, Alice."

His face was suddenly closed; the anger that had been there was gone. Cold and emotionless was the facade he now presented her.

"I only wish to know if Barty is—"

"The answer is no."

"Of course, if that is your wish. Forgive me for asking."

"It is." His words came out covered in ice.

"Can you tell me why?"

"I have told you why, because I have no wish to."

"Because you have no wish to is not an answer. I'm asking you because we are friends—"

"Will you stop, Alice. Stop asking questions, stop pushing me and others. Just be a young lady enjoying her first bloody season!"

The words had exploded from Nicholas with such force, Alice's mouth fell open.

"I'm sorry if I have hurt you, Nicholas. That was not my intention." This reaction was something more than just anger at her, she was sure of that.

"We barely know each other and yet you feel you can ask this of me!" His eyes were wide, and he was breathing rapidly. Something was very wrong.

"Forgive me, I should not have—"

"Damn you, I cannot go inside that place!" He fell back on the seats, but Alice stayed on the edge of hers.

"Why?"

"Alice." The word was anguished, and in that moment she knew whatever waited for him inside Bastil's was something that had hurt him deeply. A stain on his soul that he'd never been able to wash away. The part of his past no one would share with her.

"Please forgive me. I will of course go home and speak with Wolf. My tenacity, I'm afraid, often is my failing. That plus my naive belief." She tried to make him smile; he didn't.

He sat there for what seemed like minutes, just staring at her, his eyes running over her face and settling on her lips. They started to tingle as she remembered their kisses.

"No." The word came out softly, and suddenly Nicholas was back. Sanity had returned to his eyes and he was calm once more. "I will do it before you court more trouble."

"No!" Suddenly it seemed like a very bad idea for him to enter Bastil's. "I cannot allow it, as I can see just the thought of entering that place distresses you."

His smile was small and held no humor. "I can do this... must do this. It is time."

Alice reached for his hand as he started to leave the carriage. "No. I forbid it!"

"You forbid it, when minutes ago you wished it."

"You fear that place, Nicholas. Tell me why, please?"

His eyes held hers steady, then went to the gloved hand she had curled around his wrist.

"I fear myself most."

"I should not have asked this of you." Alice felt a desperate need to keep him with her. She sensed the vulnerability in this man. She wanted to protect him, if only from himself. "No. We shall leave," Alice said, still holding his wrist. "You are right, it was foolish of me to come here with Kitty and Bids."

"Your friend's name is Bartholomew Stillwater?"

"How do you know that?"

"The signature was Stillwater on the letter, and his name is Barty. It was not hard to conclude." He smiled again, this one a little stronger. "Now I shall be back shortly."

"I don't want you to go!" The words exploded from her this time.

"And yet you did, and as I have explained, if I do not then you will find another way to reach your friend."

"But that was before I realized you fear this place. I will go home now. Please do not go in there."

He eased his hand from her grip.

"This is a demon I must one day face, Alice. I have realized in the last few minutes that today is as good as the next to do that. I shall return shortly. Do not under any circumstances leave this carriage or open these curtains. Do you understand me?"

"How could I not, with my hearing. Of course I heard you clearly."

His lips twitched.

"But the question is, will you obey me?"

"Are you sure, Nicholas?" Alice had a deep sense of foreboding inside her.

"I am. Do not move from that seat."

"Barty has brown curls that stand off his head and is... is a rather scruffy-looking fellow, for all Verity is always trying to tidy him up. He does not wear clothes as you do."

"As I do?"

"Elegantly. Barty tends to come untucked easily."

"I had never thought of myself as elegant, but I shall thank you for that compliment, Miss Sinclair. And if you will remember, I have seen your beloved Barty before."

"Of course, and he is not my beloved." Nerves gripped her. "Nicholas, I don't think you should go in there."

"But I will."

"Be careful." She grabbed his arm again.

"I will be all right, Alice, I promise."

She didn't want to let him go. Their eyes caught and held, and then he leaned closer and took her lips in a soft kiss.

It seemed to last so long, and yet was too brief.

"I should not have done that."

"Again."

"Again. Now be a good girl, and I shall return soon." And then he was gone, and she drew in a large, shaky breath.

"In you get." The door opened seconds later, and in came Kitty. "Do not leave again if you please, Mrs. Trent."

"Very well, Lord Braithwaite, as long as that fool driver doesn't antagonize me further, I shall do as you say."

Kitty settled herself on the seat across from Alice.

"I shall tell him to behave," he said solemnly, and then with a final look at Alice he turned to leave, but stopped, his eyes finding hers once more.

"I will be extremely angry if you leave this carriage, Alice, please remember that." He left, closing the door softly behind him.

"Well!" Kitty said.

"Well what?"

"That man." Kitty waved a gloved hand in front of her face. "He's so handsome and aloof. Exactly what one expects a lord to be."

"You saw him in *The Trumpeter*."

"I know, but today he seems even more lordly."

"I don't think that's a word."

"It should be."

"Surely he is no different from the peers you've already met in my family?"

Kitty twitched the curtain and pressed her eye to the opening. Alice made herself stay where she was instead of doing the same. Because if she did, she'd call Nicholas back to the carriage.

"Well yes, he is like them, but then as I stated when Rose first introduced me to them, they are not what I would term the average standard of noblemen."

"There is a standard?"

"Perhaps the duke, but not the others. There's a certain something dangerous about them. Rebellion is in their blood, I think."

"But not Lord Braithwaite's?" Alice said to the back of Kitty's head.

"Well, I think he has it in him, but he's more contained than the others, and so much more...." She turned briefly and waved a gloved hand about again. "He has an aloofness bred into his bones that is often so appealing. A woman just itches to ruffle him up slightly, don't you think, Alice?"

"You're married, should you be speaking like that?" Alice felt uncomfortable with Kitty's words and loathed that it was jealousy making her feel that way. The man disturbed her deeply, there was no way around that fact.

"Oh, no one could surpass Mr. Trent in my affections, but it does not stop me from looking."

Alice gave up and moved to Kitty's side to look through a tiny crack in the curtains. They could not see much, only the back of Nicholas as he stood looking up at the establishment called Bastil's.

"He has superb shoulders."

He did. He could also kiss every thought from Alice's head.

"His tailor has done a splendid job with his clothing; it fits him to perfection."

It did.

"What do you think he is doing standing there like that?"

"I don't know," Alice said, but she did know. He was gaining the courage to walk inside. Whatever had happened to Nicolas Braithwaite inside the walls of Bastil's had tainted him irrevocably, and she, Alice Sinclair, had asked him to go back in that hell and find Barty.

"I feel ill."

"Why?"

"I asked him to go in there, Kitty, and I don't believe he wishes to."

Rather than make soothing noises, Kitty snorted. "Do you really believe a man such as he could be made to do anything he wished not to?"

"That is true." Alice felt marginally better.

"He's moving," Kitty whispered.

"Sssh now, we must not make another sound. It would not do for anyone to come upon us."

Kitty nodded but stayed where she was. Alice, however, could not watch and sat once again.

What she needed to do was listen very carefully and

follow Nicholas's voice as he moved through the establishment.

Dear lord, she hoped he encountered no trouble, as Alice didn't think she could live with herself if that was the case. Especially considering how much he was already suffering just walking in through the front door.

"Lord Braithwaite, it is a pleasure to have your company in our establishment once more." He was speaking to someone.

"My visit will be brief, Mr. Hedges. If you'll excuse me, I am here to collect someone."

His voice was cool and calm, as she knew his eyes would be. But what was really going on inside Nicholas Braithwaite's head? The guilt nearly choked her.

"He said I was reckless and naive. In fact, he said quite a few things, Kitty."

"Did he? Well, he's possibly right, but I think spirit is vital in a young woman.

Oh dear."

Alice watched Kitty close the curtains quickly.

"What have you seen?"

"Don't look out there!" The words were a furious whisper.

"Why not?" As the words left her mouth, the carriage door was thrown open.

"God's blood, Alice Sinclair!"

"Dear lord, I am doomed." There in the doorway stood her brother. Big, dangerous, and in a towering rage.

"W-Wolf?"

He climbed in, followed by James and Cam.

"Stay outside, Dev, there is not enough room," Wolf snarled.

Alice had seen this particular version of her brother

precisely three times in her lifetime, and each moment was etched in her memory.

"Speak now, and by God you had better make it good!" He sounded like thunder rolling in over the meadows of her home.

"Firstly, I tricked both Kitty and Bids, so they are not to blame."

"Of that I have little doubt."

"I was not tricked," Kitty scoffed, clearly not cowed by Wolf.

"Kitty," he warned.

"She was safe the entire time and has virtuous reasons for being here, Wolf. I would ask you to hear her out."

"This should be good." He folded his arms. James and Cam remained silent, their eyes on her. Cam, however, winked.

"Barty is in trouble and inside that gambling establishment," Alice said. "Verity wrote to me several times with her worries. I talked with him and saw her concerns were founded, yet he would not consider returning home. Her last letter spoke of her desperation that her brother had landed in danger in this place, and that he had nearly spent all their money. I came here and heard him inside."

"And what were you going to do with that knowledge?"

"Ah... well, as to that—"

"Speak!"

"Don't yell at me!"

"I am furious with you! We"—he jammed a finger into his chest, then pointed at James and Cam—"were in a business meeting, and I felt the fear that something had happened to you... was about to happen to you. Not Kate, as she does not constantly challenge me... yet."

"Really?" Kitty looked intrigued and excited. Alice felt ill.

"We don't have time for this. You have to go into that place and bring Nicholas and Barty out because—"

"Nicholas is in there?" Cam's expression was suddenly alert. "Why?"

"I asked him to—"

"What?" Wolf roared at her.

"H-he was passing and saw Bids. He found me and demanded I leave. I asked him to go and get Barty."

"You did what?" Wolf roared at her again, disgust clear on his face.

"When I realized that the prospect of entering Bastil's upset him, I told him not to. But he said he would... said he needed to."

"Dear Christ," Cam hissed, looking fierce. "We must go to him at once."

"Why?" She grabbed Wolf as he began to follow the others back out the door.

"Because he will be suffering the worst hell imaginable, and it is you who has sent him there, Alice."

CHAPTER 21

*T*he last time Nicholas had walked into this particular hell he'd been drunk and ready to lose as much money as he could. His respect for himself and anyone else in his life was nonexistent, and he was bent on self-destruction.

He had many weaknesses, as did most people, but his two gravest were alcohol and gambling. He'd lost his way at the age of twenty with the death of his father and not found his way out until many years later. The gambling fever had nearly destroyed him.

At first he'd frequented the acceptable places, those that noblemen were seen at, then, when he'd wanted more excitement, more depravity, Nicholas had gone deeper into hell, to places such as this one.

The interior had changed little: dark paneling, faded burgundy curtains that hung closed at the windows. The gas lamps were new and added to the general air of despair. The place reeked of it, even at such an hour. Reeked of lost fortunes and tortured souls. Many lives had been lost within these walls. He was just lucky his had not been one of them.

The tension inside him climbed as he proceeded slowly along the halls. Stepping inside the first room, he looked at the table. No one matching Bartholomew Stillwater sat in here.

He could do this for her, Alice, and for himself. Do this and save Barty as he'd been saved. But then he would never come back again.

"Good God, tell me it is an apparition?"

The only face he knew at the table had once been an acquaintance of Nicholas's; he'd fooled himself at the time they were even friends. After all, the man had held his coat while he threw up the entire contents of his stomach in a potted plant upon many occasions.

"Braeburn." Nicholas nodded.

"Take a seat, Braithwaite, we are one short."

Tall, and as always, elegant. The years of debauchery had not really caught up with Niall Braeburn as yet. But they would, given time; no one could sustain this lifestyle and remain unaffected. The son of an earl, he was simply waiting for the man to die so he could waste away his inheritance.

"I am not here to gamble. Good day."

"Not gamble? Surely you jest? There is little else to do here."

The four other men at the table tittered. Nicholas turned to leave.

"Come, Braithwaite, we are playing whist, your particular favorite. If memory serves, no one could best you at it, drunk or sober, which you appear to be now," Braeburn taunted.

Nicholas looked at the cards and the empty seat. He wanted to sit and play, wanted to feel that rush of blood. His mind started to run through the rules. Shuffling, dealing, taking tricks. Trump, lead, it ran though his head with ruthlessly efficiency, as if he had just played a hand yesterday.

I cannot allow it, as I can see just the thought of entering that place distresses you.

He heard Alice speaking to him, her hand on his. Clenching his fist, he felt her touch, and it gave him strength.

"Thank you, no, I have other business to attend to." He walked out and drew in a deep, steadying breath.

The next room did not yield Stillwater, so he made his way down the stairs and deep into the bowels of hell. His body was clenched so tight, he felt like he would shatter with a touch.

Women appeared but did not approach, possibly because of the look on his face. Nicholas walked into the biggest room in the establishment. The ceilings were high and yellowed with smoke. Scanning the tables, he found Bartholomew Stillwater. Shoulders slumped, clothes looking like he'd slept in them, the man was focused on the cards in his hand with a ferocity that was familiar to Nicholas.

It was like a fever in your blood when the gambling took hold.

It had to be that table.

The memory of James doing as he was slipped into his head. His cousin had been rescuing Cambridge Sinclair. He remembered that night clearly, because in the darkest recesses of his mind had been a small kernel of hope that maybe someday someone would rescue him.

It hadn't come then, but it had come... thank God.

Eyes turned to watch him as he walked. A few called out to him; not all the comments were pleasant. In fact, most were insults. He'd turned away from this, the brotherhood of hell, as he'd once termed it. He'd walked away and never looked back... until now.

"Gentlemen, you'll excuse me, please, I have business with Stillwater."

The man's head shot up to look at Nicholas. The whites of his eyes were bloodshot, and he was struggling to focus.

Barty tends to come untucked easily.

Alice had said that. Pretty, intelligent Alice Sinclair, for whom he had decided to walk through this den of depravity. Thinking of her gave him strength, even as he wished her to hell for it.

"I don't know you."

The words were said slowly, as if the effort of speaking was too great.

"Your sister sent me."

The man jerked upright in his chair.

"Verity?" He looked around the room. "Is she here?"

"She is not, and one would hope you have no wish for that." Nicholas kept Barty's eyes on him. "Come now, Bartholomew, it is time to leave."

"Take your meddling ways out of here, Braithwaite!" These words came from Lord Hardy, the man seated to the left of Stillwater.

"Stay out of this, Hardy."

"I will not. Just because you have become a sniveling turncoat does not mean Stillwater here is the same."

The blessed heat of temper began to melt the ice-cold fear in his veins that had accompanied him into Bastil's.

"Turncoat is an interesting turn of phrase, wouldn't you say, Hardy. Considering what you did in Whites that evening many years ago?"

"I say, there was no truth in that rumor!" the man blustered.

"Oh, I think there was, as you have ended up here and are not welcome in any reputable establishments. So sit in your seat and shut your mouth." Nicholas kept his eyes on Bartholomew.

"You've no right to speak to me like that!"

The rumble of discontent started to grow, and soon men had climbed from their seats to stand around the table. Nicholas was outnumbered, he knew that, but he wasn't leaving without Bartholomew Stillwater.

If not for Alice, then he'd save the man for himself... *and me*, Nicholas thought.

"Come here, Stillwater."

Barty looked confused, his eyes going from left to right and then settling on the hand of cards he held.

"Do you wish to lose everything in your life? Family and respect are included in that," Nicholas said. "Do you wish to send your sister and mother to the poorhouse?"

"We have no wish for your meddling ways in here, Braithwaite. Just because you have lost the ability to be a man does not mean we have."

Braeburn arrived and moved to stand behind Stillwater, effectively trapping him in his seat.

"Go back to your new friends... or should I say family," Braeburn taunted. "Those unusual Sinclairs and a duke who has no right to carry the title. They deal in trade, unlike the real noblemen of this world. They are a disgrace to their title."

"Disgrace is an interesting term," Nicholas said. "I had a conversation with my cousin, the duke you claim has no rights to his title. He said your father, the current Earl of Braeburn, used that exact term when describing you. Disgrace to your family was how he worded your behavior. Said if it was in his power, he would disinherit you, but as he can't he's going to live as long as he can to thwart you."

Braeburn's face mottled with rage.

Nicholas could handle any slur upon his character, as most of them he'd deserved at one time or other, but not his family. They had saved him, and in doing so forgiven him.

Their belief in Nicholas was absolute, even if he did not believe in himself.

"A word of advice going forward, Braeburn. Be careful what you say about my family. Very careful, as an insult to them is an insult to me, and I will seek retribution."

They'd told him he was family, and today he needed to believe it. He felt stronger because of them.

"Family!" Braeburn scoffed. "They should be run out of London. Merchants and bastards, and let's not forget about a distant daughter raised in Scotland who worked in a teashop!"

"You know a great deal about my family for someone who professes disgust."

"I know I want nothing to do with them!"

"Excellent, we are in agreement then. We want nothing to do with you either. Come, Stillwater, we are leaving."

"He stays!" Braeburn roared, red in the face.

"I think I should go... Verity—"

"You are a man, Stillwater. No woman should dictate your movements." Braeburn put a hand on his shoulder and held him down. He then nodded to someone, and Nicholas turned to find four men at his back.

"Remove him at once, and make sure he is taught never to return to a place where he is no longer welcome."

The men advanced.

"I say, this is a club for gentlemen. There should be none of that in here," a voice said as Nicholas rose onto his toes.

Keep moving. Attack first.

"Seems the numbers are weighted heavily against you, cousin. Perhaps we could even things up?"

Nicholas turned to find Wolf, James, Cam, and Dev behind the men. Again they had appeared when he needed them.

"Stand down!" The words came from the club's manager, a small, weaselly-looking man Nicholas had always disliked. The men walked away, leaving his family standing at his back.

"Braeburn, why am I not surprised to find you at the root of this," Cam said.

Like Nicholas, Cam would be facing his demons in Bastil's.

"Stillwater, come here," Nicholas stated. "Now."

Braeburn still stood at the man's back, blocking his ability to rise from his chair. In two strides Nicholas was there, grabbing the peer by the collar and wrenching him to one side, away from Stillwater.

"You are a sniveling individual with the morals of a rat, Braeburn. My family have more good in their little fingers than you have in your entire body. You're a disgraceful human who offers nothing to anyone. A leech on your family, and a worthless bully."

Nicholas pushed him hard, sending him backward into a chair that toppled over. He landed hard on his ass.

"Let's go, Stillwater."

The man must have seen something in Nicholas's eyes, because he scrambled to his feet in haste.

"Does he owe anyone any money?"

Three men nodded.

"Come and see me; I will clear his debts." Nicholas grabbed the man by the shoulder and propelled him out the room. James, Dev, Wolf, and Cam followed on his heels.

"This situation seems familiar," Cam drawled.

"Quite," Nicholas replied. "Many thanks again. I have no idea why you are here but am grateful for it."

"Do you remember what we talked about the other day?" Dev said.

"The senses?"

"Yes. Wolf felt there was danger and that Alice was involved in some way."

"She is safe."

"I know." Wolf grunted. "Please forgive her for placing you in this position, Nicholas, I will see she understands the ramifications of her actions."

"There is no need—"

"There is every need," Wolf gritted out.

As they were walking out the door, Nicholas said nothing further but had a feeling that life was about to get extremely trying for Alice Sinclair.

CHAPTER 22

*A*lice sat in the breakfast parlor alone, stirring her tea for the tenth time.

She had managed to avoid Nicholas for two weeks due to the fact she could hear if he was near. Well, that wasn't quite true. It was unusual, but for some reason her hearing was not as sharp when he was close. But it was still better than most.

Having said that, she didn't see him in the normal course of the day as he didn't come to visit her exactly, but her family were often recipients of his visits. Alice had made sure not to go to gatherings that she knew he'd be at. But she could not keep doing that indefinitely or questions would be asked.

She'd heard what had gone on inside that gambling hell and was ashamed of what she'd forced him, and her family, to do.

Wolf had traveled back to the house that night in their carriage, and the silence had been so thick with tension even Kitty hadn't tried to break it. Once there, he'd left to help Barty back to his lodgings. All he'd said to her was, "Get into the house, and this time stay there."

He had not yelled or lectured, only talked when he'd returned home. He'd spoken of many things, but the one that had stuck with her had been the fact that she could not meddle in people's lives and expect the consequences to come out in everyone's favor.

Alice had never thought of herself as meddlesome. She'd thought she was helpful and studious, but on the whole a good person. It seemed she was wrong.

Nicholas had told her she was foolish and naive, and that had hurt also, but at the time she'd been determined to save Barty so had pushed his words to the back of her head. The cold, clear light of the following day had dragged them to the front again.

Knowing she had forced Nicholas into that gambling hell out of duty was sobering.

"Hello, Alice." Rose walked in, radiating her usual happiness. Alice tried not to let that vex her, because surely it was petty of her to feel that way in the face of her brother and sister-in-law's joy over the love they shared.

"Good morning, Rose."

Rose was one of those women who was beautiful inside and out, again vexing when Alice didn't seem to be able to get through a day without annoying someone, it seemed. Well, she had once been like that, but no more.

That night she'd learned her lesson about doing the right thing, because the wrong thing had caused Nicholas a great deal of pain. Cam, also. And then there was the worry she'd given Wolf.

"Alice, someone is here to see you."

"Who?" Dear lord, please don't let it be Nicholas. She didn't think she was ready to face him yet.

"Bartholomew Stillwater. Do you wish to see him, dear?"

"Of course. I had thought he'd returned to Briarwood."

"He is due to leave today. I shall get Milton to show him in."

Alice paced about the room, wondering what she should say to her old friend. He was in the doorway before she'd thought of anything.

"Can you ever forgive me?" Barty walked toward her, hands out. Alice took them willingly. "My dear friend, say you will."

"Of course!" Alice hugged him close, and as she did so she knew that was all he'd ever be, a friend. "Come and sit with me, Barty."

"I have spent the last two weeks righting some of the wrongs I have done since arriving in London and avoiding you."

"Oh no, Barty. You should never avoid me. We will always be friends."

"I showed a grave weakness in abandoning my family, Alice. I am ashamed of what I became, but it will not happen again. Thanks to your intervention, I am able to return home with hope."

"Not I. It was Lord Braithwaite and the others in my family who helped you."

"But it was you who told them about me. For that I will be forever grateful, Alice."

"I am glad it is over, Barty. Verity will be pleased to have you home."

"Lord Braithwaite came to see me yesterday. It was he who told me you were there outside Bastil's. A risk you should never have taken, Alice."

"I know, but Verity was desperate."

His collar was creased and his necktie coming loose. The little imperfections made her smile.

"She had no right to ask those things of you, but I am glad

she did, for I'm not sure where I would have ended up otherwise."

"What did Lord Braithwaite say to you, Barty?"

"He spoke of what his life had once been like, how he'd lost the trust and respect of everyone he cared for due to his excessive drinking and gambling."

Alice hadn't expected that of Nicholas. She knew he was a good man, but to go and speak with Barty about such a painful time in his life could not have been easy.

"We talked for some time, and I realized that what he said was true."

"What did he say?"

"That throwing my life away would only lead to heartbreak for me and those closest. That nothing good would come from my self-destruction, and to walk away now showed courage, and he offered me his support should I ever need it in the future. Should I weaken."

Barty gripped her hand tight.

"I want to be a better man, Alice, but I'm not sure as yet how to do that. Lord Braithwaite has given me some ideas for increasing our depleted coffers, and I owe him for clearing my debts. I could not refuse him but will repay every penny."

"He cleared your debts?"

"Insisted on it, even when Wolf said he'd do it."

Why had Nicholas insisted on doing this when Wolf offered?

"He wanted to help me like the Duke of Raven helped him," Barty said, as if reading her thoughts. "He's a good man, Alice, and thinks highly of you."

"No, he doesn't, it is just that we are connected by family."

"If you say so." Barty looked doubtful.

"I know so."

"Are we still friends, Alice? Or has my disreputable character turned you from me forever?"

"You do not have a disreputable character. You would have come about."

His smile was sad.

"No. You were always stronger than me, Alice. But I am determined to get there. Determined to show Verity and Mother that I can be the man they believed I could be."

"I know you will."

He looked at her for long seconds.

"We are friends, Alice. The very best of friends."

"And will always be so."

He nodded.

"But I think marriage will not suit us."

She felt sadness, then, for the gentle love she'd always carried for this man. For the dream of the comfortable, happy life they'd one day share.

"Yes. I think there is every possibility that if we did, you would dispose of me at some stage."

That made him laugh.

"You are a managing woman, after all."

"I am not!"

The look he threw her was pitying.

"Very well, but I am trying to change."

"Why? I love the way you are. In fact, I've often wished for more of your gumption. Don't change."

"My actions have caused others pain. My impetuous nature and determination to do exactly what I believe should be done has hurt people. Lord Braithwaite is one of those, Barty. I can't allow that to happen again."

"Lord Braithwaite holds no grudge against you. Don't change, Alice. Always be true to yourself." He rose to his feet and kissed her forehead. "Goodbye, my dearest friend, and thank you for saving me."

She cried after he had gone. Cried for the dreams of marriage and a life of comfort, and for the man who was her friend.

"Alice?"

She scrubbed her eyes before facing her brother. Not that she could hide anything from him. His eyes saw a great deal more than most.

"Are you all right?"

"I just spoke with Barty."

He came into the room, stopping before her.

"H-he is going home, Wolf. We will not marry."

Big arms reached out to pull her close, and she gladly accepted the hug. Neither of them spoke for a while, it was enough to just be comforted by this brother of hers, whom she loved very much.

"Nicholas is calling by shortly. He wishes to discuss something with me, but I shall put him off if you wish to go for a walk or—"

"No! Please see him. I am to go shopping with Kate."

"That doesn't sound to me like it excites you overly." Wolf gripped her shoulders as she began to move away. "You have been the model sister for two weeks, Alice. You're scaring me."

"Why? I thought this is what you wanted?"

"I want you to be happy and safe. I don't want you to be someone you are not. Yes, I want you to show caution and not place yourself in situations that could harm you and your reputation. But I don't want your personality to change. It upsets me to see you this way, so perfect it is nauseating."

"And yet you were angry with me for what I did... have done, so I am trying to change, and now you tell me you do not like that change. And they say women are fickle."

Wolf sighed.

"I don't want you to be unhappy, Alice. Can you understand that?"

"I want to go home to Briarwood, Wolf. I understand the rules there, and I fit. London is not for me."

"Why?"

"Because I'm different—"

"As are we all. Surely it is better to be with people who understand you than in Briarwood without us?"

"I want to go home."

She'd thought about this. Thought about her growing awareness of Nicholas and the mistakes she'd made in London. Going home would mean she could avoid him, and people knew her there. She could once again be plain, boring Alice Sinclair.

"No. You will stay for the remainder of the season."

Alice took a step back, away from Wolf.

"But I am unhappy here."

"Unhappy surrounded by love?"

"My lord, Lord Braithwaite has arrived."

"Thank you, Milton. Please take him to my office, I shall be there shortly. We will continue this discussion later, Alice."

"I don't believe there is anything to say. Now I must go, as Kate will be waiting for me."

Ignoring Wolf, she walked from the room, looked left and right, then ran to her bedroom to collect her bonnet. Pulling it on quickly, she tied the ribbons, grabbed her gloves and the basket of knitting she wanted to deliver to Lilly's house in Temple Street for the children, and stepped back out the door.

She then walked quietly along the hall to the stairs.

"Hello, Alice."

She squeaked in surprise at the deep words from behind but didn't turn. Instead, raising a hand, she hurried down the next set of stairs.

"Good day to you, Lord Braithwaite. I must go, as my family is awaiting me."

"Alice, if you'll—"

"Can't stop!" Alice cut him off, then leapt the last three steps. She stumbled forward, gripping the basket tight, and managed to stay upright.

"That was elegant," Kate said as she arrived at her side.

"Let's go." Alice urged Kate forward. He was coming downstairs; she could hear his footsteps.

"Alice, I just—"

She grabbed her sister's arm and stepped outside with the maid following. She then hurried them to the carriage.

"What's the hurry?" Kate asked.

"No time to wait, there is shopping to be done."

"You loathe shopping, and Nicholas—"

"No, I don't loathe shopping," Alice cut her sister off. She then exhaled as the door shut and the carriage rolled away.

"You do. You said last time that you would rather spend the entire day with Mr. Brussel, and as he smells fusty and spits when he talks. And of course there is his love of eels—"

"Yes, yes, I take your point." It was infuriating when your sister had the memory of an elephant.

"Do you know what I think?"

"No, and I don't want to." Alice looked out the window instead of at her smirking sister, who looked pretty in cream and apple blossom.

"I think," Kate never took instruction well, "you are avoiding Nicholas. He and I talked about that very thing."

"Please tell me that's a lie." Alice felt ill at the thought.

"Very well, that's a lie. Of course, you running out the house today to avoid him merely confirms my belief."

"I did not run."

"You did, with Nicholas on your heels."

"I seriously dislike you sometimes," Alice sighed as she had no other words.

"No, you love me."

Alice found herself laughing.

"Are you all right, Alice?"

She took the hand her sister held out to her.

"I am, Kate. I promise, but I would rather speak on another matter."

"Very well."

She needed new gloves, and Alice a bonnet. They would also be going to the bookstore.

Stepping from the carriage, they discussed a time for its return, then walked along the street. The next hour was spent thinking about something other than what she'd done to Nicholas.

"Good day to you, Miss Sinclair."

They were wandering along the street when Miss Krimpton, Miss Haye, and Miss Morton greeted them.

"Good day." Alice and Kate curtseyed. "This is my sister, Miss Kate Sinclair."

"Are you to visit Mrs. Bonshire's?" Miss Krimpton asked.

"Yes, that is our next destination," Alice said. "I require a new bonnet."

"Ours also. Come, we shall go together."

Alice had conversed with these women once, and they were harmless enough, if a little silly.

"I was just telling Amelia and Jane that my mother wishes me to marry in my first season, Miss Sinclair. My sister and she did, so it is expected."

Beside her, Kate made a choking sound. Alice pinched her arm.

"But surely if you do not meet a man you wish to marry then you cannot do so, Miss Krimpton?"

Alice had thought it a sensible question, but the three

women tittered in that way that suggested they knew something Alice did not. It annoyed her immensely.

"What do wishes have to do with anything, Miss Sinclair? It is expected."

She looked around the faces of each; they all nodded. Dressed in the latest fashions, they looked pretty and innocent, untouched by the reality of life that many people were forced to live. Yet they believed marriage was the only bright light in their future. Alice sent up a silent thank-you that Wolf did not feel the same way.

"But you cannot wish to spend your life with a man you do not like?" Alice did not use the word love for fear of suffering another bout of tittering.

"Love will come later, Miss Sinclair. It is the way of things," Miss Krimpton said with a worldly air that suggested she knew more than she actually did.

"Right" was all Alice could manage, as the entire conversation was most unsettling. "Thank you for enlightening me."

"If these are an example of the people I shall meet in society, I'm not sure I want to enter it." The words were whispered by Kate. Alice ignored them, even though her sister had a point.

They entered the milliner's, and more tittering ensued, which had more choking sounds coming from Kate.

"I danced with Lord Braithwaite last night." Miss Krimpton sighed. She seemed to be the leader of the three and did most of the talking. "He is on Mother's list."

"List?" Alice absolutely did not feel a jolt of panic at the mention of Nicholas.

"Of prospective husbands," Miss Krimpton said, drawing her shoulders back in preparation of the pearl of wisdom she was about to share with Alice and Kate.

"You have a list?" It took a great deal to shock Alice. When you lived with a family like hers, there was not much that could, plus the things she'd heard had stripped much of her innocence away.

"Of course, we all do!"

The other ladies nodded. All now wore silly smiles. Alice pretended to scratch her ear and instead forced the earplug in her right ear deeper into the canal. These women tended to speak in extremely loud voices.

"Oh, can you believe it?" cried Miss Krimpton. "It is as if we have conjured him up!"

"What?" Kate asked, looking around her.

"Lord Braithwaite just walked by the window. In fact, he has stopped outside."

Alice moved slightly, putting herself behind a cabinet and therefore out of sight from whoever looked in the window.

"He has the most wonderful shoulders, don't you think, Amelia?" Miss Krimpton looked even more excited, if that was possible.

"Oh indeed," Miss Morton sighed.

"Perhaps, as there is a connection with your families, Miss Sinclair, you could engage him in conversation and we could join you?"

"That would be acceptable," they all agreed.

These women may appear all that was correct and sweet, but in fact they were extremely calculated and focused on their goal: marriage to a wealthy and titled man.

The women started tittering about the possibilities.

"We really are not that well acquainted," Alice said, which made their faces fall.

"Oh, he is leaving."

Alice felt a flood of relief. She would not need to stay in the milliner's for the remainder of the day now. The women went back to studying bonnets.

"Benjamin Hetherington is handsome," Miss Cantrell sighed. "'Tis quite a shame he is wed now to that woman."

"Such a shame. His brother is also handsome and quite the man of fashion."

"That woman?" Alice asked remembering Primrose Hetherington from the picnic, and quite liking her.

"She really was a nobody, and yet she snared one of the most eligible bachelors. It was distressing for us, as you can imagine."

No, I can't.

"Well, we must be off, Alice. We are to meet our family at the tea shop, if you will remember?" Kate had moved to her side.

"Oh yes, of course, I had quite forgotten the time in my enjoyment of seeing you all," Alice said. Kate moaned softly. The women smiled, more than happy with the compliment.

"Dear lord, are they all like that?" Kate asked when they had left the shop.

Alice looked left and right, then straight ahead, and saw no sign of Nicholas. If she did, she'd duck into a shop.

"I don't know them all, but some are, yes."

"You must be bored silly."

"No. There are actually some nice and interesting members of society. Granted, most of them are our family, but there are a few others. You met the Langley sisters and their husbands at the picnic."

"Yes, they were nice."

"I know my baby was alive!"

"Did you hear that?"

Kate frowned, shaking her head. Looking around, Alice saw no one nearby.

"But there is nothing that can be done, Meggie. The baby is dead, and you must start back with your sewing. Your family needs you."

"The voice is coming from over there," Alice said taking Kate's hand as they crossed the road.

"What is being said?"

"They are discussing a baby."

"Alice—"

"I feel the need to investigate, Kate."

"Very well."

Kate was used to Alice's urges, as she had them herself.

"My baby was alive, I tell you, Peg."

Up ahead was a half wall. The Sinclair sisters walked around it and found two women seated on a bench on the other side. One held a small babe in her arms, the other watched a young girl playing in the dirt close by.

"Good day."

The women looked up, and the one with the baby struggled to rise.

"No, please, stay seated, as you both look comfortable," Alice said.

They nodded, but it was the one looking at the young girl who drew Alice's eyes. Misery radiated off her in waves.

"Is that your daughter?"

She nodded.

"She is very sweet."

"I should have a babe in my arms too!"

"Meggie!" The other woman looked shocked at the outburst. "You must not speak to the lady that way."

"No, please," Alice came forward and dropped to a crouch before the woman. Kate stood at her back. "Tell me what has happened?"

"It's nonsense, miss."

"It's not nonsense, Peg," the one called Meggie said. "My baby cried, I heard it."

"Tell me your story... please," Alice said. She remembered Nicholas speaking about the woman who had birthed a baby boy, and she too had believed it was born alive, but the midwife had stated it was dead.

Unease trickled down her spine as she looked at the grieving woman.

"I had my baby, and i-it was a b-boy." Meggie sniffed as tears began to fall down her cheeks.

Alice dug about in her pockets and found her handkerchief and handed it to the woman.

"My midwife said he was dead—"

"Which he had to have been, Meggie. Surely you see that?"

Peg looked at Alice with sympathy in her eyes. She believed her friend was simply not accepting her child's death. And this could be true, but if not....

"Mrs. Adley had that man take him away before I could even hold him. If he was dead, I had a right to at least that, and what of his burial?" Meggie broke down then, and Peg slipped a hand around her shoulders and held her closer. In her arms her babe slept on.

"Mama?"

The little girl came to her mother's side, placing a hand on her leg.

"Hello, I'm Kate."

Kate crouched before the little girl and started talking softly to her.

"My name is Miss Alice Sinclair." Alice got to her feet and held out her hand to Meggie. "This is my sister, Miss Kate Sinclair." She wanted the woman's last name but wasn't sure how to get it. Offering her own was the prompt she needed.

"Meggie Todd."

"Peg Todd, her sister-in-law."

"And do you ladies live around here?" Alice asked.

"No indeed, we are from the East Side. Hobby Street, miss. I thought a walk along the fashionable shops looking in the windows would cheer my sister up."

"I'm so sorry for your loss." She squeezed Meggie's hand. "Come, Kate." She nodded to Peg.

"You're thinking about what Nicholas said, aren't you? How his housekeeper believed the child was alive when it was taken from the mother?"

"Yes."

"You have to speak with him, Alice."

"I know, I just don't want to."

"I think you're avoiding him, because—"

"Do not add anything to that because. Now we must go to drop off the knitted items to Temple Street, then we can take tea."

"Very well, but I know there is something between you."

Alice didn't answer, as their carriage had arrived. She didn't like to think about having to speak with Nicholas when she'd been doing everything she could to avoid him, but after talking with that woman, she knew she must.

Botheration.

CHAPTER 23

*N*icholas had hoped to speak with Alice today, but she'd run when he'd said hello. Literally run down the stairs, taking the last few in one leap, nearly ending up on her face. By the time he arrived at the front door, the carriage she and Kate were in was leaving.

She was avoiding him, there was no getting around that fact. He'd not brought it up with her brother, as this was between Nicholas and Alice, but it had to stop.

Wolf had said she'd gone shopping, so after leaving the house, Nicholas had attempted to find her on Bond Street, but had no luck.

He'd caught glimpses of her over the last few weeks. In the evenings she'd been elusive. Nicholas would locate her, move to intercept, but when he arrived she'd gone somewhere else. It was like some elaborate chess game and she had all the winning moves.

Her hearing, of course, gave her the advantage over him. But Nicholas was nothing if not persistent.

He'd gone to his sister's house three nights ago, and the family had all been in attendance, except Alice, who had a headache. She'd also not been at Gunther's eating ices the day he'd encountered them there.

When he'd seen the back of her head today and felt the frisson of awareness, he'd realized how much he missed her again. Missed her dry wit and laughter. Missed her sweet face and inability to hide her thoughts.

Nicholas wasn't quite sure what to do about Alice Sinclair, but he did know he didn't want her hiding from him.

Arriving at Temple Street, he knocked on the front door. Since he'd known about this house, and the other near the docks, he'd made sure to check on them regularly so his sister didn't have to. She had a family; he did not. Of course, that didn't stop her from coming here, but he gave her reports so she didn't have to.

"Hello, Mr. Davey."

The couple who ran the small house were good people who had found a home here among the children that came and went.

"Good day to you, my lord."

"Is there tea on offer?"

"Indeed there is. The kitchens will be quite busy today."

"You have other guests?"

Nicholas rested his hat and gloves on the side table in the small hallway, then headed down to the kitchens with Mr. Davey on his heels. He was sure Lilly would be there.

"Hello, Mrs. Davey."

Round and pink cheeked, Mrs. Davey was as usual wearing her apron and busy baking something. Looking to the small table he'd spent many happy hours at eating delicious food, he found Kate munching on a piece of cake.

"Where is she?"

Kate didn't speak, just pointed upward.

Got you.

He ran back up the steps before Alice had a chance to leave, as she'd surely heard his voice. Then took the stairs up to the top story where the children who were sick or needed a warm bed stayed. He found her in the last room off the hallway. Standing in the doorway, he watched her; surprisingly, she hadn't detected him yet.

Her back was to him, and he looked at the silky black hair bundled into a knot and the pale skin of her neck beneath. Nicholas didn't fight the fierce pull of longing.

Her dress was cream, and a row of buttons ran down her spine. He wanted to place his lips just above them. Taste her skin. She had a body a man would lose himself in. Soft curves that would entice him to explore. He wanted to be that man.

She was reading a story to Stanley, one of the boys who had injured himself falling down a chimney. Her voice changed with each character, and the boy was snuffling, clearly enjoying the tale.

Easing back out of the room, he went to the one next door and found it empty. Leaning on the wall outside, he waited for Alice to arrive after finishing her story.

"Goodbye, Stanley, I shall return to read you the next book soon."

She appeared in the doorway, head down, deep in thought.

"Hello, Alice."

Her head shot up, eyes wide.

"I didn't hear you?"

"So it seems. That's odd, don't you think?"

She shook her head as if trying to dislodge something.

"I—ah, good day to you, Lord Braithwaite."

She bobbed a curtsey, then went to walk by him. Nicholas grabbed her arm and nudged her into the room, shutting the door behind him.

"Not this time."

"What are you doing?" She took a large step backward.

"You and I need to discuss a few things, Alice."

She managed a smile of sorts; it was lopsided and nervous.

"Of course, I would love to discuss... whatever it is you want to discuss. We shall go down and see Kate, then—"

"I want to talk to you, not Kate."

Nicholas stayed with his back to the door deliberately. She'd make a run for it if he moved, and he didn't want to have to grab her. He would, but this was easier.

"You're avoiding me, Alice."

"I have been busy and have no reason to avoid you."

She wouldn't meet his eyes.

"Lying is beneath you."

"I need to go to Kate."

"She's eating cake and drinking tea, therefore quite happy."

Alice backed up a few more steps, then turned and walked to the window.

"You will break your neck if you attempt to leave via that route."

She didn't say anything.

"I had an enlightening conversation with Kate the other day. Do you want to know what she told me?"

"No, thank you. What I want is a cup of tea."

"She said the part of you that was fun and adventurous has gone into hiding, Alice. She said you are now boring."

"I was the serious Sinclair. I now am again."

"Why?"

She wanted to answer him, Nicholas knew that, as her top teeth were clamped on her bottom lip, stopping the words coming out.

"Alice, talk to me."

"'Tis a lovely day for a ride. We have been shopping."

She looked at his right ear and smiled. It did not reach the depths of her lovely green eyes.

The few times he'd seen her, if only from a distance, she'd looked sad, and Nicholas hadn't liked that. It made something inside him ache. Alice Sinclair was a woman of passions, but according to her sister she was now as exciting as a turtle soup. Apparently Kate loathed that particular dish.

"It's just about to start raining outside, and in minutes the streets will have turned to slush."

"It's lovely in here, however."

"In this room, or the house at Temple Street in general?"

Her eyes fired to life at his taunts, but she didn't snap back at him.

"Do you know what I respected most about you when first we met, Alice?"

She shook her head.

"Your forthright manner. It is not often a woman will call me a fool on such brief acquaintance."

"I should not have said that, forgive me."

Even her voice had changed.

"I don't forgive you."

"Pardon?" She turned to face him again.

"Alice, I know a great deal about you. I know about your hearing and I know about your family's heightened senses. I know you love to read, Kate told me that. I know you have an adventurous spirit and are loyal to your friends, which your brother told me is often your downfall."

"I am no longer that person, my lord. My actions have hurt others, so I am attempting to do things correctly. Please allow me to do so. In fact, you should applaud my actions. You told me stop this naive belief that I can simply carry on taking foolish risks and to hell with anyone and anything."

"Don't blaspheme, and I said those word at the time as I

was gripped with several strong emotions. Fear and anger being two of them."

"You blaspheme!" Her words had a snap to them that pleased him. "And you wouldn't have said those words if you hadn't meant them."

"I'm sorry if they upset you."

"They were the truth, and that is what matters, Nicholas. And you of all people should understand my need to change. My need to fit into society."

"Why me of all people?"

"Your behavior was once not as it should be but is now exemplary... or so they believe. I am attempting to be the same for the time I have remaining in London."

He had tried to be on his best behavior when required since he'd changed the way he lived his life. When you were extremely bad, with your reputation in tatters, it took a great deal for your peers to forget or forgive. There were a few who still glared at him, but most had moved on.

"Who are they?"

"Pardon?" She'd started pacing back and forth across the room to the window and away.

"You said 'or so they believe."

"Stop asking me questions."

Nicholas just needed to push a little harder; he was sure he'd have a shriek out of her in no time.

CHAPTER 24

"*Y*ou are making little sense, Alice. I had thought you the articulate sister." He sent Kate a silent apology.

"Those women!" she braced her hands on her hips.

"Which women?"

"The young ladies who have you on the top of their lists... I shouldn't have said that," she added quickly, looking horrified. "Forget my words, please."

"Lists?" Nicholas left the door and advanced on her.

"Never mind. 'Tis nothing, really, forget I spoke. I tend to ramble—"

"No, you don't, and don't take up lying as a vocation, you're hopeless at it. Your fingers are flicking."

She wanted to refute that claim but she was still attempting to be the perfect, well-behaved miss. Of course, she was failing miserably, Nicholas was pleased to note.

"Now back to these lists. Are you telling me that young ladies actually have lists with the names of men they wish to marry?"

"No, absolutely not."

"I believe we've established I am no fool, Alice. Tell me the truth."

"Oh dear."

"Oh dear?" Her head was now tilted slightly to the left.

"'Tis nothing."

"I think it's definitely something if it made you say oh dear."

"It was just something Stanley said. He has an extensive vocabulary when it comes to cursing."

"You must be absolute hell to live with," Nicholas said, awed. He'd not heard a thing. He must remember never to speak of anything he had no wish for her to overhear when she was nearby.

"How far away can you hear?"

"A great distance, and now I must leave."

Nicholas stepped to the right as she tried to pass him.

"Move... please," she gritted out.

"What will you do if I don't?" He grabbed her hand.

"Unhand me."

"You can do better than that insipid reply, surely?" Nicholas would provoke a response out of her if he had to stay in this room with her all day.

"Why are you doing this? You don't want to spend time in my company, just as I don't want to spend time in yours." The words were desperate now.

"I do want to spend time in your company."

"You can't, not after what I did to you."

Now they were getting somewhere. "Alice, you couldn't make me do something I didn't want to if you tried. I went in to Bastil's because I needed to face my demons. You made me do that, and I will be forever grateful, because now I know with a certainty that I will never again gamble within its walls. "

"You hated the thought of going in there. I saw that on your face. I made you do it."

"No. I did it because I needed to." He took both her hands in his. "At first, yes, I didn't want to, but then I realized it was time."

"I'm sorry, Nicholas. So very sorry for what you suffered because of me."

"Good God, will you listen to me, woman." He grabbed her shoulders and shook her gently. "You allowed me to face that particular demon, Alice. I feel lighter inside because of it. And I have you to thank for that."

"But—"

"I will never gamble for money again after entering Bastil's for the last time. I understand that now."

"I don't believe you."

"You wound me."

"No. I mean I don't believe you can possibly want to thank me for sending you back into that hell."

"I am happier and have been since that night."

He saw the hope then as she looked at him.

"Alice. You helped me. Yes, to enter there was terrifying, but I soon realized that place had no power over me. You and our families helped me to see that."

"Really?"

"Really."

"Wolf was angry with me."

"His anger was because of the risk you took going to such a place, Alice. Perhaps he thought of me also, but I have explained to him that I bear no grudge to you for that day, and in fact I am glad I exorcised that particular demon."

"Were you.... Did you gamble a great deal?"

Nicholas loved the feel of Alice's skin. He touched her cheek, running a finger down the silky surface.

"Yes. I was a wastrel and a vile man."

"Why? You are far from that now."

"Thank you, that is a very nice thing to say. I'm not entirely sure I can give you an answer to that, other than I gained my title and the wealth behind it at a young age and decided I was important. I then turned my back on everything my father had taught me was the right way for a man to behave. I also turned my back on Lilly."

"You must be very proud of the man you are now then, as it would take courage to change what you were."

He smiled, because how could he not when faced with Alice Sinclair. She saw the positive in every negative.

"I am a work in progress with much to atone for, but yes, I am a better man."

"A good, honorable man," she persisted.

They looked at each other for long seconds. He studied every inch of her face as she studied his.

"I try to be. You make me want to be honorable."

"Nicholas."

"Alice," he replied.

"I don't think it is wise for us to do that."

"Wise, no, inevitable, yes." He kissed her then. Just a soft, fleeting brush of his lips over hers. Sensation from just that brief contact traveled through his body.

Easing back, he held her shoulders.

"We will discuss further what lies between us, but not now. It is enough you are no longer running for the nearest hiding place when I am close."

"I promise not to do so."

"I am relieved. Now we must go to the kitchens, as I am in need of sustenance. I did not have my morning meal."

"What? Why would you not eat your morning meal?"

She was still taking him to task as they entered the kitchens.

"Good God, who didn't eat their morning meal?"

Cambridge Sinclair was in the kitchen eating cake with Kate. Toby, the boy the Daveys had found beaten on their doorstep and who now lived here with them, was sitting on the counter, also eating.

"I didn't. I had something that needed to be done."

"You must be positively weak with lack of nourishment. Eat, Nicholas, quickly." Cam waved a hand to a chair. "Mrs. Davey, we must have food for Lord Braithwaite."

"Hello, Alice, have you come to eat cake also?"

"Have you left us any?" she said, and Nicholas was pleased to hear her words had some strength to them. Pulling out a chair, he waved her into it.

"I have baked a second cake, Miss Sinclair. Mr. Sinclair often calls by for a slice."

"Are you still playing at being a lady, cousin?"

Nicholas hid his smile as he took the seat beside Alice.

"Cambridge," she ground out, shooting Nicholas a look. "I am not playing. I am a lady."

"I don't know how you've managed it for so long. Wolf said it was a miracle really, considering the hoyden you are. He has doubts it will last but is enjoying the respite. Although, he said yesterday he missed your verbal sparring matches."

"Be quiet... please."

"Oh, come now. You are like my sisters; they can't keep their mouths shut or their ladylike behavior in check for more than a few hours. It is not healthy to restrain your natural personality, Alice. Vent your spleen, girl, or it will turn sour."

Nicholas ate the scone laden with jam that Mrs. Davey placed before him. Beside it was a large wedge of cake. He consumed that next, watching the interplay between the cousins.

"Stop provoking me," she hissed.

"I am not being provoking, I am being honest."

"Shut up."

"Tut tut, Alice, that is hardly the proper way for a young lady to speak."

"You have been boring lately, Alice. I told Nicholas as much," Kate chimed in, further increasing her sister's distress.

"Wolf wants this of me!" The words exploded from Alice.

"No. He wanted you to show more caution instead of leaping recklessly into things with no regard to your safety," Cam said gently.

"I never leap into things—"

"You do, and often, cousin."

"She didn't used to," Kate added. "Alice has lost her sensible Sinclair title."

"Kate," Alice gritted out. "Be quiet." She looked to where Mrs. Davey stood. "I have no wish to continue this discussion."

"Mrs. Davey will say nothing, will you, Mrs. Davey?" Nicholas asked the housekeeper.

"Who would I tell?" The woman laughed. "Besides, I'm not one to speak out of turn."

"Alice, what we love about the women in this family is that they do not conform as others do," Cam said. "Take you, for instance. You invest in things and have that freakish ability with numbers."

"Nicholas has that, and it is not freakish, it's brilliant."

"Here, here." Nicholas raised his tea to that.

"Yes, but then he is unusual also, as he is one of us."

Nicholas munched on his cake and accepted the compliment—and the warmth in his chest too.

"Oh, good lord," she snapped, losing the starch in her spine and rounding on Cam. "I want to fit in! Perhaps I don't want to be different anymore."

Now that surprised him, and her, by the look on her face. "I want to be a better person," she quickly added. "My actions have hurt others. Now be quiet, I have no wish for anyone to overhear us."

"Why would you want to be like everyone else?" Nicholas asked. "You're special," he said to the side of her face, as she was focused on her plate. "You live with passion, Alice, and courage. Yes, sometimes they force you to do things that you shouldn't, but don't want to be different, I beg of you. Want to be unique. You and your family are so much more than other people. You should embrace that and be proud of the wonderful person you have become."

"Does anyone have a handkerchief?" Cam dug about in his pocket as he sniffed.

"I have hurt my family with my actions," Alice said softly.

"We are all fine, and extremely resilient. As you can imagine, it is taxing to have a family member as outspoken as you, but what can we do."

Nicholas couldn't hold back his laughter at Cam's words. Every member of the Sinclair and Raven families was outspoken, especially him.

"And as you can see, Nicholas is fine," Cam said, running a finger over the top of the sugar on the biscuit in his hand. He then stuck it in his mouth and made a small humming sound. "Plus, he has not always been the model of a perfect gentleman."

"Also true." Nicholas did not feel the usual panic at Cam's mention of his past. "I was a reprobate actually. I had all the vices, but I have explained that to Alice, and that she did me a favor sending me into Bastil's."

"Lilliana said you lost your way briefly," Kate said.

"Did she? Well, everything she said is right, and likely, knowing my sister, she attempted to paint me in a good light."

"Sisters," Cam sighed. "The very best of us... for the most part."

"Indeed," Nicholas agreed. He loved Lilly very much.

"But back to Alice," Cam said.

"Must we?" She looked in pain.

"Love yourself, Alice, because we do."

Cam's words were simple and effective, and very much the truth as far as Nicholas was concerned. He was fast coming to the conclusion that in fact his heart may be involved when it came to Alice Sinclair; he was just not ready to acknowledge that yet.

"Come, Kate, we are leaving."

"I thought we might be." Kate got to her feet.

"Thank you, Mrs. Davey, and please thank Mr. Davey."

Ignoring Cam, Alice curtseyed to Nicholas and left.

"She's stubborn, like her brother and mine." Cam sighed, picking up her uneaten piece of cake. "Once their mind is set, they are unlikely to be swayed. I hadn't realized she was struggling to fit in, or that she wanted to so desperately."

"It cannot be easy, Cam. Being different, hearing everything that is said."

"True, that would take some adjustment after living your entire life in a small village. At least the man she marries will be able to speak without the worry of always being overheard," Cam added.

"What?"

"Love dulls the senses. It's the same with all of us. Eden can't always hear James."

I didn't hear you? Alice had said those words to Nicholas today. Did that mean she had feelings for him? That didn't unsettle him as much as it should.

"Mind you, if her path to true love follows the same pattern as ours, she'll save a bloody Raven at some stage," Cam said. "As that has yet to happen...." His words fell away as Nicholas choked on a crumb of cake. When he'd recovered, Cam was staring at him intently.

"Has Alice saved you?"

"What?" Nicholas managed to wheeze out.

"When?"

"When what?"

"When did my cousin save you?"

"I'm not having this discussion with you."

Cam's smile was far too smug for Nicholas's comfort. "Very well, I will discuss it no more."

"Ever again," Nicholas added.

"I will say instead that it is good to see the changes in you. You have shed a layer and appear to be rebirthing."

"That sounds hellishly uncomfortable," Nicholas said, to give himself time.

"And yet true."

He sighed loudly. "Why must you Sinclairs dissect everything?"

"It's our way, we like to pick at something or someone until we have all the answers, or that something or someone is broken and battered into submission."

"You are the most uncomfortable family I've ever had the pleasure of being a part of."

"Couldn't have worded it better myself," Cam said taking the plate from Mrs. Davey and lowering it to the table before him.

Mr. Davey burst into the kitchen. "Lord Braithwaite, your house is on fire!"

CHAPTER 25

*A*lice and Kate were in the carriage preparing to depart when Nicholas and Cam ran out the front door of Temple Street. Nicholas roared his address to their driver, then opened the door and jumped in. Alice knew instantly something was very wrong. His face was tight with worry.

"What has happened?" She reached for him, needing the contact. He took her fingers in his and gripped them hard.

"My house is on fire. I must use your carriage... to call my horse now would take too much time and—"

"Of course." Alice moved over, and he sat beside her. The maid took the seat opposite with Cam and Kate. Both were looking at her. She realized why when she looked down. Her hand was clasped in Nicholas's. She released him and folded them in her lap.

"Christ, please let my staff be safe."

"I'm sure they are. Your butler is a man of action, he will have everyone out," Cam reassured.

By the time the carriage pulled up outside the Braithwaite townhouse, the tension inside the carriage was thick.

Both men leapt from the carriage. Alice and Kate followed. The smell of smoke hit them, and they could see it billowing from the windows of the townhouse. She saw that a water engine was pumping water into the house, but it was such a large place, Alice doubted it could do a great deal.

Cam and Nicholas were speaking with a group of people gathered to their right.

"The staff, Hopkins?"

"All are accounted for, my lord. Some have burns, but all made it out. But I fear we could salvage nothing."

"I care little for possessions, only that everyone is safe." Nicholas dismissed the butler's words.

Alice moved forward to comfort a woman seated on the ground. Kate too. Recently she had been studying under Essie, learning all she could about cures and medicines, and like their cousin she had a natural ability with healing.

"Neckties, Alice. Take them from Cam and Nicholas," Kate ordered her. "One of the maids appears to have broken her arm hurrying to leave the house."

She found the men near the entrance of the house. Nicholas had a piece of paper in his fist, and Cam was looking grim.

"I'm so sorry, Nicholas."

He turned, and the anger in his eyes was fierce.

"It was deliberate. Someone did this to get at me."

Alice went cold at the thought that he may have been inside, caught in the flames.

"A threat to stop me investigating the missing babies."

"I don't understand."

He thrust the note at her and walked away. Alice read the black scrawling words out loud.

"'This will be your final warning. Stop prying into things that don't concern you. Next time I will harm someone you care about. You've been warned.' Dear lord, Cam."

"I know, love. The note was delivered a few minutes ago by a scraggy little urchin who handed it over and fled." His arm came around her. "But we will keep him safe, as we will all of us."

"But his home, Cam. His life is inside those walls."

"Some of it, yes, but he has estates also. Everything in there can be replaced, Alice. People can't."

"Alice!" Kate called her.

"I need your necktie, cousin."

They made the staff as comfortable as they could. The worst injured, Alice took to their carriage.

"The others have arrived."

Suddenly the air was full of galloping horses coming down the street. No easy task on a busy day, with plenty of people stopping to watch the Braithwaite house burn.

Wolf ran to her and Kate.

"Thank God you are both all right." He squeezed them together hard. "I had a feeling you were involved."

"Nicholas's house is burning, Wolf."

"But he and the staff are all right?"

Alice nodded.

"Then nothing else matters."

"Yes, something else matters." She handed him the note. "It was deliberate."

She watched Lilly crying in her brother's arms. Alice knew that the Braithwaite siblings were watching their memories smolder and burn. Memories of parents and grandparents and childhood escapades.

"Bastards," Wolf hissed. He then stormed away to Dev and James, handing the note to them.

Alice and Kate went with the servants in their carriage back to James and Eden's townhouse. She didn't want to leave Nicholas but knew that to stay and comfort him would raise questions she had no idea how to answer.

What followed was organized chaos as they attempted to help those with burns and find places for everyone to stay. Two hours later, she had not seen Nicholas, but there was nothing more she could do for the staff, who were now all settled in their temporary accommodations.

"Alice?"

"Hello, Samantha." Alice was wandering the floor with no destination in mind; she was simply walking. The duke's house was large, and there was much to see, and for some reason she felt as if she needed to keep walking.

"Hello, Whiskers." She scratched behind a scruffy ear, and the little dog made a whining sound that said he was happy with her actions.

"Are you all right, Samantha?"

"It is very sad, what has happened to Nicholas and his staff."

"It is, very sad."

Samantha was going to break many hearts in a few years, was Alice's guess. Her hair was the color of wheat, and her lovely blue eyes were set in a pretty face.

"Where are you walking to?"

"Just walking, Samantha. I had no destination in mind."

"Then you must join us; we are toasting crumpets in the nursery. Even though we are older now, we still like to go there and do this from time to time. Wolf often joins us."

"Does he?"

She took the hand Samantha held out to her, and soon they were taking the stairs up.

"When he was injured and living at Dev's, Dorrie, Somer, and Warwick used to toast crumpets with him every morning. He didn't sleep much... sorry, you probably know this."

"I don't actually, and would love to hear more about Wolf during those days."

She'd known, of course, that her brother was wounded.

Family had written to tell her that. They'd said he was being cared for. Alice and Kate had wanted to come to London to be with him, but their mother would not allow it as she was not fit to travel at that stage, suffering from a digestion complaint.

They entered the nursery to find Warwick, the twins, and Isabella and Simon, Eden and James's children.

"Alice wants to hear about when Wolf was injured. You should tell her," Samantha said bluntly as they settled on the floor before the fire. It wasn't especially cold, but the day's events had put a chill inside her.

"He was broken when he got home, Alice, but we put him back together," Somer said.

Alice wasn't sure how long she sat there listening to the stories and eating crumpets slathered in jam, but what she learned during that time broke her heart into a million pieces.

"We didn't know," she whispered.

Whiskers, hearing the sadness in her words, climbed onto her lap for a cuddle.

"He didn't want you to know," Warwick said. "But he talked about you and Kate a lot."

"I wish we'd been here too." Alice wiped her eyes. "But thank you for sharing this with me. I understand so much more about why he didn't communicate with us now. And thank you for watching over him when we could not."

When she and Kate finally arrived home, there was not much left of the day, so the sisters retired early, both exhausted. Wolf and Rose had gone to their rooms also.

"Good night, Kate."

"Good night, Alice. Are you all right?"

They were climbing the stairs to the second floor. Alice's room was at the rear overlooking the gardens, Kate at the front.

"I am of course sad for Nicholas."

"I watched you comfort him in the carriage, Alice. You care for him."

"Kate" was all Alice sighed. "It has been a trying day, please don't make it more so."

Her sister merely kissed her cheek and went to her room. Alice closed her door and dressed for bed, then lay staring into the darkness, thinking about everything. How her brother had suffered, and how Nicholas was still suffering. Sleep began to pull her under, and her last thought was for him.

Where was he now?

Something woke her several hours later. Alice wasn't sure what. Getting out of bed, she slipped her feet into slippers and grabbed her shawl. The windows drew her. Pulling back the curtains, she saw the moon was high.

What had disturbed her? Searching the grounds, she saw nothing, and then there he was. Alice wasn't sure how she knew it was Nicholas, but it was. Walking through her brother's grounds.

CHAPTER 26

*N*icholas had slept for a few hours, rolling from side to side in a bed that was not his. He'd then risen, pulled on his clothes, and quietly left the house to check his family was safe. He'd walked around the interior of Dev's house, then gone outside to walk the grounds. He'd then made his way up the street to each of the houses a family member resided in.

"I'm clearly mad," Nicholas muttered, leaving the Raven townhouse.

The fire and the note had scared him. He'd never had to worry about anyone else before. By the time he'd come to his senses and sobered up, Dev was there to care for Lilly. Yes, he still worried about her, but she was safe... or had been. Now he'd put a threat over them all.

It wasn't his fault, he understood that, but he was still tense at the thought someone may do something to harm one of them. Looking at Wolf's house, he closed his eyes and imagined Alice slumbering. Her lovely hair free, body soft and warm with sleep.

What was he to do about her? Not that he could do

anything now with the danger hanging over him, but the fact was, he wanted to.

Letting himself in through the iron gate, he saw no one lurking around the front of the house, so he slipped down the side.

If any of his family saw him doing this, they would not be pleased. The men would protest they were more than capable of protecting them and theirs, but Nicholas was driven to do this; something inside him told him he must.

Walking to the rear, he moved deeper into the gardens that lay between Wolf's house and the manor. The smaller home he was standing behind was set up by Lord Chartley to house his mistresses. Wolf had told him that one, and it still made Nicholas shake his head. Taking the path to his left, he checked for any suspicious activities, and it was there he found the charming gazebo nestled in a stand of trees.

It seemed Chartley had thought of everything.

"Nicholas?"

He was standing in the doorway looking inside when he heard her voice. Turning, he found Alice a few feet away.

"Why are you lurking about in our gardens?"

She wore a coat pulled on over her nightdress. Boots were on her feet, and all that beautiful raven hair was loose around her shoulders, just like when she came to him in the visions. She looked like a deliciously rumpled angel.

"Go back to bed, Alice." The words came out gruff.

Of course she didn't, Alice was nothing if not consistently willful. Instead she moved closer. Nicholas felt the ridiculous urge to run... very fast in the opposite direction.

"I don't understand why you are here." She stopped close enough so all he had to do to touch her was reach out a hand. His fingers itched to run a long ribbon of black silk through them as he kissed her.

"How did you know I was here?"

"Something woke me. I looked out the window and saw you."

"You saw my face from your window on the second floor? I thought Wolf and Dev were the ones with heightened vision." His voice was remarkably calm considering his heart was thudding hard.

She didn't want to answer him.

Another thought occurred to him. "Tell me you are speaking the truth and saw me from your window, and that you were not wandering about out here alone?" The thought made him go cold. "Alice, you can't—"

"No. I knew it was you because... well, because I just did. I felt it was you." The last words were almost whispered.

He knew what she meant. It was no different for Nicholas; he felt when Alice was near.

"Alice, you need to go back to your room now." Nicholas said the words with more force than they required.

"I know." She didn't move. "Are you all right, Nicholas? The fire was so horrible for you, to lose everything like that."

"I am well. Now please, Alice. Go to your bed." Even as he spoke the words, his fingers closed hers inside his.

"Why are you here, Nicholas?"

He pulled her closer, and then backed into the gazebo, taking her with him.

"I was checking you were all safe." He couldn't come up with a convincing lie, so he settled on the truth.

"All of us? Have you been around all the houses in this street that have a Raven or Sinclair inside them?"

"Maybe."

"You have."

"I have," he grunted, uncomfortable with her words.

"That is a very nice thing to do."

"I'm not nice," Nicholas said, pulling her closer. So close

that her body lightly brushed his. "In fact, right now my thoughts are anything but nice, Alice. You need to leave."

"I know." She rose to her toes and kissed him.

It was like a flame igniting kindling. His body sparked to life. The day's emotions suddenly caught up with him. Nicholas wrapped her in his arms and kissed her with all the need and hunger he felt. His appetite for this woman was ferocious; he'd just hidden it behind a veneer of civility. The veneer was now ripped away.

"Open your mouth."

She did, and he took their kiss deeper, his hands finding the opening of her jacket and sliding inside. He cupped her buttocks and moved up her body, mapping each curve.

"I can think of nothing but you." He breathed the words against her lips.

"I am the same." Her hands were on his shoulders, touching his neck, moving wherever they could reach. His control was in tatters.

"This is folly, Alice." He gripped her waist and eased her back off his aching body. He must try one more time. "I will take you back now."

"I don't want to go back."

"Wh-what are you doing?"

She was unbuttoning her jacket. Nicholas felt a surge of lust so fierce it nearly forced a moan from his lips. He watched as she dropped the coat, and now stood before him in a white nightdress. Moonlight showed him the curves beneath. The gentle swell of her breasts, the sweet outline of her limbs.

Nicholas could smell her; soft and alluring, her scent seemed to wrap around him, enticing him.

"I am not brave enough to do the rest before you." Her hands went to the buttons at her neck. "Help me, Nicholas."

And with that one innocent plea, he closed the distance

between them again. Slipping a hand beneath her hair, he cupped her cheek.

"God help me, I cannot resist you."

He took her lips again, placing light touches on her mouth, easing the soft, trembling lips apart. He could taste her sweet innocence, and never before had he felt such an intense need to be with a woman. His body fired to life; blood flowed through his veins, urging him to pull her closer.

Her hands pushed the jacket off his shoulder, then he felt her fingers on his waistcoat. He stepped back and removed them, his eyes holding hers.

"Alice—"

"No words, Nicholas." She pressed her fingers to his lips. "Please, I want this with you."

He took her hand, kissing her fingers. "I cannot offer for you until there is no longer any danger. I will not allow anything to happen to you."

"I know that."

"But we will marry, my sweet."

"Yes."

"Be sure, Alice."

"I am, very sure."

She reached for the hem of her nightdress, and his breath lodged in his throat as she eased it up and over her head, exposing her lovely body.

"So beautiful," he rasped, mapping every inch of her with his eyes, right down to the delicate turn of her ankles. Lifting a hand, he touched the curve of a full breast, moving to circle a taut nipple with his finger. Her eyes closed as he continued the gentle torment.

"Just feel, Alice."

. . .

"I-I... it feels wonderful. I have never experienced the like before."

"I should hope not." He growled the words against her lips.

"Barty and I kissed, but it was never like this."

"I don't want to hear about you and him." He pushed the hair behind her shoulders and kissed her neck.

"I'm sure your experience is vaster than mine," she babbled. "Women are not forgiven for promiscuity like men."

Her words forced a bark of laughter from him.

"Be quiet now, Alice."

"I was just—"

"I know, now be quiet." He cupped her breasts, then lowered his head and kissed them.

"Ohhh." Alice's body jerked at the sensation. She could do nothing but feel. Every touch, every kiss heightened the growing need inside her. His gentle caresses were like a form of torture that had soft sighs and moans coming from her lips.

She felt his hands on her stomach and tensed as one moved lower.

"I will not hurt you."

"I know."

His eyes held hers as the hand descended, fingers now stroking the curls above her thighs.

"How do you know?"

"Because you are a good man."

"And yet here I stand on your brother's property about to ravish you, an innocent, and can do nothing to stop myself."

"But I wish to be ravished; that is the difference."

His fingers moved lower, and then he was there, his hand stroking her secret places. He touched the soft folds, then the hard bud between her thighs, and Alice felt the tension inside her climb to an unbearable height. It was wicked, delicious, and more than she had ever hoped to experience. Each touch, each sensation had her wanting more. She was so totally focused on the man who held her and the riot of sensations he was creating within her. And then he slowly pushed his fingers inside her, once, twice, and Alice felt the tension bubble over as wave after wave of ecstasy crashed through her.

Nicholas pulled her into his chest as she slumped forward.

"That was q-quite spectacular," Alice found the strength to say into his neck.

"Quite spectacular?" The words were hoarse in her ear.

"Exceptionally spectacular?"

"Better, but there is so much more, sweetheart."

Alice shuddered as he lifted her hair and caressed the length of her neck.

"I want to touch you too, Nicholas. I have little experience, but with your direction...."

"You do not need experience or direction, Alice, just touch me."

She unbuttoned his shirt and pushed it from his body. Mapping every inch of his chest with her hands, Alice acknowledged how fine he was. Each muscle was defined, the planes of his stomach taut.

"Barty is flabby."

"Alice," he growled.

"I am teasing you. I have never seen him without his shirt."

"Excellent. I would have to kill him if you had."

She almost believed him, but he was a good man, she reminded herself.

She kissed his brow and cheeks and then placed a hot open-mouthed kiss like he had with her at the base of his neck, which made him moan. Her hands continued to stroke his chest, down to the waistband of his breeches.

"More," he whispered, urging her lips to his for a kiss. "I need more of you, Alice."

"Yes."

He grabbed her hand and tugged as he walked backward to where a daybed stood.

"It seems Lord Chartley needed somewhere to rest as he ran between houses."

She watched as he sat and removed his boots, then returned to his feet to lower his breeches. He was beautiful, even if what she saw terrified her.

"I could never have a husband that wanted another," Alice managed to get out before her throat dried up completely.

"Is that a warning for me, Alice?"

She shook her head as her eyes went slowly down his body.

"I— You are beautiful."

"No, you are beautiful. If you must compliment me, I am handsome. Men don't like to be beautiful."

"But you are."

He reached for her, settling both hands on her hips.

"Come here, sweetheart."

Alice felt her stomach flutter at the endearment. He settled her on his thighs, hers outside his. She felt exposed.

"It's all right." He kissed her again. Slow and sensual, gently reawakening her passions. Wicked fingers touched her, stroking the tension back to an unbearable peak inside her once more.

"Be sure, Alice?" He rested his forehead on hers. "There is no going back after this."

"I-I don't want to go back. Do you?"

His laugh was forced. "Is that a trick question? Because I've wanted you since that first kiss we shared."

"Oh... really?"

"Really. Trust me to keep you safe, Alice," he whispered as he pulled her closer until she could feel him there, pressing at the entrance of her body. His hands cupped her breasts, large thumbs stroking her nipples, and she arched toward him, eager for more. He pushed inside her, past her innocence, until he was buried deep inside her tight sheath.

"It's alright, sweetheart," he soothed as she pressed her face into his shoulder. "You feel so good, Alice."

She felt stretched with him inside her, and yet she wanted this, felt so much emotion that it nearly choked her.

"Take control, Alice. Rise on your knees and lower yourself back down."

Slowly she braced her knees beside his hips and rose. "Oooh," she whispered as she sat back down. The sensation was unbelievable. Her muscles clenched around him as she repeated the action, the glide of his swollen flesh teasing her inner walls was almost more than she could take. There was pain, but also pleasure. So much pleasure.

Nicholas cupped her hips and came off the bed as she dropped down, a move that made them both moan. Soon the sound of their harsh breathing filled the small room. Alice caught her lip between her teeth to stop further sounds.

"No! I want all of you, Alice. Let me hear your cries of passion."

She did cry his name out loud as she felt it again, that wonderful rush of ecstasy. Nicholas followed, crushing her to him. He then fell backward onto the bed with her still in his arms. She felt his hand on the back of her head; it was a gesture Wolf often made. *Protection, I'm here for you.*

"Alice, are you all right?"

"I am, however, I have grave doubts I can use my legs again."

He laughed into her hair. In that moment, she felt closer

to him than anyone in her life before. It was almost overwhelming.

"We will marry, Alice."

"I'd always hoped that when the time came, someone would ask me nicely."

He lifted her high until her eyes were level with his.

"I want you for my wife, shrew." He kissed her gently. "Please."

"Oh well, as you asked so nicely."

"Besides, from what I understand about you Sinclairs, you cannot marry unless you save your future intended, and you've done that with me already. Then there's the small matter of you not being able to hear when I'm close—"

"Who told you that?"

"Cam."

"It's true," Alice said, resting on his chest once more. "And extremely unusual when you've heard everything your entire life."

"I like it."

"I do too," Alice admitted.

"But we cannot wed until the danger has passed. This goes no further than between us. I cannot have someone using you against me."

"Nicholas, I don't want you hurt, and surely it is better if—"

"In this I will not be swayed, Alice. I can't allow someone to harm you because of me."

"Oh, very well."

She did not know how long they lay there talking, but it was the most wonderful night of her life. He shared his past with her, and she heard how much the man he'd been still affected him.

"Gambling is an addiction to me, Alice."

"And you have no wish to do it again?"

"I don't and won't gamble for money. The only reason I would ever be forced to do so would be if I had no other choice."

"Then let us hope that never comes to pass. Nicholas, I met a lady today called Meggie. She lost a child also."

"Another one," he sighed.

She told him about what she'd learned.

"Mrs. Adley again."

"I don't want you hurt, but something must be done."

"I will take care, I promise, Alice. But I cannot back away from this now." He rolled until she was beneath him. She saw the emotion in his eyes as he looked down at her. Felt it in her heart.

"I know you cannot, but please be careful."

He kissed her. "I care for you very much, Alice Sinclair."

"And I you."

"It's you who come to me at night in my visions. You who demand that I find those babes and return them to their parents."

"Oh, Nicholas, really?"

"Really. You stand there in a white dress with your hair flowing around your shoulders, looking like an angel. Demanding I do something. You consume me both night and day, Alice."

"It is no different for me."

"Good. I have no wish to suffer alone."

Those words were enough for now. A promise of the future that they would share. There was no talk of love, but there was time for that. For now, she would hold her happiness inside and wait for the day when she could let it free.

CHAPTER 27

"What is the report on the damages to your home, Nicholas?" Dev asked.

He was in the breakfast parlor eating with the family... all of them. The twins, Warwick, and Mathew, who was exact image of his father but ate with the same ferocity as his uncle Cam.

"Not good, I'm afraid. The inside is completely gutted. I will need to find somewhere else until I can decide what to do."

"You can stay with us, Uncle Nicholas," Hannah said. She sat to Nicholas's right, Meredith on his knee, making eating difficult as every mouthful he put to his lips she wanted in her mouth.

"Have you told him?" Wolf and Cam wandered in, followed by Max.

"Good morning, and no I have not. I was getting around to it," Dev said.

"'Lo." Meredith beamed at her uncles.

"It has been four days since the fire. I think it time you

told him," Wolf said, picking up Hannah and hugging her close.

"Told me what? Is Alice all right, and Kate?" he added quickly.

"My sisters are their usual annoying selves."

"Mathew, is that a moth on the window?"

The boy fell for the ploy by Cam and looked left. His uncle stole the large slice of ham from his plate.

"Right then, let's go," Max said. "On your feet, Nicholas."

"But where am I going to?" Handing Meredith to Somer, he followed the men from the room.

"All will be revealed shortly."

Four nights ago, he'd made love to Alice. Sweet, sensual love that left him reeling. Left his heart full and his chest tight with need for her. He hadn't seen her since, and the longing was growing each day. But this was for the best.

He wanted Alice safe, and for that she couldn't associate with him. If whoever was responsible for burning his house saw them together, they'd know what lay between them. Their families would also know, and they would demand answers. As it stood, he wasn't entirely sure they hadn't begun to suspect, especially Cam.

"What are you not telling me?" he asked, hoping someone would answer.

"Patience, Nicholas. Now tell us, what is happening with your investigations? Has Mr. Spriggot unearthed anything?" Cam asked him.

"No. I saw him yesterday and apprised him of the latest news. Plus what Alice told me."

He realized too late where she had told him. As she lay on his chest, relaxed and sated after they made love.

"What did she tell you?" Wolf's brows drew together.

"She has not told you?" Nicholas looked away. Wolf saw too much with those eyes of his, as Dev did.

"If she had, I would not be asking."

He told them about the other woman, Meggie Todd, who Alice had come across that day she was shopping.

"How many children have been taken?" Max demanded. "We have to stop this, Nicholas."

"I know, and there are more. Every time I have a vision, Alice is holding another child."

"Alice?" Wolf questioned in a tone that suggested he wanted an answer fast.

Nicholas cursed silently. *Think before you speak.* It had never been a problem before. Alice Sinclair was addling his thoughts.

"My sister is in your visions?"

"She is, and demanding I bring the children home to their parents." Nicholas went for the truth.

"How strange." The scowl fell from Wolf's face. "Has she told you how to catch the people doing the stealing?"

"Not as yet."

"And let us not forget that Nicholas had his first daytime vision about Alice hurting herself," Cam said.

Nicholas gave him a look that promised retribution if he didn't shut up.

"Yes, that's curious, don't you think?" Dev added.

"Very. First the day vision and then the night, all having Alice in them."

"I'm killing you," he whispered to Cam as they drew level.

"You'll thank me later."

"I'll do something later."

"Extremely curious," Wolf said, looking at Nicholas with his bright green eyes.

"Care to tell me why we are walking up the street when I know the lot of you have a perfectly adequate fleet of carriages for transportation?" Nicholas changed the subject.

They didn't speak. Wolf turned down the path that lead to

the rear of his house. The path Nicholas had walked the night he'd made love to Alice.

Christ, does he know?

They walked in single file, and once they'd reached the rear, they took the path he'd trod that would lead them past the gazebo.

Surely if Wolf knows, he'd have torn me apart, one limb at a time, by now?

Add that to what he'd just learned, and surely Wolf would be raging at Nicholas?

They walked by the little building and kept moving until they reached the house of Lord Chartley.

"Are we to take tea?"

"Not quite." Max produced a key and opened the large front door. Pushing it wide, he walked inside.

"Chartley has left London with no wish to return. He wants to rent—"

"Absolutely not!" Nicholas turned to leave, but Wolf barred his way.

"Considering what I have just learned, I think you should take a look, as history suggests you and your future wife will live on this street."

"What?"

The men locked eyes. He saw no anger in Wolf's; in fact, he looked amused.

"Care to share the joke?"

"I think not. Just take a look inside, Nicholas."

"Move, Wolf."

"What harm is there in looking?"

"I am not living on the same street as all of you, Cam. Good God, society thinks us mad as it stands, this will simply add to that."

"I didn't think you cared what people said about you?"

"Come, Nicholas. Just walk with me," Max said.

"I cannot believe you think I'd join your insanity."

"But you already have. In fact, you've taken great strides." Cam slapped him on the back again. "Just a look, Nicholas."

"Lord have mercy." He gave in.

"The furniture all stays, and it's my belief that after Lady Chartley's passing, his mistresses had a hand in the decor," Cam added. "And his fashion. The man insisted on wearing lavender, and not in a good way."

"Is there a good way to wear lavender?" Dev asked.

"The man had stamina though, you have to give him that much," Cam added. "A wife and two or three mistresses have to tax a man."

"Three?" Nicholas walked into the library. The room was decorated with cream and beige satin on the walls. The furniture was well made and sturdy. Nicholas hated the spindly stuff women often favored. "Surely not."

"As you have yet to fall into the matrimonial trap, Nicholas, let me assure you that one is more than ample," Cam stated.

He would marry Alice Sinclair, and just the thought made him smile. There was always a warmth inside his chest when he brought her to mind, followed by a sharp tug of need to be with her. He wasn't sure what that meant, but he was looking forward to finding out.

They climbed to the second floor, and Nicholas refused to acknowledge how much he liked the house and that as soon as he'd stepped foot inside it had felt right.

"Just ask him, Wolf." Nicholas heard these words from Cam.

"Be quiet, Cam."

"Ask whom? What?" Nicholas turned from looking out the window that allowed him to see Wolf's house. Which window belonged to Alice? Was she in there now?

"Hello?"

As if he'd conjured her up, there she was. Nicholas made himself smile as he would to any of the women in his family as Alice walked in.

"Why are you here, sister?"

"I saw you from my window and wondered what you were doing."

She wore a simple day dress, something any number of women wore each day to go about the house. So why then did it make his body surge to life?

"It's not safe to walk about alone, Alice. I have already told you that."

He'd kissed those breasts and touched her skin. Clenching his fists, he tried to ignore the tingle in his fingers at the memory.

"It is not far to walk, Wolf, and I fail to see what fiend would be lurking in that gazebo ready to pounce on me."

His eyes caught hers briefly. The mention of the gazebo was deliberate.

"Will you tell me now why you are all here?"

"Nicholas is taking the lease on this place," Cam said.

"I have not said as such."

"Yet you like it. I watched your face as you walked through," Max said, looking smug.

"I will think about it."

"And you." Wolf pointed at her. "Go home and do things ladies should be doing instead of stalking your brother."

She poked out her tongue and turned to leave, but Wolf's words stopped her.

"Are you aware that you are in Nicholas's visions holding the missing children, Alice?"

Nicholas knew Wolf had said those words deliberately to catch her off guard. But Alice was not easily wrongfooted.

"Yes." She laughed, and it sounded natural. Nicholas knew he would need to be awake on all counts when she was his wife; she was an excellent actress. "I yell at him. I did wonder if this is because of that woman I met."

"The one you did not tell me about?"

"Yes, that one," she said calmly. "Sorry, I meant to."

Wolf looked at her, his eyes bright green. Then he sighed. "Very well. Now go home." He leaned in to kiss her cheek.

I want to kiss her cheek.

Nicholas refrained from going to the window to watch her walk back to her house. It took a herculean effort, but he moved to the door Alice had recently exited.

"You like it, Nicholas, admit it?"

He looked at Max, wanting to deny his words.

"What is it with you people, wanting everyone in the family close? It's odd, don't you think?"

"We are odd," Dev added. "I can stand at this window and see into every room in Wolf's house. Cam can smell what is being baked in the kitchens—"

"Currant buns."

"Embrace the odd, Nicholas, we've learned to," Max said.

"I can't believe I'm contemplating this." Shaking his head, he followed the men from the house, then stood and looked up at the front facade.

Yes, he felt it. This could be home.

"So," Wolf fell in beside him as they walked down the driveway and back out to the road, "you and Alice. Do you care for my sister, Nicholas?"

He tripped, stumbling forward several paces, and only just managed to save himself the total humiliation of landing face first on the street.

"I believe I have my answer. That, plus what I have learned today."

"Wolf—"

He raised his hand. "I know you are not asking for it, but I give you my blessing. God knows Sinclairs marry Ravens;

I'm just pleased she has not saved you...." His words fell away as he studied Nicholas.

"Christ! When?"

How had he given himself away?

"I have no idea what you speak of." He went for haughty. After all, he was a bloody marquis.

"When what?" Max asked as the others joined them on the street.

"Alice saved him."

"Well now, that pretty much confirms what we've suspected," Dev said.

Nicholas ignored him. "I did not say that she saved me." He had to try and save Alice from her brother.

"Your eyes told me."

"I knew that, actually," Cam added. Nicholas gave up.

"You people are odd. I've said it before, but it bears repeating."

Wolf waved his words away. "Tell me the truth, Nicholas."

"Yes, tell us," Max added.

"I'm ignoring all of you," Nicholas muttered, knowing that he was cornered, "except him." He pointed at Wolf.

"When?"

"I am not going into detail. That is for Alice to tell you should she wish it."

"Oh, she'll wish it," Wolf said.

"Wolf, I don't want you yelling at her because of something I've told you. I kept her secrets because she trusts me."

"You're defending her." Wolf smiled. "I like that."

"Like I have just said, you are odd."

"Continue."

"The first time we met, I'm not going into detail, but she stopped me from falling through a hole in the street. There was no cover on it, and it's my guess men were working down there."

"She was somewhere she shouldn't be, wasn't she?"

"She then heard some men approach with the intent of robbing me."

"Definitely where she should not be," Cam added.

"Shut up," Nicholas barked at him.

"The point here is that Alice saved Nicholas, therefore they are meant to be together," Dev said, entering the conversation. "The visions, now this. All of it makes me happy."

"As you can imagine that is my main purpose in life." Nicholas's words had the bite of sarcasm."

"And now you must take the lease on that house. I shall see about it tomorrow," Max said.

"You bloody well will not!" Nicholas roared. "I will see about it."

"Excellent." Max slapped him on the back. "I think that calls for a pint at the Speckled Hen."

"And a pie," Cam added. "Best pies in London."

Nicholas didn't argue. After all, a pie did sound good.

CHAPTER 28

$\mathcal{T}$he Hosking musicale was as comfortable for Alice as having a stomach upset. It was not that she disliked music; in fact, quite the opposite. It was simply that she did not like it played by those with no ability. Of which Lilly had told her the evening would be filled.

"There will be some excellent performers, but also some that will make you wince, Alice. Make sure you have your earplugs pressed in firmly."

"You still should have told me, Alice." Wolf was strolling down the carpeted hallway at her side, haranguing her about not telling him she'd saved Nicholas.

"And yet I did not, as clearly I was somewhere I should not have been. Now let the subject alone, brother."

Rose had decided to stay at home this evening, as she was feeling off-color and had been nauseous all day.

"God lord, Rose is with child, isn't she?" One look at his face and the smile confirmed her words.

"We'd thought to tell everyone tomorrow. But it seems you guessed."

"I did." She hugged him. "I'm so happy for you both."

"I have never loved as I do her."

Alice understood that now. Before she would have scoffed at his words, but not now. She loved Nicholas. She'd admitted that to herself as she lay in her bed after they'd made love. One day soon she'd tell him.

"You will not deter me, sister. I want to know where you were when you saved Nicholas."

"And yet I will not tell you."

Wolf had told her he'd spoken to Nicholas, and that he'd guessed she'd saved his life. He'd seen their closeness and the way he looked at her. He understood that the future for them would be together, but until then she was still under his protection.

"You will."

"No."

"Do you love him?"

She stumbled. Wolf's large hand steadied her.

"He did that when I confronted him."

"What?"

"Nicholas stumbled just like you did."

"Please tell me you did not ask him if he loved me?"

Just the thought had her heart racing.

"Have a little faith in me, Alice. I simply asked what lay between you. It is my right as your brother to do so."

Alice groaned.

"Captain Sinclair, Miss Sinclair."

Alice was relieved to be interrupted by the large man lumbering toward them.

"Lord Beecham." Wolf bowed as Alice curtsied, searching her memory for details of the man.

Five daughters, two married, and a wife who always looked weary was what Eden had told her.

"I believe congratulations are in order once more, my lord. Please tell Lady Beecham I wish her every happiness during her confinement," Wolf said.

Lord Beecham's face twisted into a scowl, jowls wobbling. It made him look even more unpleasant. From memory, her family was not overly fond of the man. A crashing bore, Cam had said. James had shown restraint, simply stating he was not a man he associated with by choice.

"I will have a son this time, Sinclair, I'll make sure of that."

"Yes... well. It is hoped that Lady Beecham will provide you with a healthy child," Wolf said, clearly uncomfortable, as any man would be discussing such a delicate issue.

Alice, however, had no such discomfort.

"You have no wish for any more daughters, Lord Beecham?"

Wolf slid a hand around her back, digging his fingers into her spine to shut her up.

"Man needs an heir, and this time I'll have one!"

"I doubt that even you can have an assurance of what your child will be, my lord."

"It will be a son! In fact, I'll ensure it happens."

"Ensure?" Wolf asked. "Surely there is no way to ensure such a thing, as my sister has stated, Lord Beecham?"

Unease slithered down Alice's spine.

The man must have realized he'd said too much.

"It is God's will, but you'll see, Sinclair. I'll have an heir this time. That reptile who calls himself my nephew will not inherit my title. Good evening." The man lumbered away, leaving the Sinclair siblings to ponder what they had just heard.

"Wolf?"

"I know, love. But it is wrong to jump to conclusions without facts."

"But those children are going missing, and Lord Beecham stated he would have a son no matter what."

"We shall talk to the others, especially Nicholas."

Walking into the room where the musicale was to be held, she tried to calm the unease inside her.

In fact, I'll ensure it happens.

A man like Beecham would do what it took to secure an heir, but would he pay for the child? Was she overreacting to what he had said because of Mrs. Potter's grandson and Meggie Todd's babe?

"Come, the others are already seated, and I have no wish to be forced to sit beside someone smelly."

"Who is smelly?" Alice asked.

"Many people. Body odor or too much scent. Then there is Lord Bexley, who for whatever reason always has an onion in his left boot."

"He does not." Alice looked around the room, searching for Nicholas.

"He does, Cam told me."

"He'd know."

They found their family, well, at least those present. Eden had been sensible enough to cry off, as had James. In fact, there was only Cam, Emily, Dev, and Lilly.

"Thank God you've arrived. I have been throwing my body on this seat for ages when someone tries to take it," Cam said dramatically. "That old windbag Tinley just attempted to." He shuddered. "The man bathes in cloves. Apparently they keep him healthy."

They sat, but she felt restless, like something was gathering in the air.

"Is Nicholas coming?"

"He is," Emily said.

She sat and waited impatiently for him to arrive.

"Good evening."

"Good evening, Captain Young."

"I have just returned to London after time with my regiment, Miss Sinclair. It is wonderful to see you again." He took the seat beside her, the one she'd been saving for Nicholas. "Allow me to say how beautiful you look this evening."

Alice felt uncomfortable at the look in his eyes.

"Thank you, Captain. The weather here has not been ideal since your departure, I fear. We have been house-bound," Alice babbled.

Where is Nicholas?

"I would like to call on you tomorrow, Miss Sinclair, and take you driving if you are free?"

"Oh... ah—"

"Sorry, Captain Young, she is driving with me. And I must beg your pardon again as that is my seat you are sitting in."

The captain regained his feet, his eyes going from Alice to Nicholas. He then bowed deeply; clearly he now understood what lay between them.

"I shall leave you both then. Good evening."

Nicholas sat. His fingers brushed hers briefly.

"Good evening, Alice." His hand touched the side of her thigh, and she felt it through her body.

"You just all but declared our connection to Captain Young, Nicholas. I thought you had no wish to do so."

"I don't like the way he looks at you. You are mine, and I've begun to realize I want people, mainly men, to understand that fact."

"Oh" was all she could manage. Inside, she felt ridiculously happy.

His smile was for her alone. Dressed in black, with a crisp white shirt and necktie, he looked vital, handsome, and he was hers.

"Was that your father's, and father's father's?" She pointed to the emerald on his finger, needing to say something, as she felt ridiculously shy suddenly.

This man knew her better than anyone else. He'd touched and kissed her. He'd made love to her.

"You're blushing."

"It's hot in here."

"No, it's not." He laughed. "Yes, this ring has been handed down to every Lord Braithwaite for many years," he said, taking pity on her.

"It's lovely."

"It will go to my son if I am blessed to have one... with you."

Alice placed the program she'd been given upon entering evenly in her lap. A large hand reached over and tweaked it slightly.

"I've missed you so much, Nicholas. More than I thought it possible."

"As I have missed you. I want to hold you, Alice, but fear that would create a scandal here. Not that I care overly, but your brother would likely thump me."

"But surely for a few bruises...," she teased him

"Heartless woman."

"I need to tell you something, Nicholas," Alice whispered as the music started once more.

"What?"

"Wolf and I encountered Lord Beecham entering the musicale."

"Can't have been very pleasant. You have my sympathies."

"Yes. He is a loathsome creature, however what he said was disturbing."

"Did he insult you?"

She saw the anger flash in his eyes.

"No, nothing like that. Wolf congratulated him on his wife's confinement. And he said something that chilled both of us."

"What did he say?"

"That he would do what it takes to ensure that his next child was a boy. That he would not have his nephew inheriting his title."

She shot him a look, but as he was now facing forward, she only saw the clenching of his jaw.

"Nicholas?"

"I don't want you involved in this, Alice."

"I am involved. But that is not the point. Do you think Lord Beecham would pay for a child... an heir?"

"I do. Come, we need some air." He leaned across her to speak to Wolf. "Your sister needs air, we shall return shortly."

Before Wolf could speak, Nicholas had her out of the chair and was walking away with her hand on his arm. He walked through a door, then out onto the terrace.

"I'm not sure this is very proper behavior," Alice felt she needed to say, even if she loved that he wanted to get her alone. "Surely tongues are wagging?"

"Let them. I want to be alone with you."

He towed her around the deck until they were assured of privacy.

"I woke with the taste of you on my lips and the memory of what it felt like to be inside you, and that has stayed with me since." He backed her into the balustrade railing and kissed her. It was fierce, desperate, and she loved it.

"I can't stop thinking about you." He held her against him.

"And I you."

"Not long, Alice, I promise. Mr. Spriggot has a lead and believes he is closing in on the men responsible for burning my house. Mr. Brown also has news on the men who are taking the babies."

"Really? But that is wonderful."

His eyes ran over her.

"You look beautiful." He ran a finger along the neckline of

her dress, dipping briefly beneath. Then he released her and stepped back.

"Good evening, Lord Braithwaite."

"Lord and Lady Krimpton."

"What has you out here alone with Miss Sinclair?" The woman did not look happy. Alice knew that Nicholas was on the top of her daughter's list of prospective husbands.

"Miss Sinclair felt faint. As I was seated next to her, I quickly helped her outside to get some air."

"But her brother—"

Alice watched Nicholas change before her eyes into a marquis. A man of consequence and power who had a lineage longer than most nobles in the United Kingdom.

"Are you questioning my motives, my lady?"

"Of course she's not," Lord Krimpton said quickly. "Come." He dragged his wife away.

"You were terrifying," Alice said, awed.

"I have walked in this world for a while, my sweet. It is, or should I say, was my hunting ground for many years."

"But not now."

"No." He touched her cheek.

"Have you had any more visions, Nicholas?"

"I have, last night in fact."

"Did I visit you again?"

"Holding yet another child. Yes."

"What did I say this time?"

"That soon I will have the answers I seek. That I will soon be asked to do something that goes against the man I have become. I must do this to free a child."

"I am worried for you, Nicholas." Alice felt a sudden urge to grab Nicholas and not let him go.

"There is no need, I am not alone." He took the hand she held out to him. "It will be all right. I started this; I will see it through. But now I have you and our families at my back."

"But what of the midwife, surely—"

"They are no longer in that residence, Mr. Brown told me. In fact, Mrs. Adley has disappeared."

"I don't like this, Nicholas. I feel as if something is about to happen. Promise you will do nothing without first notifying someone of your actions."

"I promise." He leaned in and kissed her.

She had to be happy with his words, and yet unease had started to gather inside her.

"Be careful, Nicholas."

"I have promised you I will, my sweet. Have faith in me."

She did, of course, but she felt like they were about to face something. She just had no idea what it was.

CHAPTER 29

*N*icholas did not usually enjoy musicales. In fact, they bored him silly. He knew that music had run through the blood of his forefathers; his mother had told him that as she forced him to take piano lessons. Yet he had never been overly enamored with it.

However, he had to admit to enjoying this musical because Alice sat at his side.

"Stop hissing out your breath," he whispered to her.

"I can't help it, she is terrible and keeps hitting the wrong notes."

"Push your earplugs in deeper."

"If I do, I shall need a pin to get them out."

His Alice. The woman who made his chest hurt when he looked at her. A mix of sweet and willful, she would certainly keep him on his toes.

She was dressed in apricot silk, and in her hair was woven a matching satin ribbon. He'd been aware of her before, but now... now she was in his blood. He wanted a life with her.

"If Wolf sees the way you are eyeing his sister in public," Cam whispered, "he will gut you."

"I have no idea what you speak of."

Cam snorted.

"I like the match, by the way. You are well suited."

"Of course. I live to make you happy."

"Ssh," someone behind him hissed.

"I beg your pardon, Lady Duke, but I wonder if you could enlighten Mr. Sinclair as to which symphony the music is from. He has no knowledge of such things, you understand, and everyone is aware there is no one more educated in music than yourself."

The woman nodded. "It's true I am extremely knowledgeable. Now pay attention, Mr. Sinclair."

Cam muttered something uncomplimentary, and Alice giggled. He loved that sound.

Loved?

Did he love her?

Dear lord, he believed he did. The thought shocked him enough to have him coughing. Cam reached over and slapped him hard on the back, turning the cough into a choking sound.

Eyes watering, but back under control, he glared at his friend, who could not reply as he was now attentively listening to Lady Duke.

Nicholas shot Alice a look and felt that pain in his chest.

It had to be love.

The night was over much too quickly as far as Nicholas was concerned. He'd laughed with his family and sat with Alice, their fingers occasionally touching, and he felt like a boy in the throes of his first love affair.

"You took over the house yesterday, I understand?" Alice asked as they waited for their carriages.

"I did. My staff are happy to be settled once more, as am I."

"We are now neighbors," Wolf drawled. "But I will be locking the doors at night."

"I beg your pardon?" Alice turned on her brother. "I cannot believe you would say something like that in my hearing."

"It was for your benefit," her brother stated calmly. "Excellent, here is our carriage. In you get, sister."

"Good night, Alice." He took her hand and helped her inside. "Take out your earplugs."

He closed the door and then walked to his carriage. As they were rolling away, the words were simply there, inside his head and needing to be spoken.

"I love you, Alice Sinclair."

Would she have heard? He hoped so. For some reason, he needed her to know his feelings right then.

Walking into his new home, he felt the place wrap around him in welcome. He'd never felt that way in his father's house. This would be his and Alice's if he decided to stay here, or even purchase the property.

"My lord, two missives were delivered late this evening. I have put them in the library on your desk."

"Thank you, Hosking."

He kicked off his shoes and took off his jacket, then picked up the first note before falling into his chair.

My lord I have received information regarding the case I am investigating for you. It is of the utmost importance I speak with you at your earliest convenience. Please advise when is a suitable time for me to call upon you tomorrow. It was signed Mr. Spriggot.

Had there finally been a breakthrough? Nicholas hoped so.

Breaking the plain red wax seal on the second note, he did not recognize the writing on the front.

Your interference has cost me a great deal, Braithwaite. I am now forced to leave England, but before I do, I will give you a chance to return one child to its mother. The babe is two days old. Come to Bastil's, and the stakes will be if you win, I give you the child. If not, he will go to his new home.

Surely he had not read the words correctly. Nicholas looked at the note again, but the words had not changed.

Come at 2:00 a.m.

Looking at the clock, Nicholas watched it strike midnight.

Tell no one, and alert no one. If you do, then the deal is off.

Getting to his feet, he poured himself a brandy, then picked up his cards and sat at his desk. One hour and thirty minutes later, he dressed and left the house.

"My lord, shall I wait up?"

"No, I am going to a hell, I will not be returning for some time. Go to your bed, Hopkins."

"My lord, if I may—"

"You may not."

The butler covered his shock, and yes, disappointment. After all, he had been with him during the days he gambled every night, staggering home drunk as the sun rose.

Letting himself outside, he hailed a hackney. All too soon, it stopped.

Bastil's always looked better at night, Nicholas thought as he stood outside the facade. None of the stains of debauchery were evident in this light. He knew they'd be there though, especially when he walked inside those doors.

He inhaled deeply, then exhaled slowly. He had to do this for the babe. For Alice. She believed in him to do the right thing, and surely this was that.

Thinking of her gave him strength. He started up the

steps and in through the front door. Whoever waited for him in there would likely have been playing consistently over the months if this was his chosen location. Nicholas had not. It would take all his skill to ensure he won. But he had two things in his favor: his skill with numbers, and the ability to think clearly when others could not. He'd even been able to do this when he was drinking.

"You are expected, Lord Braithwaite." One of the staff appeared before him. "Please follow me."

Nicholas said nothing, simply nodded and followed the man. They turned right, away from the usual tables, and he knew they were to play a private game in one of the rooms ahead.

He entered, and there sat Braeburn, a smug look on his face. He'd known someone who walked among the elevated circles of society was involved, but for some reason he hadn't considered this man.

Nicholas realized something else in that moment, he'd been a fool to walk in here without at least leaving a note for his family. He'd thought with his heart and not his head and doubted a simple game of cards was all Braeburn had in stall for him this night.

"Excellent. Not only will I beat you tonight, but both your family and society will be spared your vile company in the future," Nicholas said, taking the seat across from him. "Stealing infants, that is low even for scum like you."

"My father does not give me enough of an allowance. I had to supplement it somehow!"

"You will never have enough. That is how this works, Braeburn. It's an addiction."

"I am a gentleman, we do not have addictions!"

He would not win this argument.

"Why are you showing your hand now?"

"Word has reached us that your investigators have

unearthed the truth about the entire operation. All was lost anyway. I will have a good life somewhere else and be away from my father's influence. I will return when the time is right, when finally he is dead."

And this Nicholas now knew, was what Spriggot had discovered and wanted to discuss with him.

"Have you no remorse for the turmoil you have caused the families of the children you stole?"

Braeburn laughed. "They are beneath me, I feel nothing for such people."

Nicholas battled the rage that had him wanting to pummel the man. No good would come of letting his emotions rule his actions. He needed to remain clear headed if he was to get out of this with the child and his life.

"I have men stationed around the room. They will watch you, and if you win, take you to the babe."

"And if I don't?"

Braeburn didn't meet his eyes.

"You will be free to go."

Nicholas doubted that.

"Why here, like this, Braeburn? It makes no sense when you could have simply left England undetected."

The man's calm veneer slipped.

"I will beat you once before I leave!"

"Ah, so I have been yet another unhealthy obsession for you? But surely you know that you will never beat me. I am far too good for the likes of you."

"I will beat you," the man's eyes were crazed. "I have practiced, you have not."

Nicholas watched as the cards were dealt and hoped he could play with the skill he'd once had. Then he'd usually been drinking and was reckless; now he was not.

Pushing Alice out of his head, he focused. A family's happiness depended on it. He began to play.

CHAPTER 30

*A*lice tapped on the door and waited. Seconds later, there stood her brother. Rumpled, he was hastily pulling on his dressing gown.

"What has happened?"

"It's Nicholas. I fear something is very wrong, Wolf."

"Alice—"

"You once told me to be guided by what I felt. Well I feel something is wrong!"

"Sssh," he hissed. "Rose is sleeping."

"What has happened?" Rose ducked under Wolf's arm and stood before him, also looking rumpled.

"Go back to bed, love." Wolf tried to move her. "You need your sleep."

"I am carrying a babe, Wolf, not a plague. What has happened, Alice?"

"Something is wrong, Rose. And I believe it concerns Nicholas."

"We shall dress and see you downstairs shortly."

"Rose—"

"Wolf, your sister needs us, make haste," she heard Rose scold him as she hurried to her room.

"Alice?"

"It's all right, Kate."

Something in Alice's face had her saying, "I will dress and see you soon."

Alice pulled off her nightdress and threw on a chemise and the first dress she grabbed. She then pulled on a jacket that came to her ankles, and laced her feet into her walking boots.

She'd woken filled with terror. Fear had gripped her, chills wracked her body, and she'd known, Nicholas was in danger.

Rose and Wolf awaited her when she arrived downstairs.

"Do you love Nicholas, Alice?"

"I do." She did not hesitate, now was not the time for that.

"Can you hear him?"

She shook her head.

"I will go to Nicholas's house," Wolf added.

"I am coming," Alice said.

"No, you are not!" he thundered as Kate came in the room.

"Me too."

"No!"

She ignored him and slipped her arm through Alice's, who felt better for the support.

"We are wasting time."

Wolf glared at his sisters; they did not waver. He then stomped from the room with three women trailing behind him like geese behind their gander.

They held hands, with Wolf in the lead, as the night was dark and the moon obscured behind clouds. He rapped the large brass knocker when they arrived at the front door. It was a few minutes before it was answered.

"We shall look like fools if your beloved is warm in his bed."

"But he is not, as you very well know. Were Rose in danger you would not stop until you reached her," Alice replied.

He sighed, then wrapped an arm around her shoulders.

"You'll pardon the intrusion, Hopkins," Wolf said when the butler opened the door. "Is your master at home?"

The butler looked at Alice.

"No, he left the house two hours ago, my lord."

"Do you know where he has gone?"

The butler hesitated.

"If you know anything, please tell us, Hopkins. I fear something is very wrong," Alice said, trying to sound calm when inside she was terrified.

"His last words to me, Miss Sinclair, were that he was going to visit a hell and would not return for some time."

"A hell?"

"Gambling establishment," Wolf gritted out.

"No!" Alice stumbled back as if she'd been shot. Wolf steadied her. "He told me he would never gamble again."

"Come, we must leave," Rose said. "Apologies for disturbing you, Hopkins."

"If I may say, Captain Sinclair. These actions go against Lord Braithwaite's character now. He has not done such a thing in many years."

"Yes, thank you, Hopkins, good evening to you." Wolf urged the women back down the path. "Move your feet, Alice."

She held back the sob as it wanted to tear from her throat.

"I-I.... He wouldn't do this. I know he wouldn't."

"For some people it's a fever in their blood," Wolf said. "We shall set him right again, I assure you, or you will not marry him."

"No. Nicholas promised me."

Surely it was not the truth? Could she have been so wrong about him?

"The facts are before us, Alice. Come, we shall confront him in the morning," Wolf said.

"Nicholas is a good man. I believe something has forced him to go back there." Rose said, leading the way back into the house.

"Unfinished business," Wolf snapped.

"But if it is only this once—"

"He is an addict, Rose, once will never be enough," Wolf said. "Come, it is late, nothing can be done now." He urged them all back up the stairs.

"How can you expect me to sleep? Surely we need to go—"

"No one is going anywhere!" Wolf thundered.

"I don't believe he would betray himself, and me, in this way," Alice said.

Wolf looked at her with pity in his eyes.

"Sleep now."

She said nothing further, knowing her brother believed Nicholas guilty.

"Alice, shall I sleep with you?" Kate asked her as they walked to their rooms.

"No, but thank you. I wish to be alone."

Kate hugged her close, but she felt nothing, only numbness. Entering her room, Alice did not change her clothes, simply lay on her bed and stared up at the ceiling.

I love you, Alice Sinclair. He'd spoken the words to her as he drove away from the musicale tonight, and she'd believed them.

Something was wrong, she felt it deep inside her.

I don't and won't. The only reason I will ever gamble again would be if I had no other choice but to do so.

Alice sat upright suddenly as she remembered his words. Dear lord, was it possible he was being forced to gamble? But why would anyone do such a thing?

Only a threat to what Nicholas held dear would make that happen.

That I will soon be asked to do something that goes against the man I have become. I must do this to free a child.

She'd said those words to him in a vision. Dear lord, he was being forced to gamble.

"I'm a fool for doubting you, even for a second, Nicholas. Forgive me."

Alice hurried off the bed and took her coin purse out of her dresser. Tucking it in to her pocket she then opened her door and crept down the stairs to Wolf's office.

Her brother would not let her leave the house again tonight. He believed Nicholas was gambling; to convince him otherwise would be impossible, Alice knew that with a certainty. She had to do this herself, no matter that when she returned Wolf would likely lock her in her room and hide the key indefinitely.

Reaching beneath his desk, she found the key he thought she and Kate could not find and used it to open the cabinet that he'd had fitted behind the bookshelf that he also didn't think they knew about. Pulling the shelf forward, she used the key to unlock the case. Opening it, Alice took out a knife that was fitted in a sheath. Wolf had taught her how to use it, but she'd never wanted to learn to fire a gun like Kate.

Lifting her skirts, she strapped it to her thigh, then ran to the door. She had to get out of the house before Wolf woke, which he would when he felt that something was wrong.

Once outside, she ran down the street, not stopping until a hackney appeared.

"Take me to Bastil's, please."

"Begging your pardon, miss, but that's no place for a lady."

"I know, but my fiancé is there."

"Ah" was all the driver said, but the look of sympathy on his face made Alice grit her teeth.

The drive seemed to take forever, but finally they arrived. Leaning out the window, she told the driver she would pay him to wait here with her in the hackney. Alice then pulled out her earplugs and listened.

"I believe I have won again, Braeburn, which suggests you owe me an address."

Alice knew it was Nicholas who spoke those words.

"Damn you, Braithwaite. I should have beaten you!"

"But you didn't and never will. Now tell me the address where the child is so I can return it to its mother, or I'll give you what you deserve, and to hell with your men at my back."

No further words were spoken by Nicholas or the other man, and then suddenly he appeared in the doorway. He looked rumpled, hat in hand, as he stalked to where another hackney waited. He didn't look her way as he gave an address she did not recognize.

Alice told her driver to follow the hackney Nicholas was in. They rolled through the dark London streets. She saw late night revelers returning from social gatherings, and all the time she thought about Nicholas. Nicholas had been gambling to save a child. Her guilt over what she'd first thought when she'd heard he was in a gambling hell, intensified.

When the carriage stopped, she got down and paid the driver all the money she had in her reticule.

"That's where the hackney stopped. A gentleman got down and walked that way," the driver said, pointing ahead of him.

"Will you wait for me to return, sir?"

When he agreed, Alice walked slowly in the direction he'd

pointed to. Keeping to the shadows, she patted her knife, ensuring it was in place.

She could hear no voices nearby, just the occasional distant murmur.

Where are you, Nicholas?

CHAPTER 31

*I*t had taken every ounce of skill he had, but eventually he'd beaten Braeburn. The man had been shocked, sure that Nicholas had lost his skills. He'd then left Bastil's with an address and the vow that if the babe was not there he was coming for Braeburn, and there would be nowhere he could hide, even the Continent.

What surprised him as he walked though the darkened streets was that he'd left Bastil's unharmed. Of course the night was not over, and until he reached his bed he would be on his guard. Braeburn was a snake and not to be trusted.

Nicholas found the correct building. Taking the stairs up, he found number fifteen and knocked on the door. Mrs. Adley opened it.

"Why are you here?" She tried to shut it. He forced his way inside.

"Give me the babe, and then tell me who you took him from."

"The money—"

"I have no wish to listen to your motivations, as only greed could have you committing such a heinous crime.

Hand over the child... now." Nicholas kept his voice low, as he had no wish to rouse any of the neighbors. Peers were not exactly commonplace here, nor were they respected. They could turn on him should the Adleys have friends nearby.

She hurried away, and seconds later appeared with a bundle of blankets. Nicholas took the infant in one arm.

"I need the address now."

"He was from two buildings over. Bottom floor, number two." She pointed straight ahead.

"Name of the mother?"

"Glim."

"Do you keep records of the children you have stolen?"

She hesitated.

"Perhaps this will help reinstate your memory?" He pulled the pistol from his jacket pocket.

"What's going on here?" Mr. Adley appeared.

"Bring me any records of where the children you have stolen were from and have been delivered to."

"You can't come here. Why do you have that b-babe?" the man spluttered.

Nicholas pointed the pistol at his wife's head.

"Get the records now, or I shoot."

"You wouldn't dare," he scoffed.

"I'm a marquis, Mr. Adley, I can dare just about anything. What's more, it would not upset me overly to kill either you or your wife. You are both scum that I would gladly rid the world of."

"Do as he says, Syd." Mrs. Adley's voice was laced with panic. "Hurry."

The man began to move.

"Try anything at all, Mr. Adley, and you will be very sorry," Nicholas said.

The child in his arms grew restless, crying out for something. Nicholas rocked him from side to side, no easy task while holding a pistol.

"Were you and Lord Braeburn selling them to noblemen?"

She nodded. "I-I don't know the names of them that's involved."

"But the babes were sold to men who had no heirs?"

She nodded once more.

"How long has this been going on?"

"Two years."

Disgusted, Nicholas could not look at her.

Mr. Adley returned with a ledger.

He did not want to put down the pistol, so he handed the baby to Mrs. Adley while he took the ledger and tucked it down the front of his breeches.

"Give him to me."

Once he had the child again, he left without saying another word. Taking the stairs down, he hugged the babe close as it began to cry in earnest. Hurrying through the dark, he found the second building and number two, then banged on the door.

"Who's there?"

"I am the Marquis of Braithwaite."

"And I'm the Jolly Roger."

"Please open the door, I have your babe in my arms."

The door was thrown open, and there stood a man in his nightshirt, beside him a woman who had obviously been weeping. Her face was ravished with grief.

"What game are you playing?" The man stepped in front of the woman.

"Your baby was taken away last night after a man came to your door. You were told he was deformed. Is that correct?"

The man nodded.

"I have been investigating this matter for some time. Boy

babies were being taken and given to noblemen for money. Yours was to be the same."

"No!" the woman cried.

"You're lying, no one could be so cruel," the man said.

"They are, and can be. I have your babe here, please take him." Nicholas stepped inside and handed the child to its mother. "I'm sorry for how you suffered, so very sorry. There are many babies out there who have been removed from their mothers, and I will see them returned."

"H-he is our boy?" The man started to weep.

"He is."

"I-I can never thank you enough."

"There is no need. I will say good evening to you both. But be assured I will return to discuss the events of that evening."

Nicholas shook the hand the man held out to him, and then turned to leave.

Exhausted and yet somehow elated, he walked slowly back to where he hoped to find a hackney. Alice would be proud of him, and while Lilly loved him, it was different with Alice. He wanted to tell her now what he'd done, and yet that would have to wait for a few more hours.

It was as he neared the end of the lane that he heard footsteps coming from behind him. Nicholas knew whoever they were, they were coming for him. It seemed Braeburn had one more piece of the game to play.

He'd known, of course, that it could not possibly go this easy, but he'd hoped it would.

Pulling out his shirt, he tucked it in over the ledger and redid the buttons on his coat. He could not lose that... if he got out of this alive.

Strangely, he felt calm. He loved Alice and knew she loved him. He had not just found her to have that ripped away. But to get to her, he had a feeling the journey was not going to be pleasant.

He turned with his pistol in one hand as they started running.

"I will kill one of you. Which one is it to be?"

He fired. One dropped, clutching his thigh. The other three grabbed him. He fought with everything he had at his disposal, feet, fists, but eventually they overpowered him. He was then bound hand and foot and gagged.

His first thought, when he could think again, was of Alice. She'd know now that something was wrong... she would feel it, as would his family. He must stay alive long enough for them to find him.

Nicholas did not struggle anymore, deciding that he would need his strength for what lay ahead.

They carried him along the street and in through a door of what looked to be a warehouse. They took stairs down and then lowered him through a hole and into the sewers below. He was dropped like a pile of rags and landed heavily, grunting at the impact.

Their feet splashed as they walked through the sludge along a tunnel. The stench was foul, but as he could only breathe through his nose, he could do nothing about that.

"He's a bloody heavy brute," one of the men muttered.

"He's a dead weight, they's always heavier."

"He's also a toff. They have plenty of food."

Was this Braeburn's way of getting more money? Was he to be ransomed, or was this an act of revenge for beating him at cards?

They walked and walked.

"He's too heavy, I can't keep going."

"Untie his feet. He can walk."

Someone cut the binds around his ankles and then he was

lowered to the ground. Dropped, actually, into the filth once more.

"Now get up and move." Looking at the three men, he didn't think now was a time to make a run for it. One of them had a pistol pointed at him.

The passage was narrow, the walls slimy and damp. He could hardly see a foot in front of his face, but clearly the men had spent time down here and knew where they were going.

Nicholas estimated they'd been walking for over an hour by the time they stopped. The tunnel opened into a small dock. Nicholas saw three rowboats. One was manned.

"Get him in, we leave now. Kit with me, and John and Phil in the next boat."

"There's a third," one of the men said.

"We don't need it, and it's not likely anyone else will. So get in, we need to move. Lower him, then throw the blanket over him."

Nicholas tried to stop them, but they soon overpowered him and had him in the boat.

"I'll shoot you if your lift your head."

Nicholas felt something jab his side and knew it was the pistol. He stayed still, for now.

He thought about going overboard, but he wouldn't last being gagged and with his hands tied. Plus, he needed to keep the ledger dry. No, he'd wait, bide his time, and then he'd escape and go back to Alice. That thought alone motivated him.

Alice heard the gunfire and ran in that direction. She arrived in time to see the men carrying Nicholas. She knew it was him, as they'd called him a toff and she doubted there would be many of those here in this area of London.

She'd followed at a distance, not wanting to be seen, listening for the voices to guide her. Entering the warehouse, she hurried down the stairs. Jumping into the sewer had taken two attempts, but she'd done it, and hadn't squealed too many times. Possibly four or five, and those were muffled by the handkerchief pressed to her face as she followed.

Things scurried across her shoes; others made noises. Everything smelled fetid down here. The walls, roof, and floor were damp, and the space narrow. Alice did not like small spaces. It was so dark she could barely see a foot in front of her, and she hoped she didn't stand on a rodent of any kind. There was every possibility they were huge in such an environment.

You must do this for Nicholas.

Was he all right? She'd tracked their footsteps, but they had stopped somewhere up ahead. She'd then heard them speaking about getting him into a boat.

As yet she had not heard his voice, but Alice knew it was him those men had captured.

How was she to follow him if there was no boat for her to get in? Further to that was the horrifying prospect of retracing her steps. She'd be lost in minutes. There was absolutely no way she could find her way back to the street above.

Slowing as she heard the murmur of voices, she eased forward and peered around the edge of the wall. Her heart sank as she saw two rowboats leaving the mooring.

Nicholas was in one of them, but she couldn't make out which from here. Not that it mattered; what mattered was that she did not let him out of her sight.

Be brave, Alice.

Alice had always found that bravery had more appeal

when she was not alone. Strength often came from others. This time, she had to find it alone.

Her family would have realized by now something was not right. But they would not find her if Alice did not start speaking... loudly, which she could not do at the moment.

Slipping from her hiding position when the boats had moved far enough away, she found another rowboat. Looking at the vessel, Alice thought about the only time she'd been in one.

She, Barty, and Verity had been rowing down the river. She'd taken the oars and nearly tipped them all into the water.

Get in, Alice, you can do this.

Untying the rope that moored the boat, she gingerly stepped down into it. So far, so good. She then sat, and the boat rocked, but steadied. Pushing away from the side, she picked up the oars and lowered them into the water.

"Keep your strokes smooth, Alice," Barty had said. Which would likely be easier if her stomach was not churning with fear. She managed to propel the boat forward slowly, but her reach was not great and the going very slow. The second stroke she went too deep and nearly lost the oar.

Desperation had her wanting to sob, but she had to do this for Nicholas. As she tried to direct the boat forward, something happened. The current started to gently bob her along. Alice did her best to guide the boat and keep it going forward so it did not crash into anything.

They were still in darkness, but wherever they were heading would bring them out into the gray light of a London dawn soon enough.

Alice had lost sight of the boats up ahead, but could hear the occasional murmur in the distance.

Her shoulders began to ache, but she had to keep going with her feeble attempts, for Nicholas's sake. Was he suffering? Had they hurt him? Thoughts churned around and around inside her head.

Relief filled her with renewed strength as the tunnel began to get lighter, but with that came fear of exposure. Even in the weak dawn light she could be detected. Lifting the oars, she let the boat drift.

Reaching the entrance, she saw no sign of the other boats, so she nudged hers through it. Looking around, Alice had no idea where they were, but the area was less populated with buildings and people. But as she didn't know London well, that did not mean a great deal. Searching for the other boats again, she saw them heading through the mists for the bank opposite.

Torn between following and staying out of sight, she watched from the shadows as the two boats stopped. Two men got out of the first boat. Then she saw Nicholas. He was hauled roughly out of the bottom and thrown on the bank in a heap. Alice felt the wonderful heat of rage fill her as she watched his treatment. It gave her strength.

No one looked her way as they dragged him up the bank and disappeared. Alice dug the oars into the water and tried to get moving, the current assisting her once more. That, and anger renewed her clumsy efforts. Eventually she bumped into the bank on the other side. Stumbling out, she stood, bracing her hands on her knees and taking in large lungfuls of air.

She had to find Nicholas.

Hurrying up the bank, she stepped onto the narrow road. There were a few buildings, sheds and warehouses, but no sign of Nicholas or the men. Panic filled her. Making her way to one of the buildings, she hid in its shadows and listened. Nicholas must be close; he had to be. She could not contemplate losing him now she'd come so far.

CHAPTER 32

*H*is head hurt, his mouth was raw from the gag, and his wrists were bleeding, but the only thought consuming Nicholas was of Alice. For some reason, he felt she was in danger.

Something had been niggling at him. Yes, his situation was less than ideal, but the fear inside him was solely focused on her.

What risk had she taken? There was little doubting she was capable of that and more. His blood ran cold just thinking of the scenarios he'd already found her in.

He told himself over and over again that he was being foolish. Alice was still warm and safe in her bed... please God, he hoped so.

"Inside."

He was thrust through the door of a narrow building, then forced up some stairs. Another door was opened at the top and he was pushed hard in the back, forcing him forward and down to his knees. The anger that had been riding him since this had begun grew.

Nicholas had realized something about himself while

these men had walked him through those sewers and then forced him into the bottom of that boat. He wanted to live... in fact, he wanted to live very much. Once, he'd not cared overly about his life, but that had changed, and now he wanted all of it. Life, love, and yes, children with Alice Sinclair. *And I am going to have it*, he vowed silently.

The gag was finally removed, and he inhaled deeply, enjoying the rush of air against his lips.

"Why have you captured me?"

Two men stood before him. Brothers was Nicholas's guess, as they looked identical. Brown hair and eyes, short, solid builds, and not someone a person would like to meet in a dark alley alone.

"We've been paid handsomely to take care of you."

"Lord Braeburn is paying you, I presume?"

They neither agreed nor disagreed, just sneered down at him. Nicholas didn't like people sneering at him; it angered him more.

"So, he lost at cards to me in a fair game, and then sent you to kill me because of it? The man has always been a sniveling coward. He can't even do his dirty work himself."

"It's true, he's not a man I can respect," one of the men said. "There's that business with the bairns, after all. I've never been happy about that."

"Shut up, Ted."

"It's true. It's not right."

"I said, shut up!"

The man called Ted clamped his lips into a line.

"What will you do with me now?"

"You're staying here till it's dark, then you're going on a long journey."

"I'll pay you more if you release me."

"I'm paying them handsomely, Braithwaite, and I can

assure you that they may not be loyal to that fool Braeburn, but they are to me."

Nicholas was shocked to see who entered the room behind the men.

"Captain Young?"

"The very one."

Gone was the amiable look; in its place was a mocking sneer.

"I don't understand."

"Very likely, because unlike Braeburn, I have a card face. I masterminded this entire operation. We've earned a considerable amount of money over the last two years. You have put a stop to that, but we shall start again somewhere else."

"Why?" Nicholas asked him. "What possible reason could you have to torture these poor parents?"

"Money, of course. Fourth son, you understand, perpetually short in the pockets. This opportunity allowed me to change that."

"Bastard! You are sick and depraved to do such things to those people." Nicholas advanced on the man, but without his hands he could to nothing against the boot that he took to his stomach.

"Braeburn wanted you harmed and I have to say I was happy to oblige as you have caused me considerable trouble. First with thwarting my money making enterprise, and then my matrimonial prospects." The man's smile was smug. "Think about this while you prepare to meet your maker, my lord. I will be there to help your grieving beloved, Miss Sinclair, when she learns of your demise. I can now marry her and get my hands on her money. After all, she is a tasty wee morsel."

Rage had him staggering to his feet. "You will never get near her! Her family will protect her." He ran at the man, but it was too late, he'd left the building, taking his men with him, and Nicholas only collided with the door for his troubles.

"Alice." He must get to her. He couldn't let Young touch her. His sweet, lovely Alice. *They will keep her safe.* He had to keep reminding himself that. Their family would ensure no harm came to her until he returned. As long as she took no risks... but she always took risks.

He had to escape.

They'd put him inside a room on the second floor of a building. There were walls and a skylight in the roof, a chair and some crates, but little else.

He tried the handle. It was locked, of course, but he had to try. Leaning his shoulder into it merely confirmed how solid it was. Pacing across the room and back, he tried to ease the stiffness in his legs and think clearly.

He must save Alice.

When he heard the key turn in the lock, he moved back, bracing himself against the wall. Waiting to see Young's mocking face again.

"Get in there!"

Alice came through the door fast with the assistance of a hand on her back. Nicholas met her in the middle of the room, bringing her to a stop against his body. He fought to free himself so he could hold her. He wanted to seek retribution for her treatment at the hands of whoever dared to touch her.

"Let her go!" Nicholas roared at Captain Young, who stood in the doorway. "It's me you want, not her."

"But she knows where you are. I shall now have to kill you both. Such a shame, as I so wanted her money and the status of her family connections. Perhaps I shall keep sweet little Alice alive longer than you, however." He laughed, then slammed the door again.

"Alice? What the hell are you doing here?"

"Nicholas!" Neither of them could touch the other with their hands tied, but Nicholas lowered his head to hers, and for two seconds, acknowledged she was here with him. The infuriating woman he loved with every fiber of his being. Then he stepped back to glare at her.

"I want an explanation as to why you are here, madam."

"There is no time, we must escape."

She was filthy and smelled of the sewer. Her hair had come free and hung in black tangles to her waist. Dirt was smeared over her pale cheeks.

"Tell me you didn't follow me through those sewers, Alice. That you didn't take yet more risks tonight when both Wolf and I expressly forbade you from doing so."

"All right, I won't."

"Answer the question, Alice."

"What was the question? You asked quite a few."

She shot him a look, then moved her eyes slightly left. She always did that when she was in the wrong.

"Alice, now is not the time to test me!"

"Don't yell at me."

"I will bloody yell at you. Christ, woman. Those men will hurt you. They will kill us both!" Fear had his voice rising. "I thought you safe and warm in your bloody bed, and yet here you stand!"

"They will not kill you." The conviction in her words was absolute.

"Tell me how you came to be here?" he gritted out.

"I followed you to Bastil's when I realized that was where you'd gone."

Nicholas felt his anger slide into rage as she proceeded to tell him the story of her evening, starting with her belief something was wrong, then visiting his house with Wolf.

She could have been snatched off the street at any time when she left her house alone. Even now, Alice could be in the clutches of some fiend and he would never have seen her again. The fear spiked his anger.

"I cannot believe you were reckless enough to follow me to Bastil's, then here! Why did you not get help from your family!"

"Stop yelling at me."

"I will yell at you when you behave like a fool!" He couldn't seem to calm down. His insides were like a cauldron of angst, and she was his outlet. "This is not a game!"

"I know that. I will not apologize. I did what needed to be done." Her chin lifted, and she looked like an angry urchin.

"What needed to be done! I could have possibly escaped on my own, but now I must protect you while trying to free us both."

"I can protect myself."

"How?"

"We just need to stay alive long enough for the others to reach us." Her voice was subdued now.

"What others? No one knows we are here, Alice."

"They do by now and will be looking for us. The problem is we can't yell, but we will need to soon, and then Eden will find us. Cam will track us by scent, and Wolf and Dev by our colors."

"That is all very well, but how do you propose to get out of here so we can begin to yell?" He hadn't meant to sneer, but it came out that way.

"There is no need to be mean. I followed you because... well, because."

Her lip trembled.

"Alice." He moved closer, but she stepped back out of reach. "My anger is induced by fear, surely you can allow me that much?"

Unlike his, her hands were tied before her, and he watched as she bent and grabbed a handful of her skirts.

"What are you doing?"

"I just remembered I have a knife."

"You just remembered?" Nicholas watched as she revealed one pale thigh. Strapped to it was a sheath. She grabbed the handle of the knife in her hands and slid the blade free.

"Careful, I do not want any of that lovely limb harmed."

She did not smile or look at him, instead moving behind him. He felt her sawing through his bindings, and then he was free.

He took the knife, then did the same for her. When he was done, he handed it back to her, and she placed it back in the sheath, then lowered her skirts.

"We must escape now, Nicholas, before that fiend Captain Young returns. He has fooled everyone."

"I know, but I want to hold you first." He grabbed a handful of her skirt as she tried to step away again, tugging it hard. She fell against him.

"Stop fighting me, Alice."

Suddenly her arms went around his neck and held him in a fierce grip. Her face was pressed into his neck as she sobbed.

"Knowing those men touched you and could have harmed you in any way terrifies me." He held her in a fierce grip. "I want you safe always."

"I know. B-but I would take those risks again, Nicholas. We are connected now, I feel your p-pain, and distress."

"As I do yours."

"Really?" She looked at him.

"Really."

"Nicholas, I must tell you something."

"What have you done?" He cupped her face.

"I have done nothing. You sound like Wolf."

"Trouble does seem to follow you, my sweet."

"I love you, Nicholas."

He kissed her softly, pouring everything he felt into that moment.

"That pleases me greatly. Did you hear my words last night, Alice?"

"Yes."

"They are the truth. I love you also. Every infuriating inch of you."

She sniffed as he released her.

"But now we must get out of here, and the only way is up."

She looked at the skylight above them.

"But how will we get up there?"

"There are crates, and a chair. We shall try and get you out with those and a lift from me."

"I will not leave without you, Nicholas."

"You will if I order you to."

She folded her arms. "No."

"God, you are a trying woman."

"I will never change."

He barked out a laugh. "And I would wish you to be no other way, my love, but for now, today, will you please follow my orders?"

"I shall decide as you issue them."

They worked together to get the crates in place. He then placed the chair on top.

"Up you go, and I'll steady the chair, Alice."

She gave him a look but didn't argue. He helped her onto the first crate, and then the second.

"Try and stay in the middle of the chair."

"I don't have very good balance. Rowing across that river, I was convinced I'd fall in."

"Alice, I don't want to think about what you did to get to me. I'm aware you are brave for doing so, but I still want to shake you for it."

She huffed out a breath but struggled onto the chair.

"I can see up your skirts."

"I can't believe you said that!"

"Yes, you can."

She looked down at him. "I need to tell you something else, Nicholas."

"Do so while you try and open that window."

"I doubted you."

"When did you doubt me?"

She grunted as she pushed the window, but it didn't budge. Damn, his intent had been to get her out of here as fast as he could. Now he'd need to get up there and force that window open, as he was the stronger of the two of them.

"Come down, love, I will try."

Nicholas wrapped an arm around her waist and lowered her to the ground. He then climbed up the crates.

"I can't reach the chair, Nicholas."

"Go to the door and listen, Alice, unlike you my balance is excellent."

"Such an ego," he heard her mutter.

She did as he asked, and Nicholas focused on the window. The catch was stuck. He hit it several times with his fist, and it gave.

"Someone is coming, Nicholas!"

"Come here." She ran to him. "Lift your hands." He grabbed them and pulled her up. "Climb out now."

"And you, Nicholas."

"And me." He grabbed her waist and threw her up and through the window. "Move back, Alice."

Her head disappeared, and he grabbed the frame just as the door behind him opened. Pulling himself up, he climbed through the window onto the roof, slamming it behind him.

"Run!"

Alice started to the left. He grabbed her and headed right, toward the river.

"We need to find a place to hide!" she cried.

"The river. If we can get to that, there are boats, and they will take us downstream to safety."

He thought she said, "dear God, no," but couldn't be sure. Nicholas reached the end of the roof and looked down at another building.

"I will go first, then you, Alice. Do you understand?"

Her eyes were wide with fear.

"Alice?"

"Y-yes."

Nicholas jumped, landing on his knees.

"Now!"

She didn't hesitate, just leaped. He grabbed her as she landed, pulling her into his body to break her fall. Her heart thumped hard against his chest.

"Such a brave girl." Taking her hand, he ran along the roof to the end. The only way down from there was to jump.

"We are trapped."

"No, I will lower you, then you can drop the last few feet. Bend your knees as you hit the ground, it will lessen the impact."

She looked over the edge. "I don't think I can do that."

"Yes, you can, you're the bravest woman I know."

"It's an act. I'm actually a coward." Her voice was tight with nerves.

"We're all acting, Alice. It's how we play those roles that makes us different."

"Which does nothing to reassure me." She was moving away from the edge.

Nicholas grabbed her hands, giving them a shake. "You can do this."

She nodded. "But I'm closing my eyes."

He dropped to his knees. "Sit beside me." She did. He took her hands and lowered her over the edge.

"Open your eyes, Alice."

They caught his.

"I'm letting go now." It was the hardest thing he'd ever done. She fell and landed with a thud, falling backward onto her bottom.

"Very graceful." Nicholas lowered himself and gripped the edge. "Move back, Alice."

"Be careful."

He let go and also landed with a thud, which jarred through his body.

"Are you all right, Nicholas?"

"Yes. Now you need to listen carefully, love, for those men."

She nodded.

Nicholas went first, with Alice at his back, taking the stairs as fast as he could but ensuring she stayed with him. Reaching the bottom he waited, looking at her.

She shook her head.

Taking her hand, he headed for the bank.

"I can hear them, Nicholas, they are heading this way."

"How close?"

"I don't know?"

"Why don't you know? You can hear someone speaking several streets away."

He waved her to a crouch as they reached the water and started along to where the boats were.

"It's you. Remember I told you what happens sometimes when you are near?"

"Right, strangely that knowledge is not endearing now," he said, pulling her in front of him. If they were shooting, a bullet would hit him first.

"Are they close?"

"I think so."

He saw the boats then. "Run, Alice." She did, picking up her skirts and sprinting for all she was worth.

She scrambled into the first boat. Nicholas released the moorings of the other two and pushed them out into the river.

"That's very clever, I didn't think of that."

"Yes, I spent years at Eton for just such a moment."

"Sarcasm is not becoming."

"Get in the bow, Alice."

"Where is that?" She looked left and right.

"The front."

She scrambled there. Nicholas sat in the middle and picked up the oars.

"Hurry!"

He pushed off and started rowing as the men crested the bank. "Duck, Alice!" Nicholas saw a gun. Instead, she removed her knife again and stood.

"Sit, you bloody fool!"

But she didn't, instead drawing back her arm. She then threw the knife. Nicholas watched as it flew through the air and embedded itself in the arm of the man aiming his gun at them. He screamed and dropped to his knees.

"God's blood, Alice Sinclair, you are a woman of surprises. Did your brother teach you that?"

Now they were far enough away that without a shotgun they would not be reached, he felt marginally calmer. The men, however, were running along the bank, following their boat's progress.

"Wolf taught Kate and me to defend ourselves."

"At least I know you will protect me."

"Nicholas, I need to tell you something else." She dropped down into the front of the boat once more.

"Right now?"

"Yes."

"The same something you tried to tell me before? The conversation started with 'I doubted you,' I believe?"

The men were still running beside them, and Nicholas knew that at the first opportunity they would either fire at them or get in any vessel that could put them on the water. He had to get them to the opposite side, and fast.

"Tonight, when we went to your house when I knew something was wrong, Hopkins told me you had gone to a gambling hell, and I was angry."

She looked close to tears. After what she'd just been through, it was this that was breaking her.

"Because you believed I'd lied to you?"

"Yes. I'm sorry, at first I was not thinking rationally."

"But then you realized I hadn't lied, presumably, as you are here with me now?"

"I was lying on my bed thinking of you when I remembered something you said to me."

"What?"

"Two somethings, actually. First, you said the only reason you would ever gamble again would be if you had no other choice but to do so. Second, you said I told you in a vision you would soon be asked to do something that goes against the man you have become."

"I remember."

"I'm sorry for doubting you, Nicholas."

"It is all right to doubt me occasionally, Alice, as long as you don't make a habit of it."

They reached a bridge, and he watched the men run over it.

"Nicholas!"

"I see." He tried to stop the boat and head for the bank, but the current was swift.

"It's all right now, Nicholas, they are here," Alice said with a wide smile.

"Who?"

"Our family."

And suddenly there they were. Running across the bridge from the opposite side. Wolf was in the lead, with Dev on his heels. James came next with Cam and Max. The men took one look at the approaching storm and fled.

Wolf leaned over the side and shook a fist down at her.

"You, Alice Sinclair, are in so much trouble!"

"Oh dear."

"Don't threaten the woman I love!" Nicholas roared back. Alice's mouth dropped open as she looked at him.

"I do love you."

"I know that, but you've told all of them." She pointed at their family, who were smiling down at them... all except Wolf, who was scowling.

"They already know, love. There are not many secrets in our family."

Alice laughed, and it was such a wonderful sound Nicholas found himself joining in.

CHAPTER 33

*A*lice sat in her brother's office, across his desk from him.

"To have left the house like that, Alice. What were you thinking? It was reckless and foolhardy!"

It was the fifth morning after her dash out of the house in the middle of the night to find and rescue Nicholas.

This lecture had been going for twenty minutes so far, and she had already been the recipient of many others. Wolf just found new and inventive ways to say the same thing each time. Alice sat quietly and appeared to be listening, when in fact her mind was wandering... more accurately, it was focused on Nicholas.

Where was he? When was he coming to see her?

"To wake in fear like I did that night... I tell you, sister, it is not a feeling I would ever wish to recreate."

"Why did you not tell me you were badly wounded in the war, Wolf?"

"Pardon?" He looked confused.

"Dorrie, Somer, and Warwick told me they cared for you, Wolf. Why did you not tell me... us how you were suffering?"

"You could do nothing for me, Alice."

"I would have found a way to come to you. To know that you were without us... it hurts deep inside, Wolf."

"Alice." He gripped her hand. "You could do nothing for me."

"I could have been there for you."

"I know, but I did not know how to tell you, and then it just seemed better that I didn't, as I knew you would worry."

"Oh, Wolf." Alice felt the sting of tears.

"I'm all right now, and I'm sorry you had to find out."

"Don't apologize. We knew, you know, Kate and I. Felt your pain, but were helpless to do anything, as Mother would not travel. She said your letters stated you were all right."

"I never thought of that, you being able to feel my pain." She gripped his hand hard. "But I'm still bloody angry with you."

The door opened then, and in walked Nicholas. Her heart leapt at the sight of him.

"I hope you're not haranguing my fiancée?"

"She deserves to be harangued, and you have not asked me for her hand."

"Why is she crying?" Nicholas glared at Wolf.

"Happy tears," Alice managed to get out.

"She is reckless, and I have been telling her so."

"For five days," Alice added.

"If you listened, I would not need to."

"Reckless, yes, but also brave and fearless," Nicholas said, looking only at Alice. "I want to marry her."

"Very well, I agree, and now I'm leaving, as this is making me nauseous. Please excuse me."

She heard the door close behind Wolf.

"Alice." He said her name as he lifted her into his arms and simply held her. "I've missed you."

"Where have you been?"

"There was much to deal with. It took me from London briefly. But now I am back and won't be leaving you again."

"I would like that."

"We are to go to James's house shortly, it is Eden's birthday."

"So I gather with large families, someone is always having a birthday." He kissed her softly.

"Tell me that Captain Young has been found, Nicholas. Wolf would say nothing on the matter, only that you would call to see me when you were able."

"Both Young and Braeburn have been captured by the authorities trying to flee England."

"But what of the children, Nicholas? What is to be done about them?"

"I was given a ledger with records of the babies they have taken. There are many. I have handed it over to someone who will do the right thing with the information. But right now, will you come for a drive with me?"

"Of course."

Alice ran to her room and tied on a bonnet, then collected her gloves. He was not in the foyer when she reached it. She went outside to see if he was beside the carriage.

"Come into the carriage, Alice."

She heard his voice and stepped up and into the carriage. In his arms were two babies.

"I don't understand."

"That one is Jane Budd's son, and the other is Meggie Todd's." He indicated each by nodding at them.

Alice stood and looked at the screwed-up little faces on the infants. Then could do nothing to stop the tears.

"Y-you are a good man."

"You make me want to be a good man, my love. But please don't cry when I cannot hold you as my arms are full."

She reached for Meggie's son and took him, gently settling him into her arms. She took the seat next to him.

"I collected them from the homes they'd been placed in. The people who had paid for the infants did not fight me when I told them of the incriminating information I had against them. James and Cam came with me."

"I hope the others find their way home also."

"As do I, my love, as do I."

The babies slept as the carriage rolled through London, and Alice rested against Nicholas, content for now to be close. They arrived at Meggie's house first.

The door opened after the second knock.

"Meggie," Alice said, holding out the babe. "This is your son. We have brought him home to you."

The woman burst into loud sobs and took the babe, thanking them profusely through her tears. Nicholas said he would return tomorrow and explain the circumstances. For now, she needed time to be with her son.

They reached Jane Budd's house a few minutes later, after a short carriage ride. This time it was Nicholas who knocked on the door. Alice stood back and watched.

"I have your son, Jane," he said when she opened the door.

"Can it be true?"

"Here, take him into your arms." Nicholas handed over the babe. "There will be time for questions tomorrow." He took Alice's hand. "Good day."

"At least we have seen two home to their families."

Nicholas pulled her onto his lap for the drive to James's house. He kissed her thoroughly.

"I want to marry you now."

"I feel the same way, but will you mind waiting for a few weeks? Mother has always wished for a Christmas wedding."

"If we must. James said to me today that he would like us to wed at Raven Castle. How do you feel about that?"

"I like the idea very much."

She rested against him, and there was no place she would rather be than in his arms.

"Nicholas, you must know that now you are redeemed."

He knew what she meant, but as he was busy kissing her neck, he did not answer immediately.

"Nicholas." She tugged his hair.

"Ouch."

She cupped his face, holding his eyes.

"Tell me you know my words for the truth? Tell me that your demons are gone and you see the man I do?"

"I'm not sure my demons will ever truly be exorcised, Alice. But I do feel freer. It is not only what we have done that has redeemed me. It is your love also."

"I have always known you are the very best of men."

"Now that's not entirely true."

"Perhaps not entirely." Alice smiled. "I shall say then, that now I believe you are the very best of men."

"And you are the very best of women… if a little head-strong at times."

The family had all gathered in James's study, as they often did. After giving Eden her birthday present, a pair of fine lace gloves from Alice and toffee from Nicholas, all wanted to hear the full details of what had happened since they had last seen him.

They were welcomed with hugs and kisses. Nicholas left Alice briefly to look at James's books. He found the one he wanted by the gold lettering on the spine.

"Nicholas! What are you doing with that book?" Eden looked in a panic as he approached.

"I thought it may come in useful for Alice. *Housekeeping for Those in Need*," he read the spine.

"Dear lord, he's opening it." This came from Lilly.

"We are doomed." Emily sighed.

Rose giggled.

Essex made a lunge for the book, but he simply lifted it out of her reach.

"What is going on?" James was looking confused as were the rest of the men in the room. Alice was looking anywhere but at the women in her family.

"Oh simply tell them, it is done now," Eden said, folding her arms.

Opening the book, he cleared his throat.

"Entry by the Duchess of Raven. Nicholas will marry Miss Gillett by season's end. I bet a new bonnet on the outcome."

"What?" James looked stunned. "That woman with the high-pitched laugh? Good God, what has he done to deserve such a fate?"

"Entry by Emily Sinclair. Nicholas will marry Miss Hannah by season's end. I bet a pair of silk stockings."

Cam crowed with laughter; in fact, he was soon laughing so hard he was crying.

Nicholas continued to read the names. Rose was next, then Kate.

"Entry by Alice Sinclair. Nicholas will marry Miss Krimpton by season's end. I bet a pair of gloves." He lowered the book and glared at her. "Miss Krimpton. I had no idea you could be so nasty. The woman would be like condemning me to purgatory."

"I didn't like you then." She looked smug.

"I cannot believe you lot had a betting book right here in my study." James was now looking proud. "The women in this family really are remarkable."

"The last entry is from my sister but dated four days after the others."

"You added yours later?" Eden did not look happy. "Surely that is cheating?"

"I don't see how it can be when at that stage he had not declared his love for anyone," Dev said, coming to his wife's defense. Lilly said nothing but looked quite happy with herself.

"Entry by Lady Sinclair. Nicholas will marry Miss Alice Sinclair by season's end. I bet her wedding gown."

He handed the book to Max, who along with the other males in the room huddled over it.

"How did you know?" He went to his sister.

"You were different from the start with her. I saw it in both of you."

Alice moved to his side, slipping her hand in his.

"I knew you would love each other."

They spent the day with family, celebrating Eden's birthday and the love they now felt for each other.

In the early hours of the morning, Nicholas found Alice waiting for him in the gazebo, his own garden nymph. His love, his life.

She flew into his arms, and there in the moonlight he made sweet love to her, knowing that when the sun rose, she would have his heart as he had hers, and theirs would be a bright future filled with everything he'd never believed he'd have.

"I love you, Nicholas." She arched into him as he entered her body.

"And I you."

After that, no more words were needed. He was finally complete.

THE END

SEDUCTIVE DANGER

Thank you for reading TEMPTING DANGER. I hope you enjoyed Nicholas and Alice's story. Book 6 SEDUCTIVE DANGER in the Sinclair and Raven series is available now!

Can a touch of magic and a holiday miracle bring these two destined lovers together?

Rory Huntington has vowed to live his life relying on no one, but when he's betrayed and left for dead, a determined raven-haired beauty rescues him, and he must put his trust in her to keep him safe. Kate Sinclair leads him back to his estranged brother and a family he wants nothing to do with. He's drawn into the yuletide festivities against his will and soon captivated by everything about her. Rory desires Kate more than any woman he's ever met, yet he cannot pay the price she asks, forgiveness of the past and reuniting with his family.

Join the Sinclair and Raven families as they celebrate the wedding and festivities of Christmas at Raven Castle.

From USA Today Bestseller Wendy Vella comes an exciting Regency series about legend, love and destiny, with a hint of magic.

DEVILLE BROTHERS SERIES

From USA Today bestselling author Wendy Vella comes a sizzling new series full of passion, scandals and intrigue. Tasked with protecting the King, the Deville brothers are part of a secret alliance forged centuries ago, but when it comes to affairs of the heart they are yet to be tamed.
Seduced By A Devil

Desperate for his help

Gabriel Deville, Earl of Raine, has never met a woman like Dimity Brown. Mysterious, alluring and utterly infuriating, she has no respect for him. In fact, the piano teacher treats him like he is the underling, not her. His beloved sister, however, calls her friend, and when Dimity disappears, he cannot refuse his sibling's urgent plea to find her.

Gabe's first shock is finding Dimity in a seedy tavern, dancing on the bar. The second is seeing the feisty young woman vulnerable and scared. He soon realizes that what he feels for her is a great deal deeper than anger and he will stop at nothing to keep her safe. Earning her trust and uncovering her secrets will be a challenge, but securing a place in her heart will be the biggest challenge of his lifetime.

Powerless to resist

Dimity had believed her life would never be anything more or less than it currently was, but then her father dies, and everything changes. She is thrown out of the only home she has ever known, and finds a letter in her father's things that turns her life completely on its head. Penniless, confused and desperate, she has nowhere to turn until Gabriel Deville steps back into her life.

Lord Raine is arrogant, ridiculously wealthy, and far too dangerously handsome. Despite the sparks that had always flown between them, their interactions had been coldly civil. When he insists she accept his help, Dimity takes it, certain she can resist him, and what is growing between them long enough to unravel the secrets of her past.

Can they overcome their differences and society dictates to forge a life together?

Books in the Deville Brothers Series

Seduced By A Devil
Rescued By A Devil
Protected By A Devil
Surrender To A Devil
Unmasked By A Devil

ABOUT THE AUTHOR

Wendy Vella is a bestselling author of historical and
contemporary romances
such as the Langley Sisters and Sinclair and Raven series,
with over two million copies of her books sold worldwide.

Born and raised in a rural area in the North Island of New
Zealand, she shares her life with one adorable husband, two
delightful adult children and their partners, four delicious
grandchildren, and a sweet little pup called Tilly who rules
the home.

Wendy also writes contemporary romance under the name
Lani Blake.

Sign up for Wendy's newsletter
www.wendyvella.com/newsletter